PRAISE FOR S  T0029350

Cinder-Nanny

"Diana and Griffin's slow-burn closed-door passion is authentic."

—*Kirkus Reviews*

"*Cinder-Nanny* is a definite must-read. This cute play on the age-old fairy tale will surely worm its way into your heart and leave you feeling all warm and fuzzy."

—*Harlequin Junkie*

"Wilson's ability to weave a sweet tale of two people, each of whom needs what the other has to offer, is magical."

—Bookreporter

The Paid Bridesmaid

"Combining a fast-paced plot with a slow-burning romance, this is sure to give readers butterflies."

—*Publishers Weekly*

"Wilson's (*Roommaid*) funny, sweet stand-alone about marriage, friendships, and mistaken identities is full of witty dialogue, endearing characters, and fast-paced narrative. Will appeal to fans of feel-good romances, rom-coms, and plots about weddings and social media."

—*Library Journal*

The Seat Filler

"Wilson (*Roommaid*) balances the quirky with the heartfelt in this adorable rom-com."

—*Publishers Weekly*

The Friend Zone

"Wilson scores a touchdown with this engaging contemporary romance that delivers plenty of electric sexual chemistry and zingy banter while still being romantically sweet at its core."

—*Booklist*

"Snappy banter, palpable sexual tension, and a lively sense of fun combine with deeply felt emotional issues in a sweet, upbeat romance that will appeal to both the YA and new adult markets."

—*Library Journal*

The #Lovestruck Novels

"Wilson has mastered the art of creating a romance that manages to be both sexy and sweet, and her novel's skillfully drawn characters, deliciously snarky sense of humor, and vividly evoked music-business settings add up to a supremely satisfying love story that will be music to romance readers' ears."

—*Booklist* (starred review), *#Moonstruck*

"Making excellent use of sassy banter, hilarious texts, and a breezy style, Wilson's energetic story brims with sexual tension and takes readers on a musical road trip that will leave them smiling. Perfect as well for YA and new adult collections."

—*Library Journal*, *#Moonstruck*

"*#Starstruck* is oh so funny! Sariah Wilson created an entertaining story with great banter that I didn't want to put down. Ms. Wilson provided a diverse cast of characters in their friends and family. Fans of *Sweet Cheeks* by K. Bromberg and Ruthie Knox will enjoy *#Starstruck*."

—*Harlequin Junkie* (4.5 stars), *#Starstruck*

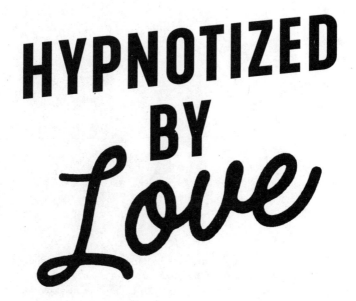

HYPNOTIZED BY *Love*

SARIAH WILSON

Montlake

This is a work of fiction. Names, characters, organizations, places, events, and incidents are either products of the author's imagination or are used fictitiously. Otherwise, any resemblance to actual persons, living or dead, is purely coincidental.

Text copyright © 2024 by Sariah Wilson
All rights reserved.

No part of this book may be reproduced, or stored in a retrieval system, or transmitted in any form or by any means, electronic, mechanical, photocopying, recording, or otherwise, without express written permission of the publisher.

Published by Montlake, Seattle

www.apub.com

Amazon, the Amazon logo, and Montlake are trademarks of Amazon.com, Inc., or its affiliates.

ISBN-13: 9781662514227 (paperback)
ISBN-13: 9781662514210 (digital)

Cover design by Caroline Teagle Johnson

Cover image: © sarayut Thaneerat / Getty; © Margarita Chastikova / Getty

Printed in the United States of America

For Kollin,
even though you don't like kissing books

CHAPTER ONE

"What did they say?" my identical twin sister, Sierra, asked me as I slumped into the chair across the table from her. She'd told me to meet her at Starbucks after my meeting, and I was regretting that. I didn't want to be in public right now. I wanted to go home and curl into a ball.

I took off my blazer, and not surprisingly, I was sweating everywhere. I had been trying to look professional, and instead I was a swampy mess. I wondered if that had played any role in the committee's decision. Only a fool like me would wear a blazer in June in Florida.

"Savannah?" Sierra was waving her hand in front of me, trying to get my attention.

"Censured," I said, letting out a long breath. My sister pushed a Paradise Drink toward me, and I sipped at it. Not even pineapple mixed with coconut milk could soothe this gaping wound. I was in trouble, and I hadn't done anything wrong. "I'm officially censured."

I didn't like how heavy that word felt in my mouth. Even though the air-conditioning was on, I pulled my blouse away from my skin, trying to create some kind of breeze to cool down my overheated body.

"What does 'censured' mean?" she asked.

"It basically means I'm on probation. That if something else happens, I'm in danger of losing my certification."

Sierra managed to look angry, frustrated, and concerned all at once. That was the thing about having an identical twin—it was like having a living mirror. Not just in the physical sense, where I was constantly reminded that we had the exact same features, the same dark brown hair and matching dark eyes, but in having a person who constantly reflected your own emotions back at you. Because I was also angry, frustrated, and concerned.

But mostly angry.

"Even if you lost your certification, you could still practice, though, right?"

I shrugged a shoulder. I could. But there were so many dishonest and untrained people in my field claiming to be hypnotherapists that having that certification felt really important to me. Yes, technically I could still practice hypnosis with people, but being a member of the professional organizations that I belonged to and was accredited with mattered to me in a way that I wasn't sure I could explain to Sierra.

When I didn't answer, she asked, "What did Camila say about it?"

That question felt like a hot knife skewering my stomach. "I think she's disappointed." Camila had been my mentor and the person who'd started me down the road of my profession. She seemed to believe my side of the story but had admonished me to remember what she'd taught me.

I read Camila's text out loud to Sierra. "It isn't fair, but like I've told you—you have to be very careful. Going forward you'll have to avoid even the appearance of evil. Don't give them any more ammunition." Camila had responded after I'd messaged her to let her know how the meeting had gone. I hated this feeling—like I'd somehow let her down. She'd always been so proud of me in the past.

And I couldn't even talk things out with her or make a game plan to move forward. She'd texted me from the airport because she was taking a flight to Peru for a retreat and would be incommunicado for the next couple of weeks.

"What does she mean by 'the appearance of evil'?" Sierra asked.

I set my phone down on the table. "I don't know. I'm guessing anything that can be construed the wrong way. Maybe I should drop my male clients. Or start recording our sessions. Just to protect myself."

Something I would have to look up—whether I was even allowed to do that. I had no idea what the law said about it.

My sister leaned across the table and put her hand on top of mine. "I don't think things are that dire."

She hadn't been in that meeting. "They might be." I let out a long sigh and played with my straw. "How were things at your job today?"

Sierra was an emergency room nurse, and despite her tendency to share the grossest parts of her day, I wanted to change the subject and not think about how close I'd come to losing everything I'd worked for.

All because a man I'd romantically rejected had lied about me and made it his mission to try to ruin my career.

My sister was in the midst of making me clench up as she described her last patient, and the object he'd had in a particular orifice, when our friend Bridget arrived.

Bridget asked, "Am I interrupting?"

"Yes, thankfully," I told her. We'd all been friends since high school but had grown closer after we'd moved back to our hometown around the same time. Bridget had taken over her mother's flower shop and had decided to set a state record for most men dated in a single year.

She flashed a smile at me, knowing all too well the kind of grisly story Sierra had been sharing with me. As always, Bridget was a tiny, bright blonde blur, never holding still for very long, shifting and moving in her seat as she settled in.

"I want to hear all about what happened today with you, Savannah," she said as she dropped two shopping bags on the floor.

But I didn't want to dwell on the situation. "It went fine. I'm censured. On probation. But I still have my certification."

Her face turned a light red, and she shook with the rage I was trying to keep contained. "How can they let him get away with this?"

The *him* in question was Timothy Grainger, a man I barely knew. He had come in as a potential client, but during our initial interview, there was something off about him. I couldn't quite put my finger on what it was, but I told him I didn't think we would be a good professional fit and gave him the names of three other hypnotherapists that I'd recommend. As I was walking him out, he asked me on a date. I politely told him I wasn't interested and thanked him for coming in, sent him on his way, and naively thought that was it.

Timothy didn't let it drop, though. He continued to stop by and wanted to speak to me. He called a few times but didn't leave a voice mail. I considered contacting the police, worried that things might escalate. But then he just stopped showing up, stopped calling.

I was so glad that it was over.

But my relief had been premature, because instead of harassing me in person, he moved to doing it online. He started leaving negative reviews of my business. He seemed to be creating a new account every day, and there was nothing I could do about it.

Then to make matters worse, he decided to hit me where it would hurt most. He contacted the Florida Board of Professional Hypnotists and filed a formal complaint against me, alleging that I was the one who had harassed him. He said that I had asked him on a date and made him uncomfortable. And I didn't have any evidence to the contrary— he'd never sent a text or left a message. It was my word against his, and the Board had to err on the side of caution, given all the negativity surrounding our jobs.

Camila had been the one to remind me that our profession was already so constantly maligned that the Board members wanted to be seen as if they were treating the accusation seriously.

And I was the one who had to pay for his lies.

The one good thing I had going for me was that an online client I'd worked with, a young woman named Ginger, turned out to be a social media influencer and told her millions of followers that I'd helped with her anxiety after half a dozen sessions. I'd had so many people sign up for online sessions that it made the annoying thing Timothy had done mostly fade into the background.

Until today, when I'd been forced to deal with it again.

Bridget was still on her rant about it, drawing my attention back to her. "Bad things should happen to him. I hope all the protruding parts of his body wither up and fall off! I feel like we should be doing something. Egging his house, at least. Keying his car. Something."

The last thing I needed was to be arrested for vandalism. "Unfortunately, people don't always get the comeuppance they deserve right away. I do believe that he'll get his, though."

She crossed her arms and shook her head. "That doesn't seem like enough. Karma's not reliable enough for me."

I needed her to de-escalate. "It's over. I just want to move past it and think about something else. I don't want him to have this much control over me and my thoughts."

"Which I support, but I went online and gave you so many stars that people are going to have to pledge allegiance to them."

"You've never been a client," I reminded her.

"So? Neither was Timothy and he's lying every day, and I can lie for your benefit. Plus, everyone lies online. See also: all of social media." Bridget repositioned her purse on the table, and her Chihuahua, Lulabelle, shook while staring me down. Bridget cooed at her. She took her dog with her everywhere, including on her dates. I knew that dog had seen some things. It was probably why she always seemed so nervous.

"We should talk about something else." I didn't want to give Timothy any more words or headspace. He didn't deserve them.

"Savannah's right. And since we're changing the subject," Sierra said while nodding at me, "do you want to hear about the compound fracture that came in this morning? I'd never seen a bone sticking that far up out of the—"

I gagged slightly and hurried to ask, "How are things going with Joseph?" Joseph was the guy my sister had been dating for the last few weeks.

She grimaced slightly. "Not well. Things have just been . . . off when we're together. Like, we had dinner last night and he told me I wasn't allowed to eat carbs in front of him, since he's gluten-free, and he threw away my pasta."

He threw away her food? I internally screamed for a second.

"Allowed?" I repeated. "You told him he doesn't get to dictate what you eat, right?"

"Unacceptable," Bridget chimed in. "Get out now."

I didn't normally go straight to recommending ending things, but nobody got to tell my sister what she could and could not eat. Especially given the disordered eating issues she still had. She'd worked so hard to overcome those thoughts and impulses, and that jerk Joseph knew about them.

Trying to keep my cool, I said, "I know you don't like breaking up with people, but there will be bread and men with nice personalities who treat you kindly waiting for you on the other side. If you want, I'll pretend to be you and break up with him."

"That's okay. I can do it myself," she said with a wave of her hand. My offer had been a hundred percent serious. People could never tell us apart, and we had spent years switching places. We still managed to trick our dad on a regular basis, even though our hair was completely different lengths.

So I'd happily call up Joseph and tell him where he could stick his gluten. "You are a much better person than me. I've always admired how easygoing and even keeled you are. I would have stabbed him by now."

"You would have," she agreed. "I guess I could tell him that we've grown apart. That we're not as close as we were."

"Right. He grew into someone controlling and self-centered, and you grew into a person who doesn't care for that. I can see where that would make you not as close as you used to be." I clamped my lips together so that I wouldn't say more. Sierra could be stubborn, and I didn't want to inadvertently add anything that might push her back into his wheatless arms.

So I turned toward Bridget. "And how are things going for you? Any new men we should know about?"

She gave Lulabelle a doggy treat and frowned slightly. "There was a guy last night, but it was no big deal. Just a onetime thing."

"I feel like you should text us whenever you bring a random guy home. For safety reasons," Sierra said, and I nodded.

"Oh, I couldn't do that. Think of my data plan," she said with a wink, and I couldn't help but laugh.

"Maybe we should go out this Saturday," Sierra said. "We could have an actual girls' night out."

"I can't. I have a date Saturday night," Bridget said.

"Who with?"

"I don't know yet. And speaking of dating possibilities . . . I heard a rumor today. One that I think will particularly interest you, Savannah."

I raised both of my eyebrows at her expectantly. "Me?" After my recent brush with quasi-stalking and harassment, I wasn't really in a dating kind of place.

"Mm-hmm. Guess who I heard is back in town?"

"No idea," I said. Our little beach town loved gossip more than anything, but during the tourist season, everybody was more focused on earning as much money as they could before things got quiet again.

I had no idea who she meant.

But before she could fill me in, the bell rang on the front door and I happened to glance over.

Mason Beckett walked in.

My heart leapt into my throat and I gripped the edge of the table so tightly my knuckles turned white. I hadn't seen him in six years.

Not since he completely wrecked my entire life.

Camila had told me to avoid the appearance of evil, as if she'd somehow intuited that the horrible offspring of Satan and a snake was going to waltz right back into my Starbucks.

Mason's being here felt like an omen of doom. I knew that my life was about to be completely upended.

CHAPTER TWO

Red-hot rage filled me, making my limbs quake. How could he just stroll in here, to my favorite hangout, like he hadn't made me the laughingstock of our entire high school?

I closed my eyes quickly. Part of my job was helping people to not feel the way I was feeling right now. I needed to relax, calm down. I did some breathing exercises, but my skin still tingled with angry anticipation of the moment when I'd open my eyes again.

"There he is," Bridget said with a sigh. "Mason Beckett. My soon-to-be Saturday date."

"Huh," Sierra grunted. "Was he always that hot?"

"He's definitely gotten yummier with time."

Not able to help myself, I opened my eyelids slightly to look at him. He stood in line, waiting for his turn. A detached part of my brain that wasn't sharing in the full-body panic at seeing him again evaluated what Bridget had said.

Mason seemed taller. Definitely broader, like he'd grown up and filled out. His hair was a lighter brown than I remembered, a caramel color that suited him. He wasn't looking at us, but those soft, lying hazel eyes of his were indelibly burned into my brain. He had on a light blue button-up shirt with the sleeves rolled up over his forearms and a pair of khaki pants, looking every bit the bestselling author I knew him to be.

He seemed cool and casual and not even a little bit sweaty, and it made me hate him more.

"Cool timing, universe," I muttered under my breath. Like I hadn't been punished enough today?

"Did you say something?" Sierra asked, the concern evident on her face. "Are you okay?" She was older by three minutes, something she constantly reminded me about, and apparently thought that gave her the right to be the mother hen in our relationship.

"I'm fine," I said, still gripping the table. Bridget was oblivious to our conversation, making eyes at Mason's back.

"Are all of my teeth still in my mouth?" I asked my sister. This was lining up with so many of my nightmares. This was usually the point when I would wake up drenched in sweat.

Well, the sweating part had already happened, but part of me hoped this was some kind of fever dream that I'd snap out of soon.

She shot me a strange look, and Bridget announced, "I'm in love."

"With Mason?" I asked incredulously. "I guess it's easy to be taken in by him when he's not wearing his dalmatian fur coat."

Another strange look from Sierra. There were definite disadvantages to that twintuition thing that she and I shared. She knew what I was thinking and feeling even when I didn't say it.

She was the only one who knew how I used to feel about Mason.

But instead of making my waking nightmare worse by exposing things I wanted to keep hidden, she said to Bridget, "You've been in love with seven different men this year already."

"Yes, but Mason might be top three. Maybe even The One."

"Are you on a dating app right now?" Sierra demanded, and Bridget stopped midswipe to say, "I'm just browsing."

"You had me worried for a second," my sister said. "I thought you were considering an actual relationship."

"Maybe I don't like being single," Bridget said defensively, still looking at pictures of available men.

"The only reason you're still single is because all the men in the world got together and had a meeting," Sierra said teasingly, and Bridget laughed. Normally I would have laughed, too, but all of my focus was on Mason.

I was glad we were at a place that didn't have any cutlery, because I was definitely feeling a little stabby.

"I can commit for brief periods of time, as long as it's followed by very long stretches where I'm allowed to date whoever I want," Bridget said. "And I honestly don't really believe in relationships, and you should always stand behind your beliefs. So maybe a short fling."

That had me seeing red all over again, followed by a sick, sour taste in my mouth. "Hooking up with Mason Beckett would be a mistake."

Bridget didn't seem to notice my tone. "You're probably right. He is the kind of mistake you'd only make five, maybe six times."

Then she set her phone down and smoothed her skirt down. "How do I look? Do I look like I'm about to land my dream date?"

Another flash of anger that made my retinas feel like they were going to bore holes into his back.

Sierra said, "You look fantastic. Like you're about to add another notch to your bedpost."

"They're not so much notches at this point as they are just one long, deep groove," Bridget said with a saucy wink.

Did Bridget not remember what had happened? How could she be joking about going out with Mason?

But she misinterpreted my incredulous look.

"You are wasting your side-eye. I am not ashamed. I hope he's wearing socks, because they're about to get knocked off," she said and then made her way over to Mason.

I wrenched my gaze away. I wouldn't watch this happen. I had to leave. But it was like my legs wouldn't work. As if I really were in some horrible nightmare that I couldn't convince myself to wake up from.

Sierra cleared her throat. "I'm sorry that I keep asking this, but are you okay?"

Shaking my head, I tried again to do some calming breaths, but it wasn't working.

Sierra put her hand on my knee. "I'll support you in whatever you decide, but if you want my two cents, I think you should talk to him. Let him explain what happened. It's been six years, Savannah."

"Thanks, Mom," I said sarcastically, and she immediately stopped. I had no intention of talking to Mason Beckett and didn't want to find out what had happened, and no one was going to convince me otherwise.

Not even my twin.

Something our mother hadn't been able to understand or respect.

"You have too many enemies," Sierra said.

"He's my only enemy."

"Not if you count people who drive the speed limit in the fast lane, make small talk on airplanes, take up two parking spots, or spoil the endings of books you're reading."

"Everybody hates those people," I mumbled.

"And that Timothy guy."

Definitely him, too. But right now, in this moment? I hated Mason a lot more.

Even I could admit that it didn't seem rational.

I heard Bridget returning to the table. I glanced up in time to observe that she was smiling brightly, and some hot barb twisted in my heart.

"He said no!" She said it with so much delight that I thought I'd misheard her.

"Mason said no? To going out with you?" Sierra said it with as much disbelief as I was feeling.

Disbelief and something else.

Relief.

Men didn't say no to Bridget, so I'd been expecting an entirely different outcome, and now I was relieved that he hadn't said yes?

It had to be because I wanted to protect my friend.

That, and nothing else.

"He did. And he did it so kindly that it didn't even feel like a rejection. He's just like I remember him. A real prince."

"Yeah, the prince of darkness," I mumbled as Bridget just shook her head at me. I wanted to ask her if she remembered all the bad stuff about him, but realized that she wasn't going to listen.

"Game on. This is going to be fun." And when Bridget got that determined note in her voice, I knew for sure that there was no way to dissuade her.

The hunt had begun.

For a tiny moment, I almost felt bad for Mason. But then I realized it was just indigestion and it quickly passed.

He was a grown man. He could deal with his own problems.

"Isn't that his mother?" Bridget asked, and sure enough, Heather Beckett had joined her demon spawn. He kissed her on the cheek and then handed her the drink he'd ordered for her.

She said something to him and then went over to the barista at the counter. It didn't surprise me—Heather was very particular about how she wanted things done.

A trait her son had inherited, and one of his more annoying qualities.

"He's coming this way," Sierra hissed to me. "Be cool."

"Yeah, this is when that happens," I retorted sarcastically.

"Then at the very least aim for civil while knowing that I have bail money on me just in case."

She intended to make me laugh and break the tension, but instead I took it as encouragement when I shouldn't have.

He didn't meet my gaze as he approached the table, and I found myself holding my breath. I could get through this. I could behave in front of his mother, because the absolute last thing I needed was a lecture from my own mom about how I'd embarrassed her and the Sinclair family name in front of the entire town of Playa Placida.

I would stay cool and collected and rise above this. I'd be aloof. I wouldn't let him see how much he still bugged me.

His voice was deeper than I remembered. Smooth and rich, like poisoned honey. "Sierra. Hello again, Bridget." He nodded at them.

Then his fiery gaze landed on me. "Savannah Sinclair." He said my name with so much disdain that I was outraged. How could he be angry with me? I was the wronged party here. He was the one who had spread lies about me, not the other way around.

"What are you even doing here?" I hissed the words at him.

So much for my great plan to remain aloof.

"Currently? Feeling unwelcome."

Bridget leaned forward toward him, peering up at him from under her long lashes. "Fancy seeing you again so soon."

He didn't respond to her overture. He didn't even look at her. His gaze stayed locked on mine.

"What brings you back home?" Sierra asked it in a friendly, conversational tone, but I knew she was ready to ride shotgun for me.

Still keeping his eyes on me, he said, "I'm visiting my mom for a little while. I'm not really sure how long."

It had never occurred to me that Mason might be here for an extended period of time. I'd thought he would come in, completely ruin my day, and then crawl back into whatever hole he'd emerged from.

I unexpectedly found myself speaking again. "Decided to take a break from living under a bridge and shaking down goats for gold?"

His eyes lit up with interest and he smirked at my jab. Like I amused him.

That was somehow worse.

I had honestly forgotten this overwhelming sense of visceral hate. It had been years since I'd felt this way. Not even Timothy's false reporting had made me this upset.

There was something else there, too. The one feeling I'd never told anybody about, besides Sierra. And even though I would have denied it with my last breath, that staggering chemical attraction I felt toward him hadn't gone away. It was every bit as bright as my anger.

I was breathing hard, practically panting, and I didn't know which emotion was making me feel this way. I did not want to be attracted to him. I had willed myself for years to let it go, making up the lie that he wasn't as handsome or as smart as I'd remembered.

There was a time I would have offered up my firstborn child just for the chance to go on a date with him.

That was before, though.

And I would never be that naive again.

His mother, Heather, joined us. "Hello, girls! How are you today?"

Everybody said hello to her. I might have added a greeting as well, but I was still locked in this staring contest with Mason and I planned on winning.

"I need your help," Heather said. "I've been trying to get Mason to donate for the silent auction for the PTA fundraiser. He's such a talented writer that I thought somebody would love to have him evaluate a manuscript. Don't you think that's a good idea? You should help me talk him into it, Savannah. Since you're the one finding donors."

I absolutely did not want to talk him into it. I wanted him to steer very clear of this event.

"Mom"—he sounded embarrassed—"I already said no."

Bridget smiled. "That seems to be Mason's word of the day. 'No.'"

His mother looked like she was about to ask what Bridget meant when Heather's phone rang and she glanced at it. "I have to get this. Savannah, I'll see you at our session tomorrow."

She waved to me, and Mason added, "Yes, Savannah. I'll see you tomorrow."

There was a promise there that was both repulsive and enticing.

What was wrong with me?

They left and Bridget stood up. "I need to head home. If I'm going to win Mason over, I've got some optimistic shaving to do."

She reached for her purse and said, "Come on, Lulabelle. Let's go."

Her dog made a wheezing noise that might have been a bark, and with a quick wave, Bridget was gone, too.

Sierra said, "Do you think she realizes she shares way too much personal information with us?"

"No, I don't think she does." My words sounded echoey in my head because my brain was fixated on what Mason had said and what it had meant. I couldn't focus on anything else.

As if she could read my thoughts, my sister asked, "Why are you seeing Mason tomorrow?"

"Trust me, I'm not."

"Maybe he knows something you don't."

I shrugged. It didn't matter. "To be honest, I don't care what secrets Mason has. I'm not planning on ever seeing him again and will, in fact, be going out of my way to avoid him."

"Hmm." My sister made a noise like she didn't believe me. "Well, if nothing else, at least he made it so you stopped thinking about Timothy."

Yes, I'd stopped thinking about the man who was trying to ruin my career to focus on the man who'd tried to ruin my life.

That felt like a real out-of-the-frying-pan-and-into-the-fire kind of situation.

I needed to stop thinking about both of them. Especially Mason, because he was going to make my blood pressure rise to a dangerous level.

He'd see me tomorrow. Ha. As if.

Mason Beckett was *not* going to see me tomorrow, and I'd do my best to make sure of it.

CHAPTER THREE

When I got home that night, I managed to successfully evade my mom (who had left me eleven voice mails) and snuck into my bedroom. I hated having to live at home again, but it was a necessity so that I could finish up my master's degree in mental health counseling.

Sierra was waiting for me in my room, which was a good thing because I needed to complain about Mason Beckett and what he was doing back in Playa Placida, what he'd meant by everything he'd said, whether or not Bridget would be successful in getting him to go out with her. I ranted for an unusually long period of time, with Sierra's eyes getting bigger and bigger.

She made several sympathetic sounds, nodding as I spoke. She did eventually try to change the subject a couple of times, but I was stuck. I only wanted to talk about Mason.

Which was why I was avoiding my mother. She would only want to talk about Mason, too.

And why we should end up together.

A conversation I was not in the mood for.

At some point, my twin had snuck out of my room, and I was so busy ranting I hadn't even noticed.

I decided I should just go to bed to forget about all of this and deal with it fresh in the morning. That did not happen, though. I tossed and turned all night, running over in my mind what he'd said and what I'd said and how Bridget was determined to date him.

Why did that bother me so much?

When the sun rose, I still didn't have an answer, and now I was exhausted. I got up early, hoping to avoid my mother completely. If it had been a typical day, she already would have been awake to get to her job. Both she and Heather were elementary school teachers and worked in side-by-side classrooms.

I knew what they would have been gossiping about today if school were in session.

But since it was summer break, my mom was sleeping in, and it gave me the chance to make a clean getaway.

I was going to have to face the music at some point, but the longer I could delay it, the better. Mostly because I needed to get my own emotions under control and figure out what was going on with me before being confronted about it by my mother.

My phone buzzed, and I checked it at a stoplight. My mom had sent an indecipherable text. It was the fifth one she'd sent me since the Starbucks Incident. Along with two emails and all those voice mails.

I didn't respond. I didn't have to. I knew what she would say. She'd tell me it was time to get over whatever had happened in high school with Mason and move on. Water under the bridge, that kind of thing.

And it wasn't because my mom was worried about my eternal soul or wanted me to be a good person. No, she was best friends with Heather Beckett and had been since they were little girls. We spent every holiday with the Beckett family; almost every day after school had been spent at either their house or ours. Mason was an easy addition to the tight bond that Sierra and I shared. So our mothers had joked most of my life about either me or Sierra ending up with Mason.

Or both of us. I didn't think they were particular about it.

But they stopped with their sister-wife jokes when it became clear that Mason and I were more alike. We loved reading and writing, while Sierra was more interested in dancing and science. Mason and I had both been on our high school volleyball teams and had traveled to away games together. As we got older and our interests grew more developed and aligned, it became our mothers' personal mission to get me and Mason to fall in love.

The problem was, it sort of succeeded on my end. I had a mad crush on him. He always treated me like his kid sister, even though we were the same age. He wouldn't let any of his friends date me or Sierra, a fact we didn't discover until years later.

It was humiliating to have such a massive unrequited crush. It made me sad and desperate, mostly to get his attention. I started competing with him—to become the editor in chief of the newspaper, the head of the yearbook staff—because I knew he wanted those positions. To get the best grade in our AP English class. I tried putting streaks in my hair, changing my clothes. I so wanted him to see me in a different light.

None of it worked. If anything, it seemed to annoy him.

There was one night, though, when it seemed like it might have worked. One desperately romantic night where I thought things were going to change. He acted like he was interested in me. But then we went back to our regular lives, and it was like I had imagined the whole thing.

But then . . . he officially asked me on a date. It was after an away game, our junior year. We got back to school and he walked me out to my car, like he always did. Then he said, "Hey, Sinclair, what do you think about you and me going to the spring formal together?"

My throat constricted so tightly I seriously thought I might pass out, my heart rampaging against my rib cage. I managed a "Yeah, that would be fun," which was so much better than what I wanted to do, which was run around the parking lot in triumph, both hands aloft, shouting that I was the champion and Mason Beckett was going to be my boyfriend.

It had been an honest miracle that I'd been able to drive home, because I was shaking so hard that I didn't think I'd be able to make it back safely.

The night of the dance arrived quickly. Sierra went with a senior boy. I'd focused most of my attention on her that evening. She hated dressing up, while I'd always enjoyed it, and it was good to have the distraction. My parents had gone out on a date. I hadn't told them about Mason asking me, and I had to assume he'd done the same, or else our parents would have been in the living room trying to take a thousand pictures of us together.

Sierra and her date left, and I waited and waited.

And waited.

He never showed. He never called, no text, nothing. He completely ghosted me.

I was beyond devastated.

And our playful rivalry? It wasn't playful any longer. I wanted to beat him at everything that I could. He thought he could break my heart and still be my friend? It wasn't going to happen. I was named editor of the paper, but he got head of the yearbook.

He never explained, never apologized. It was like it had never happened, him asking me to the dance and then not showing up. And I didn't have the strength to confront him. I was so riddled with my own insecurities and issues that asking him why he had ditched me was beyond my capabilities.

Our friendship was over.

My twin was outraged on my behalf, and she uncharacteristically begged me to let her yell at him, but I didn't want to make it a bigger deal. It was already humiliating enough.

I definitely didn't want our mothers to find out. I wanted it to just go away.

It didn't stop me from having feelings for him, though. As much as I wanted those to go away, too, they didn't.

And it was probably the fevered imaginings of a heartbroken teenage girl, but I would have sworn that I caught him, more than once, looking at me with regret and something else, like maybe he shared some of those feelings.

I hadn't given him a chance to explain, though. I blocked him on my phone, my email, all of my online accounts. I didn't want to speak to him at all.

There were some texts from a number I didn't recognize and a couple of generic emails that I suspected were from him, but I couldn't prove it. They just said things like "Hey, how are you?" As if I didn't know he'd sent them, like I was just going to forgive and forget. I could never really figure out why he'd sent them. Had he thought we were just going to move on and pretend that things were okay between us?

But there was no way he'd wanted to resolve things, given what he'd done next.

The lies he'd told, the rumors he'd personally spread.

It was unforgivable, and I wasn't ever going to get over it.

That didn't really match up with the whole Zen/good-vibes thing I was going for with my practice, but that was reality. My twin was the one who let things go easily and forgave just as quickly.

Which was part of the reason why pasta-tossing Joseph had lasted so long.

Me? I was petty. I could fully admit to it, being able to hold a grudge. Well, not a grudge so much as the ability to perfectly retain all of the necessary memories/facts to prepare me for my next encounter with Mason Beckett.

Not that those memories or facts had done me much good. I'd sat there like a rage-filled monster, unable to speak, and could only just growl at him menacingly.

No wonder he'd smiled at me. He'd probably recognized a kindred spirit.

I really did want to be the bigger person. I was just failing miserably at it.

To soothe my wounded psyche and ignore my current shortcomings, I mentally ran through my schedule. I was all booked up this morning. I had a session with Heather and then an intake for a new client, followed by an online session and then lunch.

It only took a few minutes to drive to our small downtown area. It was mostly filled with shops for tourists, and my office was just off the main street in a very old building.

I climbed up to the second floor and let myself in. I had just put my things down when I heard the reception-area door open and then voices.

As in, more than one.

And there in my waiting room?

Mason Beckett. Again.

This was starting to feel like some kind of cosmic prank. I was about to snarl at him and ask what he thought he was doing when I realized a beat later that his mother was also in the waiting room, ready for her session.

"Heather!" I said, trying to smile. I was probably failing.

"Good morning!" she said, standing up and walking toward me. "I hope you don't mind, but I told Mason he could tag along and observe. Is that okay with you?"

No, it most definitely was not okay with me, but what was I supposed to say? *No, take your evil offspring and go?*

"Sure. Come on in."

Heather chattered away, like she normally did. My mom was more of an introvert, and I'd always assumed that one of the reasons her life-long friendship with Heather worked so well was that Heather paved over any possible awkward silences with constant conversation.

Sariah Wilson

She lay down on the couch while I sat in my chair. I tried to listen to her story, but instead I was hyperaware of Mason observing my office and then heading over to sit in the corner, where he could keep an eye on me.

He probably thought I was scamming his mother and was here to verify his suspicion.

This was going to result in another onslaught of negative online reviews.

I took in a deep breath, telling myself to ignore him. I'd been observed in many sessions. This wasn't anything special or different.

It didn't feel that way, though.

I needed Mason gone.

Heather was in the midst of telling me about her neighbor's carport collapsing on top of the new SUV they'd just bought when I gently interrupted her and asked if she was ready to begin.

"Yes! Oh, and I want you to know that I've been listening to that recording you gave me. I've noticed a big difference with my insomnia. I am definitely falling asleep faster and staying asleep. I should have come to you a long time ago!"

Mason shifted loudly in his chair, as if he wanted to say something, but he didn't.

I started the induction sequence and we moved through it quickly, heading to the deepener and into the place where Heather felt safe and relaxed.

It was always easy to tell when she'd entered the trance state, as the chipper, chatty Heather became silent, her answers to my questions monosyllabic.

Not able to help myself, I glanced at Mason. He had his arms crossed and was staring daggers at me.

I turned my attention back to his mom. I wasn't here to hate on stupid Mason; I was here to help Heather with her problem. While I talked about overcoming anxious thoughts and the importance of sleeping a

24

full eight hours and how her body needed that, I heard Mason making little noises of disbelief in the corner.

Red bursts of anger fizzled through my blood. Shaking my head slightly, I tuned him out completely and focused on his mother. We did the guided imagery where she remembered a time when she'd slept well, and I encouraged her subconscious mind to retrain her body to get the rest that she needed.

"As soon as you get in your bed, you are able to easily let go of all your worries and concerns from your day. You will allow your body and mind to relax and to sleep well and fall asleep quickly," I told her.

Another snort from Mason.

I had to swallow back my retort.

We went through the remaining steps a tad faster than we might normally, partly because Heather had done it so often that it wasn't necessary to take my time, but mostly because I really wanted Mason out of my office. That whole situation with Timothy had already made me doubt myself and my abilities.

I didn't need Mason doing his best heckler impersonation and making everything worse.

I finished up, properly closing out the session and bringing Heather back to full awareness. I could always tell the moment it happened because her eyes popped open and she immediately began talking about her neighbor, picking up right where she'd left off.

Feeling a bit rude, I had to interrupt her again. I had another client scheduled, and I needed Mason to go so that I didn't say something unforgivable to him in front of his sweet mother. "I'm sorry, but I wanted to tell you that I think our next session should be our last one," I said. "It sounds like everything is working the way it's supposed to."

I hoped Mason wouldn't show up for that one, too. I wasn't strong enough to refrain from throwing things at his head if he continued to silently mock me.

His mother beamed at me. "You have already helped me so much. That's why Mason wanted to come with me today. He didn't believe it."

I bet he didn't.

"It was great to see you," I said, pointing my comment solely at Heather. "I'll see you again next week!"

She said goodbye and stood up. Then, oddly enough, she put a hand on my shoulder and said, "Be nice, please. And say yes. For my sake."

Before I could ask what she meant by that, she left my office.

But Mason stayed put.

For a moment I couldn't speak. He was looking at me so intensely— with anger? Desire? Something else entirely?—that I felt . . . trapped. Like his gaze was holding me in place.

It was as if he were touching me, and all he was doing was looking at me. I had actual goose bumps.

Despite my resolutions to be the bigger person, I lashed out.

"What are you doing?" I asked him, rubbing my hands along my exposed arms, willing the goose bumps to go away. "You can go now. Feel free to show yourself out. I have another appointment."

He nodded. "Yes, you do. And I'm your ten o'clock."

CHAPTER FOUR

This was why Heather had asked me to be nice and say yes. They both knew they were going to spring this on me, and I was totally unprepared for it.

"That's not . . . you can't . . . I won't . . ." I sputtered, unable to form complete sentences. There was absolutely zero chance I was going to hypnotize Mason Beckett.

My plan was to steer clear of him entirely. Not to be forced to spend another minute in his lying-dirtbag presence.

"Always so articulate," Mason mused, that insufferable smirk on his face. "I saw that video about you on social media. The one where you cured that girl's anxiety." He didn't make air quotes with his fingers when he said *cured*, but I could hear them in his tone.

"And so you tagged along today to what, try and catch me in the act of gaslighting your mom? You heard her. I'm helping. Sorry to disappoint. And, again, please feel free to go."

He stayed put.

"My mom has dealt with insomnia for a long time. Ever since her mom died. She's had a lot of sleepless nights. I know it's affected her day-to-day life."

His voice had altered, softened. It put my guard up, making me completely suspicious. He only talked to me like that when he wanted something. "And you're right. She does seem to think that you've helped her."

Seemed to think? "It's not in her head. There are so many medical studies that prove the efficacy of hypnosis. It is especially helpful with insomnia, which is backed by scientific research. You can look it up yourself if you want. I'm not a witch doctor or a quack or whatever other insult you've got geared up. I take what I do seriously. I know it works."

He held up both hands, like he was surrendering. To placate me, but I wasn't in the mood to be placated.

"So let me see for myself."

"I don't really mix business with revulsion."

At that, he got up and walked over to the couch, close to where I was seated. The setup was intended for my clients to lie down and relax, with me close to their heads so that they could hear me more easily.

But Mason sat on the couch directly across from me so that our knees were almost touching. This shouldn't have made me feel woozy. It should have fed into my anger, but I was leaning hard into the total disorientation.

I held my breath as he studied me. I really had forgotten how handsome he was. How much more handsome he'd become as a man than he'd been as a teenage boy.

"Show me." He said the words so softly, and his invitation made my heart sputter. "Let me see what it is you do."

"No thanks," I managed after swallowing hard. "That's not how this works. I don't have to prove myself to you."

His eyes were just as I remembered them, a light hazel color, but so intense that they overwhelmed me.

He'd always been able to make me feel like I was a bit hypnotized, and it was happening again now.

"Please," he said in a pleading tone that undermined all of my good intentions.

I had to get control of my rebellious hormones. "I don't think it's a good idea for you to be my client," I said with as much finality as I could muster.

"Because I stood you up for a dance seven years ago?"

"That's not . . ." Did he really think that was the reason I was mad?

"It's why you hate me, right?"

I let out a scoff. "You know full well what you did."

"I know I didn't come over that night."

Now I was mad all over again. "It's cute that you think I've been angry with you for this long over you ghosting me."

"You think I'm cute?" he interjected.

"That's not what I . . . you're totally misunderstanding . . ." I pulled in a deep breath. "Despite your god complex, you didn't invent the concept of being a selfish jerk. I haven't been losing sleep over not getting the great privilege of going to a dance with you. I'm sure I'm not the first girl you stood up."

"You were. Still are."

Why was he saying that? Was *you're the only woman I've ever stood up* supposed to be romantic or something? "Are you trying to make me feel special right now?"

"No. I wanted to explain." He flexed his hands, and for one heart-stopping second, I thought he was going to reach for my hand, but he didn't.

I tried to tell myself that I was relieved, but I could taste the disappointment at the back of my throat.

"Explain," I said, curling my fingers tightly in my lap so that they wouldn't get any funny ideas. Mason was the worst. My brain completely understood that fact, but my body was fully out of control right now.

He let out a sigh and reached up to rub the back of his neck. It was a gesture so familiar that it made my heart wince. He only did that when he was stressed or upset.

Maybe it had been a calculated move, but it had the intended effect. Part of my defenses came crumbling down, and I hated that it happened.

"I was an idiot mess of hormones?" he offered with a wry smile that had the same effect on me as the neck rubbing. "I really wanted to take you to that dance. I was about to tell my mom that I had asked you when she started in on one of her tangents about how we were going to end up together and get married, and I'll admit, it freaked me out. My parents were in the midst of their divorce and I had a pretty negative view on relationships at that point. I wanted one dance to have fun with you, but our moms were planning our entire future together. I realized that if they knew that I'd asked you, I'd never hear the end of it. And I wasn't ready to be in a serious relationship. I was a coward that night. I should have called you and told you, but instead I ran and hid."

"Why didn't you just tell me?" Since my mother was equally bad, I would have completely understood.

"My only excuse is that I was a seventeen-year-old boy. As a species, we're not exactly known for our ability to communicate. I regret it, though. I'm really sorry. If I had known how much it would hurt you, that it would ruin our friendship, I never would have done it."

How was it possible to be touched by his apology and still hate him this much? "That wasn't what ruined our friendship."

"Then what did?"

I blinked slowly. Was he really going to make me say it? Make me relive it? While pretending he had no idea what I was talking about? I wasn't interested in playing this game. I didn't owe him an explanation. I wasn't going to embarrass myself any further.

"I'm not going to be a client. Let me have just one session," he said, as if he realized I wasn't going to say anything else. "And then I'll go, and you'll never see me again."

Why was he pushing this so hard? I had a mixture of raging emotions—I still wanted him to leave, and I was latching on to his offer as a way to make him stay away from me permanently.

Which would be excellent, considering how many swirling, tingling, inexplicable things he was making me feel.

There was another part of me that wanted to prove myself. To show him that I was professional and good at my job. The competitiveness I'd felt toward him hadn't disappeared, apparently. "I don't think—"

He must have sensed my hesitation, because he moved in for the kill. "The Savannah Sinclair I knew never backed down from a challenge in her life." He seemed to move closer, leaning forward with his hands folded together between his legs. His knee accidentally brushed against mine, his fingers so close that he could touch me, and it took all of my willpower not to wildly rear back. I wouldn't let him see how much he could still affect me.

I knew what he was doing.

I knew it, and yet it was still working. The backs of my knees were sweating. As if wanting him were some teenage muscle memory that I couldn't shake.

Like I was becoming that girl again, head over heels for him, ready to do anything he asked.

The best thing was for him to go. I opened my mouth to say as much, but no words came out.

"I read an interview where you said everyone is hypnotizable," he said.

Some frantic part of my brain loudly worried, *Why is Mason reading interviews I've done?* But the rest of me was focused on the slightly flattered feeling that he had looked me up. That he wanted to know about me, even though he had to realize how much I despised him.

31

"I said 'almost everyone.' Some people can't do it," I found myself saying, against my will. Heaven help me, but I wanted to impress him. So many people looked down on what I was doing now, as if it were less than. Especially when comparing me to Sierra. We both helped people, but in different ways. But she was the noble one, the trained medical professional, and I was the woo-woo sister. "Most people move in and out of a trance state all day without realizing it."

"Really?" He looked skeptical.

"If you've ever zoned out while driving, when you're daydreaming, or been so caught up in a book or movie you blocked everything else out, that's a hypnotic state."

Mason looked slightly surprised. "So if that's happened, then odds are you can be hypnotized."

I nodded.

He smiled at me then, a real smile that made the edges of his eyelids crinkle. "Then I'm a great candidate. Let's hypnotize me. Show me what you've got, Sinclair."

Mason hadn't called me by just my last name since high school. Again, I was melting and felt powerless to resist. Where was that steel backbone of mine? "There isn't enough time. When I have a new client, I do an introductory session where we talk about how hypnosis works and what the client wants to change, and then we set up a hypnosis session for later."

"If you check your schedule, I'm your eleven o'clock appointment, too. We have plenty of time."

In disbelief, I picked up my phone and pulled up the app with my schedule on it. A Felix Morrison had signed up for the ten o'clock session, and Johnny Diamond at eleven o'clock. I felt really stupid. Those were names of characters from the TV show that Mason and I used to watch together, *Late for Class*.

We used to sit too close to each other, our hands nearly touching, our shoulders occasionally brushing. I used to read volumes into our interactions, even though Mason hadn't been writing a single word.

I looked up at him, that intense flame still burning in his eyes. This had to stop. I couldn't revert back to my teenage self, and I most definitely could not get caught up in Mason's charm.

It sounded like the best idea was to do what he asked. I knew how persistent he could be when he wanted something.

Shame he never wanted me, some part of me sighed, and I dismissed it.

It was easier to go along with it and give him what he asked for. Then he could go away and I would no longer have to think about him, or try to figure out what cologne he was wearing because it smelled really, really good, or contemplate the five-o'clock shadow that lined his sharp jaw, how it was the same caramel-and-light-brown color as his hair but had flecks of red thrown in, and wonder what it would be like if he kissed me, how that scruff would rub against my skin, and I literally gasped, shocking myself out of that daydream.

It didn't help things that Mason was staring at me like he knew exactly what I'd been imagining.

His heated gaze dropped down to my lips, and they burned in response.

"Why?" The word was strangled, and I had to clear my throat. "Tell me why, and I'll do it."

At that, he leaned back slightly, breaking the physical spell he was weaving between us. "Let's just say that I'm writing an article about hypnotists and thought you'd be a good place to start."

My cheeks flushed slightly. Of course. Of course this was about his job and not about . . . whatever might have existed between us.

Nothing ever existed between us, I reminded my overheated lady bits. Yes, he might have wanted to take me to that dance, but he hadn't. And then he'd spread a rumor so vicious and so mean that, to this day, people in our hometown still side-eyed me.

I was nothing but a means to an end for him.

Then I thought of his sweet mother, who had been so kind to me my entire life. She'd asked me to do it. And I could do this for her sake.

He wanted me to do a session for some story? Fine. He wasn't the first journalist I'd worked with.

Hypnotizing him would be a small price to pay if it meant that he'd leave me alone, and if it would make his mom happy.

Because having him this close again was reminding me of things I did not want to remember.

As well as things I shouldn't be wanting.

"I'll do it," I said, wondering if I was going to regret this.

I should have known that I would.

CHAPTER FIVE

"Good," he said with a grin that made me immediately regret my decision. "Do you want me to lie down?"

Why did that sound suggestive? I wanted to fan my face but refrained. The air conditioner was working, right?

"No, first I need to explain the process to you."

I launched into my introductory session monologue. I told him about the different stages of consciousness, said that this wasn't a miracle fix-it cure-all, that he would remain in control.

He asked, "Does this mean you're not going to get out some old-timey watch, swing it back and forth in front of me, and then make me quack like a duck?"

"Only if you want me to, and it'll cost you extra."

"Was that a joke, Sinclair?"

It had been. One I hadn't intended to make. I was not going to slide back into our old friendship like nothing had passed between us. Maybe he'd had an understandable explanation for ghosting me, but I wasn't about to allow him to deviously charm his way back into my good graces.

Slipping back into professional mode, I said, "Clinical hypnosis is not stage hypnosis. It isn't mind control. You won't do anything against your belief system. Your critical mind will stop you from doing anything you're not comfortable with." If I were a gambling woman, I would have bet that his critical mind would not only keep him safe but also keep him from being able to be hypnotized at all.

"Okay." He nodded. "Are you going to make me believe a bunch of things that aren't true?"

Was he not listening? "No. I won't be able to do that. I'm not going to be able to deceive you, manipulate you, or exploit your vulnerabilities."

He raised his eyebrows playfully. "I bet you're disappointed by that, given that I'm the one here."

Little bit, if I was being completely honest.

"Although I guess it's a good thing you can't make me give you my PIN number. Because if you actually had that ability, my guess is you'd probably be living on some tropical island by now."

Now he was the one teasing me, and it was unsettling. No wonder he'd called me out on it.

The awkwardness I was feeling had me gesturing toward the candy bowl I kept out on the coffee table. "Do you, um, want some M&M's?"

That smile of his was back. "There's literally a fairy tale warning people about eating candy found in suspicious locations."

So now I was a child-eating witch? It was hard to muster up too much indignation because I'd thought worse about him. Heck, I'd said worse about him.

And somehow his remark made me feel more like myself again.

Ignoring his jab, I went back to the task at hand. I explained that he wasn't going to black out, that he wouldn't have amnesia and forget everything. He would be aware and feel like he was conscious, even though he was hypnotized, and that I'd maintain his confidentiality.

I had said this speech so many times that it was easy to go through the whole spiel without hesitating, without tripping over my words. Because internally? That's what was happening. My brain was all over the place, trying to make sense of what was going on, that I was voluntarily spending time with Mason Beckett.

Who was comfortable enough with me that he was making jokes.

"The most important thing for you to know is that you'll be in control of the session and I'm just here to help guide you. All hypnosis is basically self-hypnosis, and I'm here to facilitate that."

He raised an eyebrow at me, and I caught a whiff of his disbelief. "You're going to help me hypnotize myself?"

"Your subconscious mind isn't something you can turn off and on with a switch. It's always there, listening and responding. Hypnosis is shifting into another state of consciousness where you'll be focusing your attention and reducing your peripheral awareness so that you can better concentrate."

"I don't know that I'll be able to shut off my peripheral awareness while you're in the room."

I felt my face heat up and wondered if I was turning red. I didn't know how to take that statement or how to react.

It had been so easy before. I hated Mason Beckett, and it was all very black and white. I never could have predicted that I'd be responding physically like this to him.

Then whatever slightly kinder thoughts I'd been harboring quickly went out the window when he shook his head and said, "I can't believe you think this stuff actually works. I feel like I should be congratulating you on your cult and telling you I look forward to the eight-episode documentary on Netflix."

"I know it works," I said indignantly, trying to keep my hostility in check. "I've seen it and personally experienced it. Even the American Psychiatric Association says it is a 'powerful, effective therapeutic technique.'"

He grinned. "I'd bet that's not the first time you've had to say that."

It was not, but I wasn't going to give him the satisfaction of agreeing with him. Especially not when I was so annoyed by him and his stereotypical, condescending views. "Normally I'd ask you about why you've come to see me, what your goals are and what you think is holding you back, but given that you're here to write an article, I don't think there's a point."

The kinds of things that made people get stuck were stuff like low self-esteem and low confidence, and I didn't think either one of those was an issue that he'd ever had to deal with.

"No, go ahead and give me the full experience. What do people typically come to see you for?"

"There's a lot of different reasons. I help people with everything from insomnia, like your mom, to stress and anxiety, addiction, phobias, pain control, panic attacks, PTSD, behavioral control issues. Stuff like that."

He looked like he was about to make a snarky comment but managed to refrain. Instead, he asked, "What would you treat me for?"

Mason's question felt very strange, like it was a test. The truth was, I didn't know him now, as the person he'd become. It was weird to be with someone who felt so familiar but strange at the same time. "I don't know. Are you still irrationally terrified of alligators?"

He straightened up at that, squaring his shoulders. "That's a normal and sensible thing to be afraid of. Alligators are cretaceous leftovers, and from an evolutionary standpoint, it is entirely rational of me to want to avoid tiny dinosaurs."

"Growing up in Florida probably really helped with that," I said, pressing my lips together so that I wouldn't laugh. I ducked my face so that he wouldn't see my smile.

But he did. "Sinclair! Are you almost smiling? Should I run a stroke protocol?"

Ignoring his teasing, I said, "Okay, so no to overcoming a phobia. What about relationship problems?"

Why was that question hard to get out? I didn't care who he dated.

"I do just fine in that department," he said with a confidence that was definitely on this side of arrogance.

"Really? I heard you were almost engaged until she dumped you."

He frowned. "I wasn't almost engaged. And I broke up with her because she had issues."

"I'm assuming one of her issues was that she couldn't stand you. Which I understand, by the way."

"Ouch. Incoming." He said it playfully, but there was something in his tone that made me wonder whether or not I'd actually hurt him. "You heard, huh? Have you been keeping tabs on me?"

The truth was that when I'd heard he was nearly engaged, it was like someone had gutted me. Which made zero sense. I didn't want him to know how close to home his words hit and just shook my head.

He added, "You always did use to watch me. Even when you were angry at me."

Him exposing that truth to the light made me want to scurry away and hide. The only way out of this was to pretend like his words didn't affect me. "Studying an opponent is not 'watching them.'"

He leaned forward again, and it took everything I had not to scoot back six feet. I was not going to show him any weakness that he could exploit. "What did you like watching me do?"

It sounded like an innocent question, but the way he asked it had images surging through my head like a memory tsunami. Even when I'd loathed him the most, I hadn't been able to keep my eyes off him. The way his body moved when he played a game of volleyball, the sound of his voice as he drove home a point during a debate, finding him in the library, where he'd be reading a book, lounging in a chair, taking up all the space around him.

I'd even been disgustingly fascinated by watching him eat. The appetite he had, the way he seemed to enjoy everything put in front of him. How he was with his friends, the times he would laugh so hard that his entire body shook.

Desperately aching over the fact that I was the one who used to make him laugh that way and missing it more than anything.

There was something seriously wrong with me.

"I've been rethinking all of my life choices," he announced, interrupting my thoughts. "Reevaluating what led me here."

"Sitting in front of your worst enemy, asking her to hypnotize you?"

Another wry smile. "That's definitely on the list."

His statement made me think of yesterday, and how in the short time I'd become reacquainted with him, all of his choices seemed to be negative. "Maybe what you need is to do things differently. Instead of always saying no to people, try saying yes. That's what I could focus on in our session."

"Turning me into a yes-man? Sure. Let's do that." There was no conviction behind his words, and I knew that his attitude was most likely going to affect this outcome.

"You doubting the entire process and what we're going to work on will ensure that it will fail, just so you know. When you talked about whether or not people could be hypnotized, there is a small percentage who can't be, and it's mostly due to doubt. Something like five to twenty percent of people are highly suggestible and easily hypnotized, and everybody else fills in the rest of the curve."

"So you think it won't work on me?"

"The main focus of hypnotism is to get you to shift your perspective, and it comes down to two things. Consent and belief."

He blinked quickly at me. "So I have to believe in you like you're Santa Claus?"

Not able to help myself, I rolled my eyes. He really was bringing out my worst teenage self. "Believe in the process, not me. Besides, I'm not going to be bringing you any presents."

He gave me a sly smile. "But you are concerned with whether or not I've been naughty or nice."

If I kept rolling my eyes like this, they were going to eject from my skull. "I think we both know which list you belong on."

"Yes. One hundred percent nice," he announced.

I couldn't help myself. I laughed. Not a joyful, you're-so-funny laugh but one of pure shock that he'd said something so profoundly untrue.

"Now you're the one who doesn't seem to believe me," he said.

"You're right. I do not believe that lie you just told."

He smiled at me. "Maybe a bit naughty. But I've found that most women tend to enjoy that."

I'd enjoy it, that annoying part of me offered, and I had to again remind myself that we hated him. "I can do hypnosis for that, too. To make you less of a womanizer."

"Ah, so you're going to save me from myself. I get why you do this. You always did like rescuing people."

Now it was my turn to frown. "That's not true."

"It is. You were the one who found the lonely kids at school and sat with them at lunch and invited them to hang out with us. Sierra was the same way. You were always tutoring people and spending extra time practicing with your teammates."

That he thought nice things about me was, again, disconcerting and unsettling.

Almost like he was trying to throw me off balance. Was he attempting to get me to mess up so that he could write an article proving that I was a fake? Distract me so that I'd confess this was all made up?

Then, as if he were trying to prove my suspicion, he said, "As for the other part of what I need for this to work, I may not be able to give you my belief, but you'll always have my full consent. For anything you'd like."

That was definitely flirting, and it wasn't allowed. Words jumped to the tip of my tongue, and I wanted to tell him that I'd refused to work with Timothy and that he'd repeatedly hit on me after I rejected him and how unethical it all was, but I knew that Mason would find a way to turn it back around on me. If he was going to write an article, there was no way I was going to give him even a hint about the whole censure situation.

It would be like pouring chum into shark-infested waters.

This was different. This was a one-and-done situation. Mason wasn't going to be a client and wouldn't be back in my office ever again.

And this flirting wasn't real. He was only attempting to throw me off my game. I had to remember that.

But he was making it hard to keep my wits about me. I started to speak, but he was staring at me.

Not that that was new—he'd been staring at me a lot lately—but this was different. It was more . . . assessing. Like he had a question and was searching my face for an answer.

I tried to keep my breathing even and steady, but it was hard to do. His eyes moved slowly, as he leisurely took all of me in. My pulse was racing, like the time I accidentally had two energy drinks in a row and thought my heart was going to explode.

It made me feel vulnerable, utterly exposed to him. As if he could see through me, into my soul, and there was nothing I could do to stop him.

No barrier I constructed, no wall I erected, would be strong enough to keep him out.

Then his expression shifted and he appeared satisfied, like he'd found what he'd been searching for, and his face broke into an annoyingly glorious smile.

I didn't know what to make of that, so I cleared my throat and began the session. "Let's get started. Your head needs to be supported. You're free to lean back or lie down."

It was amazing how normal my voice sounded, because I was shaking from that thorough visual examination he'd just given me.

Another slight smile from him and then he lay down on the couch. He put his right arm behind his head and his left hand against his chest. Another gesture so familiar to me that it was painful to see. That was how he always lay down. And I'd been foolish enough once to imagine myself curling up beside him, that left arm wrapped around me, holding me close.

The thought made me ache all over again, which strengthened my resolve to stay mad.

I couldn't let him affect me this way. But I was also finding it a bit impossible to speak. I didn't trust myself.

"This feels a little like the calm before the storm," he announced, shattering the silence.

"Says the storm generator," I retorted, once again forgetting to stay professional and not let him bug me. If nothing else, at least his remark loosened my tongue and got me talking again.

He closed his eyes, giving me the chance to study him for a moment. This was truly pathetic, but I decided I'd take one last look and then get this out of my system. He really was handsome, and time had been overly kind to him. The angles of his face seemed slightly sharper, the muscles in his biceps a bit larger, his shoulders wider and stronger than I remembered.

And he was so tall he barely fit on my couch, his feet dangling over the edge.

As a tall woman, I'd always appreciated that about him.

"By the way," he said, opening one eye, "in case you do wipe my memory in order to steal my PIN number and I forget to tell you later, you look really pretty today."

All of the oxygen left the room.

CHAPTER SIX

He closed both of his eyes after his shocking announcement.

My first totally irrational thought was that Mason had somehow read my mind and knew that I'd been appreciating his finer physical qualities.

Too bad they're attached to a lying dirtbag, I said internally, but nothing inside me believed that. All of my cells were too busy responding to all of his gorgeousness.

I thought of Camila and her warning. How I had to avoid even the appearance of wrongdoing, and here was Mason complimenting me before a session. Technically it was fine, but if the wrong person overheard him, I might be deemed unprofessional. Despite what his mom had asked of me, my instincts were urging me to kick him out. Now.

The problem was I didn't want to make him leave. Even if I suspected him of trying to trick me, of possibly using me, of not being sincere, without even counting what he'd done to me years ago—

None of it seemed to matter.

I wanted him to stay.

And I had no idea how or when my perspective had shifted.

Mason Beckett cannot read my mind, I whispered to myself as I steeled my nerves and willed myself to begin.

The M&M's sitting on my coffee table were calling to me, and I wanted nothing more than to grab a handful and pop that hard candy goodness into my mouth, letting the sugar rush soothe me. I also had an emergency sugar stash in my desk drawer, but Mason would a hundred percent notice and would most likely have something annoyingly true to say about it.

"You saw me do this with your mom, but the first step is to have you relax. So I want you to take three slow deep breaths, and each time as you exhale, start to feel yourself relaxing fully."

I was using my hypnosis voice—gentle, calm, purpose driven.

"Clear your mind. Let go of any worries or stresses you're carrying around right now. First, I want you to be aware of your arms. Flex, feeling them, and then relax. Let them get more and more comfortable. They feel limp and loose. As you breathe out, you are more relaxed. Slow your breathing and focus on that sensation of relaxation."

I watched as he tensed his arms and then let them go.

"Good," I said. "Focus on your shoulders. Feel any tension and then let it go, sinking into the couch, breathing out anything that would weigh you down."

This time he didn't respond as well. If anything, he looked more tense, holding himself rigidly in place.

"You're supposed to be relaxing." I shouldn't have scolded him, but it almost felt deliberate. Like he was trying to provoke me. That was probably another irrational thought, but since my day was full of irrational and illogical things, why not one more?

He opened his eyes to peer up at me. "I'm sorry, but it's hard to relax when I have to worry about whether or not you're going to stab me while my eyes are closed."

I tried not to sigh. "I promise to not stab you while you're in my office."

"And after?"

"The offer only extends as far as these four walls."

"Noted. So . . . relaxing. What are you going to do to help me fully relax?" He said it softly, with a look in his eyes that made my mouth go completely dry.

How did he manage to make such an innocent question sound suggestive? My imagination was running wild, and I didn't know what was wrong with me.

It had been a long time since I'd actively loathed someone. Was it supposed to feel so much like lust?

"I'm already doing it," I said through clamped teeth. My knee sweats were back. "Like I said, this is called progressive relaxation."

"So we're going to do my entire body?"

Again, unbidden images. I hadn't been to church in years, but what from I remembered, lust was a sin, and if that was correct, I needed to stop it. Living in Florida had made me realize that I couldn't end up in hell.

"Yes, because that's how this works. Now be quiet."

A small smile and he closed his eyes again. "Whatever you say, Sinclair."

I used my hypnosis voice again and directed him to focus on feeling the tension in his chest, to concentrate on breathing slowly, and my gaze slipped over to the letter opener on my desk.

He made me nuts. I'd never, ever even considered harming another person before.

But nobody got under my skin like Mason.

I was kind of on autopilot as I tried to figure out this strange hold he had over me. I was an adult woman. It was ridiculous to be responding to a man who had hurt me so deeply just because he was objectively hot. I wasn't seventeen any longer. I didn't need to let my hyperactive ovaries be the boss of me.

"Good," I told him automatically. "Very good." I always assured my clients as we went through this exercise.

He crossed his arms across his chest, and his entire body tensed up. His eyes flew open, and that look, the one that felt so much like desire, was back. There was a heavy, charged moment that passed between us until he smiled and said, "I wish I'd known that all I had to do to get you to talk nicely to me was do a session of hypnosis with you."

Although I knew he didn't mean it that way, it made me feel like he was taking advantage of me, and I was back to wanting to maim him. I pressed my lips together. "This isn't going to work unless you listen and stop talking."

Now he looked smug, and that impulse to do something to wipe that smirk off his face was a bit overwhelming, but I refrained, even though my letter opener was right there, because I had promised I wouldn't stab him.

He let his eyelids drift shut and then said, "You're eyeing your letter opener, aren't you?"

"I'm not!" I protested too quickly.

That made his smile bigger.

I hated this feeling. Like he knew me better than anybody and could see right through me.

I couldn't stab him because Sierra would probably be the one who would have to clean his wound when I took him to the emergency room, and she'd be mad. Not to mention the paperwork and the fact that I absolutely would lose my certification.

It wasn't worth it.

Instead, I returned to getting him to relax, having him concentrate on one body part at a time. It turned out to be a very bad idea, as it allowed me to watch him flex repeatedly and wonder what he did to work out these days. He most likely didn't play volleyball any longer. The gym? Did he run?

Such a terrible path to go down.

I preferred doing face-to-face sessions with clients as opposed to online ones, but right now I could have used a few miles and some computer screens between us.

Because I didn't understand my warring impulses. How was it possible to want all of his blood to be outside his body but also want to climb on top of him and kiss those firm lips of his?

The worst part was that I couldn't look away from him because I had to make sure the relaxation technique was working.

Which it finally, fortunately, did.

He relaxed completely into the couch, his arm dropping down and his body slack and loose. I started the deepener process, telling him to imagine a staircase and to count each step as he went down, starting with ten until he reached one, reminding him to relax his body, to concentrate on my voice, to let go.

Shifting into this phase somehow made it easier to get myself back on track and focus. I told him to open a door at the bottom of his staircase and to imagine, just beyond the door, a place he loved, one so beautiful, peaceful, and warm that he would always feel serene, relaxed, and completely happy when he thought of it.

"I want you to take it all in. The more details you allow yourself to see and experience, the deeper we'll go into your subconscious. Can you see it?" I asked.

"Yes." His voice sounded different, slower and deeper, and it reminded me of his mother's when she would reach this stage. Like he was well and truly hypnotized.

Heather definitely fell within that small percentage of people who were highly hypnotizable, so it would make sense that her son would be suggestible, too.

But the larger part of me assumed that he was messing with me. I'd accused him yesterday of being a troll, and now he probably was actually trolling me.

"What do you see? Hear? Smell?" I asked, fully prepared for him to say something stupid.

His voice retained that low and relaxed tone. "I'm at a pond, sitting on the edge of an old, weathered dock, my legs dangling over the side. There are fireflies dancing around me, frogs croaking softly, crickets chirping. The water makes a hushing noise. A rowboat is tied up nearby, rocking back and forth. There's a bonfire in the distance, but I'm surrounded by bright twinkling stars and a sky so dark that I can't tell where the night starts and the water ends. Dark cypress trees dot the edge of the pond, Spanish moss swaying slightly in the breeze. It's warm, but there's a hint of a chill in the heavy air. I smell campfire smoke and perfume that smells like wildflowers."

My heart leapt up into my throat, choking me. I couldn't breathe. I sat there, waiting for him to open his eyes and say, "Gotcha!"

Only he didn't. He stayed in his trance state while perspiration broke out on my hairline.

He was describing one of my best memories. Both the boys' and girls' volleyball teams had traveled for an away game, but there was a hurricane warning in our hometown, so the decision was made to stop at a cheap hotel to wait it out. I remembered the look in Mason's eyes when he'd knocked at my door, telling me to come with him, that he'd found something cool he wanted to show me.

Some of the kids were standing around a firepit, a massive fire blazing. Mason led me away, taking me by the hand. It was the first time he'd ever held my hand. I remembered the rush I'd gotten from our fingers being intertwined, giddy at him finally touching me in a way that was more than just friends.

He took me to that dock, not far from the hotel. It was perfect, secluded, romantic. I hoped he'd kiss me, but he didn't. We just sat and talked, holding hands, until the sun came up.

That night made me fall even harder for him. I was so sure we were soulmates. Meant to be.

No wonder he'd made the *New York Times'* bestseller list. He had painted me a picture so vivid and perfect that I was right back there in that place with him again.

"Are you alone?" I asked, not able to help myself.

A ghost of a smile flitted across his mouth. "No. There's a beautiful girl next to me. Someone I've loved my whole life."

If I'd had a hard time breathing before, it was nothing compared to this suffocating, smothering feeling. Like I'd never be able to breathe again.

Loved. Past tense. My heart clenched.

He'd had feelings for me?

Was that why he'd spread that rumor? He'd somehow mistakenly thought I didn't feel the same way about him, so he'd lashed out at me as some kind of petty, immature vengeance?

My head was spinning, a million different emotions whipping through me so quickly I didn't have time to figure out what I was feeling. I needed to put all that aside, though, and concentrate on the session.

If for no other reason than to prove to myself that I could be professional with someone who made me feel anything but.

I talked to him about what this place would represent for him, how he could return here when he was feeling overwhelmed or stressed. That it was safe, his sanctuary, and no one else could be there unless he invited them in.

Now that we'd established a safe place for him, I asked him where he felt it in his body when he said no to things.

"My chest."

I instructed him to imagine pulling those feelings from his chest—the ones that always said no, the parts that were afraid to experience things—and wrapping them up into a ball in front of him.

"What does it look like?"

"A rolling storm," he said.

"Drop that ball into the rowboat, letting it float away on the water. You don't need those feelings. Something interferes with your ability to say yes to things. A feeling. As that rolling storm drifts away from you, can you see what that feeling is?"

He waited for a few beats and then said, "Yes. Fear."

Interesting. I never would have pegged Mason as a fearful person. Mostly because he had so much unearned overconfidence that it hadn't ever occurred to me. "What are you afraid of?"

"Different things. I'm afraid of being used. My last girlfriend didn't care about me and used me."

This . . . felt like information I shouldn't have. She'd used him? How? Why? It didn't really matter in the current situation, but I wanted to know more, and I wasn't sure where that impulse came from.

"What do you need to soothe that rolling storm? To conquer that fear?" I asked, edging away from my nosiness about his love life.

He didn't answer for so long that I thought he'd fallen asleep. Then he said, "To be seen and loved for who I am."

That felt very insightful, and was the sort of thing someone might say in their fourth or fifth session with me. I again allowed myself the possibility that Mason was screwing around, but instead of saying as much, I went on with my usual dialogue, telling him things like his subconscious mind would listen intently and that he would overcome his fear and start to say yes. That it would feel good to say yes and he didn't have to worry what others thought. "You are strong enough and confident enough to do the things you want to do."

There was a split second where I thought about how honest and insightful he was being and wanted to ask him why he'd done what he had to me. Where things had gone wrong and why. Get him to explain when he would be truthful with me.

But that definitely would not be okay. This session was about him and his needs, not mine. Plus, his answer wouldn't really matter or change things. What was done was done, and there was no going back.

I coughed slightly and then said, "Say yes. Try new things. See how good it makes you feel." I paused and then, unable to help myself, added, "And call your mother more. She misses you."

I thought he would have some kind of snarky comment in reply, but he didn't say anything.

"Mason?"

No answer.

He had either fallen asleep or gone into a deeper state, something called profound, or hypnotic, somnambulism. If it was the first one, it wasn't surprising that he'd come in here and pass out, but if it was the second, then that meant he'd be even more receptive to what I was telling him.

I'd never had a client go that deep before. But from what I'd been taught, I knew it was an opportunity to do more guided suggestions and positive reinforcement because he would be so much more receptive. I told him to remember times when he felt brave by saying yes, when he took risks and how powerful that would feel.

"It will be easier to say yes because you're opening yourself up to new things and new possibilities. You will do things that scare you because you're no longer going to allow fear to run your life."

I gave him a few more helpful statements in anticipation of winding down and moving on to a proper awakening so that I could send Mason Beckett on his merry way.

But before I could begin the final stage, the building's fire alarm wailed loudly, the shrieking sound piercing the air. I jumped out of my seat, my heart slamming wildly against my chest. I covered both of my ears and looked down.

Mason wasn't moving.

CHAPTER SEVEN

Well, at least this proved he wasn't faking it. He lay there like Sleeping Beauty, completely still and apparently unaware of the noisy commotion around him.

The fire alarm had never gone off in all the time I'd been renting this office space, and I wasn't sure what that meant. Real or not? I wasn't about to stick around and try to figure out whether it was a false alarm.

I needed to do a proper closure with Mason, but there was no time. And I couldn't just leave him, because it would be bad if I let Mason get burned up.

Even lying backstabbers deserved better than that.

I stood and began to shake his shoulders, ignoring how big they felt under my hands. "Mason, you have to wake up. Mason."

Still nothing. Since I'd never had a client enter that somnambulism state before, I didn't know the right thing to do here. I knew eventually he would just wake up on his own, but we didn't have time.

So I shook him harder. Maybe I'd get to slap him in order to wake him up. That idea cheered me up a bit. But then I thought I smelled smoke, and I wasn't entirely sure if it was from a potential fire here at the building or if I was still thinking of that dock memory that he'd conjured up.

"Mason! We have to go! There might be a fire!"

When I said the word *fire*, his eyes opened quickly. He blinked at me a few times and seemed really disoriented. Another hypnosis patient might have come out of the session just fine without the awakening, but if Mason was as suggestible as he seemed and had gone as deep as I thought, this could be bad.

I needed to close out the session. But later.

"What's going on?" He almost sounded drunk, his voice thick with confusion.

Tugging at his arm I said, "Let's go. You have to get up. The fire alarm's going off." Now I was starting to feel a teensy bit panicked. If there was an actual fire, I had no idea where it was at or how bad things might be. We just had to get out of the building.

He was still groggy but managed to get to his feet. He leaned heavily against me as we walked toward the exit, and I cursed the fact that I was on the second floor. We had a rickety old elevator, but I wasn't willing to chance it. Fortunately, the stairwell was clear and safe, and I helped him down each step.

There was a burning sensation where his side pressed against mine, and I didn't know if it was from the fear that we might potentially be trapped in a fiery inferno of death, or if it was from being this close to him, touching him again. I swore under my breath. He really did smell amazing.

We made it to the street level and went out onto the sidewalk. Most of the other tenants were gathered there, and I heard the wailing of fire trucks headed toward us.

The building tenants weren't the only ones standing around watching. Everybody nearby poured out onto the street to watch. A lone police officer, the first person to respond, was trying to herd us away from the building to make room for the incoming fire trucks.

I looked up and didn't see any smoke, didn't smell anything. I wondered if it actually was a false alarm.

Vivian, the interior designer who had an office on the third floor, said, "This is your fault, Moe! I told you to knock it off with that hot-plate nonsense."

Moe was a nervous-looking man who worked as a pet therapist up on the fourth floor, and he was wringing his hands as he said, "I like to have tea, Vivian!"

"Then buy it from a barista like the rest of us!" she snapped back. She noticed me and Mason, and her annoyance turned into a smile. Vivian was new to town and had only been here for a few months. I had welcomed her to the building with a plate of cookies, and we'd been friendly ever since.

"Savannah! Who is this?" she asked. "A new client?"

How was I supposed to describe Mason to her? I couldn't exactly say he was nothing more than a pain in my butt. "This is Mason. And I guess you could call him a client."

My shoulders were being squeezed, and I noticed that Mason was smiling at me and sort of hugging me. I quickly stepped away from him. If Vivian noticed my unease, she didn't say anything. She just smiled at him in that way that every woman under the age of forty seemed to smile at him. She said she'd see me later and then walked over to the officer across the street to ask a question.

"Feeling more awake?" I asked Mason, ignoring the aching feeling I had. As if my body were missing his warm touch.

"I am!" He sounded downright giddy. "Why are we outside?"

"Apparently there's a fire, and the alarm went off. Our hypnosis session got interrupted. Hypnotic states range from light to really deep, and I think you went really deep."

He raised both eyebrows at me playfully. "I don't do anything half-way. What did you do in there? I feel amazing. Euphoric."

Considering I hadn't gotten to the part of the process where I would have told him that he'd wake up feeling refreshed and exhilarated, it was surprising. "I didn't see any huntsmen bringing you the heart of your enemy, so I'm not sure why you're so happy."

He grinned at me, and I felt the corners of my mouth wanting to rise in response, so I pressed my lips together tightly.

"I'm shocked you didn't leave me behind," he said, his voice teasing.

"Yeah, that makes two of us."

Then he said something that nearly knocked me off my feet.

"Come to dinner with me."

Sure I hadn't heard him correctly, I said, "What?"

He enunciated each word carefully. "Come. To. Dinner. With. Me."

"Are you asking or demanding?"

"Asking."

It was very bad that part of me wanted to say yes. I settled on, "Uh, no, thank you."

I thought it was very big of me to add the thank-you part of it. Sierra would have been proud of me.

Mason didn't seem even a little bit deterred. "You want to say yes."

His words slammed into me, making me feel off kilter. "What? I so do not."

He looked up at the top of the building. "I've known you my entire life, Sinclair. Don't lie to me. Don't lie to yourself. I think we should talk things out. Over dinner. I'll take you to Flavio's and get you enchiladas."

Mexican food had always been my weakness, and this wretch knew it.

"Let's bury the hatchet," he suggested. "And not in my back, like your look suggests."

"I'm not the backstabber," I told him. "And I'm not going to dinner with you. It would be totally unprofessional of me to go out with you. Do you even know—"

He had gotten me so worked up that I almost told him about getting censured and how dating someone who was just a temporary client might get me into real trouble. Mason wanted to write an article. I didn't need to feed him things he could hold against me.

I'd like him to hold me against him, some rebellious part of me thought, and I groaned. I did not need commentary from my clearly deranged hormones.

The fire trucks pulled up in front of the building, and firefighters rushed inside.

Heather joined us, a shopping bag in hand. "Oh my goodness, what happened?"

"There might be a fire, and Sinclair here heroically rescued me," Mason said.

"I didn't—"

But Heather still hugged me, even though I hadn't actually done anything. "Thank you so much!"

When she released me, Mason said, "I've been thinking about it, Mom. And I've changed my mind. I want to sign up to do an item for the silent auction."

"That's wonderful!"

He had locked his gaze with mine, his eyes dancing with mischief and delight that he'd caught me. Because I was in charge of the auction and would have to interact with him again to set it up.

Why was he being like this?

Heather said, "I'll let you two work out the details. Savannah, I'm supposed to meet your mom for lunch. I'll give her your love!"

I couldn't help but sigh in frustration as she walked away. Who knew what Heather would share with her? This was like watching a car wreck happen in slow motion but being powerless to stop it.

Mason had moved closer to me. "Let's work it out over chips and salsa."

So tempting. I crossed my arms. "I said no."

"I've heard saying yes feels better."

Was he making fun of me and what I'd told him? "Are you mocking me?"

"What do you mean?"

"You're saying what I told you. From our session."

He frowned slightly. "Honestly, I don't remember much past you telling me to be quiet and relax."

Now I was the one frowning. That was concerning. I'd never had a client not be able to remember a session, especially one that had just happened. I needed to do some more research. I wished Camila were reachable. I could have used her guidance.

"I'm not going to dinner with you," I told him. "Not now, not ever. Never."

"Never's a long time, Sinclair."

We were joined by some other tenants, and Bridget was pushing her way through the crowd.

"What's going on?" she asked me.

I filled her in on the necessary details, but it didn't matter, because she was too busy making googly eyes at Mason.

Who seemed to enjoy the attention.

She took a step toward him and rested her hand against his chest. "You poor thing. It must have been so scary."

If she weren't one of my closest friends, I would have added her to my List of Enemies at that moment.

"It was," he said, flirting back. "I probably need some consoling. Did you want to go out with me tonight and talk about it?"

But when he said this? He was looking directly at me.

Like it was a challenge.

Only I didn't know what game he was playing.

"I'd love to!" she said, and I could hear the triumph in her voice. "What did you have in mind?"

"I was in the mood for Mexican, but now I'm thinking something a little bit more . . . exhilarating. Maybe Murphy's Alligator Emporium and Restaurant."

My eyes widened in surprise.

"Isn't that the place where you can feed and pet the alligators?" Bridget asked, and Mason nodded.

None of this was making sense. He was doing the auction, going out with Bridget after he'd told her no, and wanted to pet an alligator?

I put a hand over my stomach. Oh no, I had done this. I was too good at my job. He was saying yes to everything, including stuff he was afraid of.

"You're going to touch tiny dinosaurs?" I asked him incredulously.

He shrugged one shoulder. "You're welcome to join us, if you want."

Bridget nodded too enthusiastically at me. "Yes, Savannah, that would be fun! We could all hang out."

I did not understand what was happening right now. If she wanted to conquer him, why was she including me in her plans?

"Tonight at seven o'clock? I'll meet you there?" he said. His questions were probably directed at Bridget, but he was looking at me when he asked them.

"I'll see you there at seven! Let me give you my number."

He handed her his phone, and she input her digits. "Text me soon," she said, waggling her fingers at him. "I have to get back to my shop."

She shot me a look that I couldn't interpret and walked back across the street with an exaggerated sway in her step.

One of the firefighters came out and announced that it had been a false alarm, that a wiring issue had triggered the sensors and an electrician had been called to fix it. We would most likely be allowed back in the building tomorrow.

Great. I was going to have to reschedule all of my afternoon appointments.

I really wished that I had enough money to hire an assistant. It would make my life so much easier.

And instead of keeping all of that information inside my head where it belonged, I was apparently muttering it out loud, because Mason said, "I could be your assistant."

"No, you couldn't."

"Do you want to go get lunch with me?"

What was wrong with him? "Lunch with one girl, dinner with another? No thanks. I'm nobody's second choice."

"You weren't my second choice." His words had so much heft that I felt a little flattened by them.

I stood there, clutching my phone, not knowing how to respond. What was he doing to me?

"So no to lunch. I guess I'm going to the gym and then I'm feeding alligators. Thanks for the session. See you later, Sinclair."

He walked away, and I sat down on the curb to try to pull myself together. I faced away from him so that I wouldn't watch him walk away. Even then, I still couldn't help but look over my shoulder at him.

And because it was me, of course that was the exact moment he turned around and caught me staring at him like the deranged weirdo I was. He waved with a cocky half smile, and I cursed the day that he was born.

He was so infuriating.

I pulled out my phone and started doing some quick research on hypnotic somnambulism. The more I read, the more alarmed I became—because I hadn't closed the session the way I should have, Mason might now be a danger to himself.

I wanted to call him, but I didn't have his number. And who could I ask to get it? Both Heather and my mom would read too much into it. Bridget might feel territorial and not give it to me.

I was going to have to crash his date.

CHAPTER EIGHT

"You did what?" Sierra asked.

I had put on one of my favorite sundresses and a pair of espadrilles. I usually dressed up when I went out, but I didn't want Mason to think I'd made any effort for him. But I couldn't bring myself to wear something grubby. This dress was older, so it was my one concession.

"I hypnotized Mason, and I think I did something to him. Because of that fire alarm, I didn't get to properly close the session and wake him up the correct way. We had to flee the building."

"So you're saying there was a premature evacuation?" She laughed at her own joke while I glared at her.

"Now I think he's really suggestible and is going to say yes to everything."

"Why is that your problem?"

"Because I broke him," I said as I went through my jewelry box, looking for a pair of gold hoops. "I temporarily wrecked his defenses. If I took a shell off a turtle, I'd have to help him because he wouldn't have his protection."

She was eating potato chips and finished chewing the one in her mouth. "If you pulled a shell off of a turtle, I'm pretty sure it would die."

"That's not the point!"

"Maybe not, but now all I can think about is shell-less turtles, and it's making me sad. Along with the serving size on this bag. Fifteen chips is one serving? I eat fifteen chips while standing in the pantry trying to decide whether or not I want chips."

It made me deliriously happy that my sister could joke about eating. That she was eating mindlessly without worrying about calories. She mocked serving sizes now, but I could remember a time when she wouldn't have let herself eat chips and would have scrutinized every calorie and bite of food that she would allow herself to eat.

My eyes felt a little misty, and I shook my head in an attempt to clear my vision. "That shell-less turtle is going to hang out with Bridget and alligators."

That got Sierra's attention. "Both are going to eat him alive."

"Exactly."

"Meh, he's a big boy. He doesn't need you to save him."

That reminded me of something Mason had said in our session. "Do you think we want to rescue people?"

"From alligators?"

"No, in general. Like we have some need to save people. I mean, you are a nurse."

She shrugged and ate another chip. "I like my job. If that means I have some savior complex, so what? People get helped either way."

Right. Mason needed help, and given that I was the one who had done this to him, it felt like my responsibility.

I couldn't tell Sierra the thing I was most worried about, because he'd said it in confidence. That he'd been used by his last girlfriend and didn't want it to happen again.

And I adored Bridget, but she would a hundred percent use that man all up and then toss him to the side. Although maybe that's what he was after, and I should just step aside and let him have his fun.

Unfortunately, I had this thing in my head called a conscience, and it made me feel like I should intervene.

At least for the next twenty-four hours or so.

"Does this mean he's stuck this way? Always saying yes to things?" Sierra asked. "Like, are you going to have to be his babysitter for the rest of his life?"

That sounded like my version of hell. "There are Buddhist monks who spend their whole lives trying to stay in a deep trance state and never achieve it, so I think it's safe to say that Mason Beckett is not going to be stuck this way. He'll be back to his old obnoxious dirtbag self soon enough. But I think for the next day or so, given what I suspect, I have to watch out for him."

She chewed her chip thoughtfully, looking at me like she didn't believe me. "So you're just going to crash their date? Bridget's not going to like that."

"They both invited me."

Her eyebrows shot up her forehead. "They both invited you? That's . . . entirely abnormal. Explain to me how this happened."

"Mason asked me to go to dinner with him and I obviously said no and then Bridget showed up and he asked her out instead and they said I could come."

I knew how weird it sounded, and Sierra's look confirmed it. "He asked you to go to dinner with him?"

"Right. But I shot him down."

A long pause and then she said, "By going to dinner with him tonight anyways?"

I was trying to put my necklace on, and that made me stop, my hands hovering behind my neck. She was right.

He had gotten me to go to dinner with him even though I'd said no. Sneaky jerk.

"Why do you think he wants to take you to dinner?" she asked when I didn't respond to her correct and now blatantly obvious observation.

I shut the clasp and made sure the pendant was hanging correctly. "He said something about talking things over."

"Why does he want to talk now?"

"Good question. I have no idea." Because there was nothing he could say to undo what he'd done.

"Mom said something about him maybe moving back to Playa Placida. Maybe he wants to apologize in order to make sure the next forty Sinclair/Beckett Christmases won't be awkward."

Mason might be moving back home permanently? That was entirely unexpected and an unwelcome thought. I had been operating under the assumption that this move was temporary and he'd be flying back to New York in the not-too-distant future. "We're not going to be spending the next forty Christmases with Mason. He's going to meet someone, I'm going to meet someone, and there will at least be buffers if we do all get together."

"Are you, though? Going to meet someone?"

Now I turned to stare at my sister. "What is that supposed to mean?"

"Let's just say I've never seen you as worked up about a guy as you are about Mason Beckett."

I read her subtext loud and clear, but I wasn't interested in traveling down this twisted road with her, so instead I just got mad. "I can't believe you just implied that I like Mason. Do you know what he said to me today?"

"What did he say?"

"He said hypnosis was a cult and that I'm a fraud."

"Well, you showed him, didn't you?"

That made me pause. "I guess I did. And I did a really good job of it! You should have seen him out there saying yes to everyone after my 'fake' hypnosis convinced him it was a good idea. Yes to the silent auction! Yes to Bridget! Yes to petting alligators!"

"You should have asked him for some money," she said jokingly. "And he shouldn't have said the cult thing, because that wasn't nice, but he's not the first person who's said something like that to you, and usually you don't get this upset. Which means something else is going on. What is it?"

Having someone know you so well was both a blessing and a curse. It made it very hard to hide things from them.

"He also said . . ." I was trying to think of what I could share with her, what he'd said outside the confines of the actual session. "He said I was pretty!"

It was such a stupid thing to repeat that I was mortified as soon as I'd said it. Obviously, that wasn't a bad thing, but it had bothered me.

Sierra confirmed how idiotic it was when she said sarcastically, "What a jerk! Want me to beat him up for you?"

She didn't have the whole context, so she wouldn't be able to understand why it made me mad. I couldn't tell her about the other things he'd said that had left me floundering. Like when he'd said that he loved me. Because I'd been obsessing over that pretty extensively for the last few hours and had tried to come to a logical conclusion about it.

Mason hadn't said that he was *in* love with the girl next to him on the dock, just that he loved her. And there were so many other kinds of love besides romantic love. He could have loved me as a friend. Or in a platonic you're-a-pseudo-sister-to-me kind of way.

I had initially assumed he meant romantic love, but that was because I was just projecting, using my own past feelings and emotions to explain his. I couldn't jump to conclusions and most definitely couldn't tell Sierra about it, because I had to keep it confidential.

It wasn't until Sierra spoke that I realized I'd just been standing there, running all of these things through my head. "Did you at least get any good gossip?"

"Like what?" I asked.

"Did you ask him why he made up that rumor?"

"No."

"Why not?"

That made me pause and consider why I wasn't going to ask Mason about the rumor. There was the fact that I had decided long ago that what he had done was unforgivable and it wasn't my job to let him relieve his guilty conscience by confessing and apologizing. But it was more than that.

I'd given him so much power over me, over my heart, that I was terrified to ever let that happen again. What if he had some reasonable explanation? Not that I could think of one, but what if? I'd seen today just how easy it would be to fall back into something familiar but exciting with him.

There was no way I was going to let that happen. He'd already ripped my heart out of my chest once—there was zero chance that I'd let him destroy me again. I wouldn't go down that road a second time. I didn't think I could handle it.

But I couldn't share any of that with my sister. So instead I opened my closet door and pulled out a bin from the top shelf to find the purse that would match with this dress. "So he could just lie about it more? No thanks. I'm full up on lying men at the moment. He can spin his sob stories somewhere else and leave me alone."

My sister had her gaze pointed down at my bedspread, tracing a flower shape with her finger. It briefly occurred to me that her finger probably had grease on it from the chips when I realized that there was a reason she wasn't making eye contact with me, and it made me feel anxious.

"What?" I asked.

"I don't think you want him to leave you alone."

That was almost as ridiculous a statement as me saying I was angry about him calling me pretty. "Are you serious? I very much want him to go away."

"I don't know." She still looked down. "You've been talking about him nonstop since you first saw him."

"And? Seeing him and being around him is traumatic. I'm processing."

"Okay. Whatever you say. But you do seem a little jealous of his date tonight with Bridget."

Of all the inane things that my twin had ever said to me, that had to take the cake. "I am not jealous. I turned him down, and then he settled for the next best thing."

Crap. I did sound jealous.

Her eyes lifted. "I would probably be the next best thing, given that I look just like you."

My heart froze completely and then began a low thudding in my chest. Was this why Sierra was acting this way? Did she have feelings for Mason? Had she always wanted to be with him and I was standing in her way?

"Do you like him?" I asked in a strangled voice.

"Ugh, don't look at me like that. Of course not! No, Mason has always been like a brother to me. I do *not* want to date him. I'm still technically involved with Joseph."

At that declaration I relaxed, not realizing that my entire body had tensed up. "I thought you were going to break up with him."

"I am. I just haven't gotten around to it yet."

"Then don't text him cute, couple-y things like you're still together."

"For sure." She nodded. "But for argument's sake, what if I already did?"

"Sierra," I said with a groan, "don't make me drive over to his house and end this thing myself. You deserve so much better."

"I know, I know. I'll end it. Soon." At that, she got up and brushed her potato chip crumbs all over my floor. Which meant I'd have to vacuum before I left, because the ants outside were just waiting for an excuse to come marching in.

While in the past I might have complained to her about it, I didn't do that anymore. I was just happy that she was eating, and eating something she was so obviously enjoying.

I went over to her and wrapped her in a big hug. She mumbled a protest but then hugged me back.

"I just really love you, okay?" I said, willing myself to not start crying, my chest aching from how much I loved her. My sister was the best. I was so proud of her and the progress that she had made. She might have been misguided where Mason was concerned, but she was an incredible person, and I was so glad that she was my twin.

"You're such a sap," she said, then let me go and headed for the door. "Have fun crashing someone else's date."

"I was invited," I reminded her.

She paused in the doorway and looked back at me. "Keep an open mind, would you? Sometimes things aren't what they appear to be."

Given that Sierra wasn't the kind of person prone to making cryptic statements, I wanted to ask her what she meant, but she was already gone.

Which was probably for the best. If she was pro-Mason, I didn't need to hear about it. I glanced at myself in the mirror, and that teenage girl inside me, who absolutely refused to stay quiet, wondered if Mason would like what he saw.

I didn't dress up for him, I told her and gave myself a satisfied nod. I'd dressed up partly because I enjoyed it but mostly because if I was going to wade into the belly of the beast, I needed to have a certain amount of confidence.

No more delaying.

Time to go bust up a date.

CHAPTER NINE

I intentionally arrived early at Murphy's Alligator Emporium and Restaurant. It was about half an hour north of Playa Placida, and it was one of the biggest tourist traps in a fifty-mile radius, which was really saying something because Florida was lousy with tourist traps.

The outside was beautiful, though. Just beyond the parking lot, there was a long wooden bridge built over the alligator and crocodile enclosures, which were surrounded by big, leafy tropical trees.

Standing on the bridge was a bit like being inside a giant jungle, the artificial stream bubbling beneath my feet as it coursed through the enclosures.

Given that it was nighttime, the animals were all very active, and I heard the sounds of them sliding into the water or their tails dragging along the ground as they moved through the enclosure. This was when they hunted in the wild, and even though I didn't share in Mason's irrational fear, as a native Floridian I had learned to always keep my distance.

"Waiting for someone?"

I turned to see Mason somehow looking even hotter than he had earlier that day. He was again dressed in loose and casual clothing and looked far more comfortable than the ninety-two-degree weather with one hundred percent humidity should have allowed for.

"You look nice," he said.

Not pretty? I wanted to sarcastically ask, but I didn't.

Even if he sucked as a human being, my mom would have been furious with me if I didn't observe the social niceties with the son of her best friend. "And you . . . have clothes on."

It was the best I could manage.

He flashed me a grin. "I usually have clothes on."

That's a shame, that voice inside me said, and I sighed because it was very frustrating to have a part of myself that was immune to logic and the fact that I hated him and only cared that he was hot. "Yes, managing to wear clothes in public is one of your best qualities."

"You wouldn't say that if you'd ever seen me without them."

My temperature spiked at his words, and I felt even sweatier and hotter than I had just a few moments ago.

No doubt about it, that was most definitely flirting. I might have been a bit clueless when it came to men, but even I couldn't miss that extremely obvious overture.

I cleared my throat, uncomfortable. It made me think of our session and how I had assumed that he was flirting then to mess with me. Was he still doing that?

If so, why?

But I didn't ask my question. Instead I remembered why I was here. I felt like I should warn him about tonight before he did something that he might regret. "I knew you'd be early."

"I knew you'd be early," he countered.

Again it bothered me that he knew me so well. Or was it how well I still knew him? Either way, I was annoyed. "I got here when I did because I needed to talk to you."

He looked hopeful at my words, and I clarified. "Not about our situation. More about what happened earlier today."

A couple on a date approached us, and Mason had to move closer to me to allow them to pass by us on the bridge.

My pulse went into overdrive when his chest brushed against my arm, and I peered up at him. The blood in my veins seemed to thicken just because of his nearness, and an undeniable electricity sparked between us. I shivered despite the heat as a wave of desire speared my stomach. Goose bumps broke out on my skin where he was touching me, and I hysterically wondered if he could feel it.

I saw his Adam's apple bob up and down and the hungry look in his eyes.

Like he wanted me.

Even though he hated me.

A moment passed, then another, and despite the fact that the couple had already entered the restaurant, we stayed put.

What was that cologne? I was going to buy a bottle and pour it all over my pillow.

"Sinclair," he murmured, and the sound of him saying his pet name for me made molten heat swirl in my abdomen. When he'd called me Sinclair in high school, it had always made me feel like he saw me as one of the guys—just his buddy, nothing more.

But him saying it now made me feel the exact opposite, like it was an endearment he used only for me, and there were all kinds of emotions and sensations that thought caused inside me. I had to end this. I put a hand against his very broad and strong chest, immediately regretting the impulse because I wanted to keep exploring.

I forced my hand to push against him slightly, making it so that I could move away. I turned, hoping he couldn't see my reaction.

There were so many things wrong with this scenario, the first being that he was a total slimeball, but just as big of an issue was that he was a client. I couldn't step out of line and give the Board a reason to rescind my certification. Behaving inappropriately with a client was their biggest no-no.

But probably most importantly, he was literally here to go on a date with another woman.

He closed the gap between us but thankfully didn't get as close to me again. I wasn't sure I would have been able to handle the way he overloaded my senses a second time. I was turned away from him, looking into the enclosure, although it was a bit too dark to make out much.

"Do you know how to tell the difference between an alligator and a crocodile?" he asked, and I was grateful for the distraction. For anything that would make it so I wouldn't have to acknowledge what had just happened between us.

"It's the snouts, right? Something about the way they're shaped?" I turned my head over my shoulder to look at him, and that was a big mistake.

Because he was sporting the most mischievous, charming grin I'd ever seen, and I had to lean forward against the railing for support. "No. You can tell the difference because one you'll see later and the other you'll see in a while."

It took me a second, but his joke registered, and I couldn't help myself. I laughed.

His grin grew wider as he laughed with me, and I had forgotten how much I'd once adored that sound. It was deep and hearty and fun.

"I made Savannah Sinclair laugh. I feel like someone should give me a gold medal."

That set off a warning signal. This was wrong. All wrong. None of it was okay. "Mason, when I mentioned why I got here early, it's because I needed to talk to you. I came here tonight because you're under the influence."

"Under the influence of what?"

"Of my exceptional skills and your high suggestibility. Like I mentioned after our session, you went into a really deep state of hypnosis called somnambulism, and I didn't get to end it properly with the awakening stage and bring you out. You were really groggy and disoriented when I had to wake you up due to the fire alarm. I was telling your subconscious to say yes to things, and now you're out here saying yes to everyone and everything and possibly putting your life in danger if you try to hold an alligator and it's all my fault."

He looked more amused than concerned. "So you're saying I don't have free will and my mind's playing tricks on me."

"I know how it sounds, but maybe a little bit."

"Well, thanks for the warning. Do you do this sort of thing often? Put people into really deep trances and then follow them around?"

"Never. I don't have any personal experience with it. I've heard about it. I mean, there are people who are so receptive and have so much practice slipping into deeper states that they can have surgery performed on them without any anesthesia."

He shot me a half smile. "So you could have stabbed me and I wouldn't have known."

"Well, we all have our regrets."

That got me a laugh, and he sounded like I delighted him. "So I'm under your spell?"

"It's not a spell. It's not magic. It's more like an open loop that either needs to be closed or to let the suggestion wear off. I could do another quick session with you and close that loop." Why hadn't it occurred to me before to offer this to him? It was perfect. I could get him back to his normal terrible self and then go on my merry way and let him enjoy whatever gross things he and Bridget were going to do to each other.

"No thanks," he said. "No more hypnosis for me. I've got a hot date tonight."

I'd tried a general warning, but he needed to know the specific threat that Bridget might pose. If he wasn't going to let me undo it, he at least needed to know what was going on. "Bridget is not like you remember from high school. She's a . . . manizer."

"What is a manizer?"

"A man who is a player is a womanizer, and so the opposite of that . . . Bridget is a manizer."

He crossed his arms and leaned against the railing, that amused smile growing bigger. "Isn't she supposed to be one of your best friends?"

"That's how I know! I love her, but she is going to chew you up and spit you out, and you . . ." How was I supposed to tell him that I wanted to protect him from being used without sounding like I was betraying what he'd confided in me and promptly forgotten about?

"I what?" he prompted. Like he knew what I was thinking. "Are you worried about me, Sinclair?"

"I'm not . . . that's not even . . . you don't . . ." I let out a big breath. "You're the one who decided to surround yourself with man-eaters tonight, and I might be the only thing keeping you safe."

"Are you going to protect me?" His voice was low, sexy, and it made my toes curl. "How are you planning on doing that?"

It was a little comical to imagine that I could keep him safe. Even with all my murderous thoughts today, I knew it wouldn't take much for him to fend me off. Like, he could so easily disarm me and then just grab me up in his big, strong arms, crush me against him, twirl me back against a wall, and then savage my mouth, and I . . .

He took a step closer, letting me feel the warmth of his body, which derailed my wild thoughts that were veering into a place they shouldn't, and I shivered again.

"Although I wouldn't mind seeing how you planned to protect me. Would you throw your body across mine?" He asked it so innocently, but he somehow managed to have me considering the possibility.

"You're not acting like yourself," I said, and I wasn't sure which one of us I was actually directing that statement toward.

He patted his chest, sporting a look of mock confusion, and said, "Funny, I feel like myself."

Of course he would take me literally. "That's not what I meant. You were passing out yeses today like they were candy. Which is unlike you."

"Like M&M's? Which are your favorite," he said.

They were my favorite candy. "You don't know that."

"I do." He was right, but I didn't want him to be. Which made it so that I couldn't think of a good retort.

My ability to formulate a response went away completely when I noticed that measured look of his was back, the one where it felt like he was assessing me and looking for a specific answer. I should have told him to knock it off, but instead I just glared at him.

Then he said, "You know, for someone who claims to hate me, you seem to be voluntarily spending a lot of time with me."

Claimed? Did hate him, thank you. "Against my better judgment."

"Uh-oh. Did somebody hypnotize you to do it?"

He was not in the least bit funny. "No, you don't have a shell. You need protection."

"You lost me."

With an exasperated wave of my hand, I said, "It's a whole thing about you being a shell-less turtle, but basically by tomorrow afternoon, you will be back to your old self that we all know and hate, and you can shoot down random women who ask you out and tell your delightful mother no to everything she asks you to do."

Mason seemed to take my rant very seriously, mulling it over, and then said, "Do you know why I said no to my mom when she asked me to donate a prize for the silent auction? To evaluate someone's manuscript and give them writing tips? Because I feel like a total fraud."

There wasn't anything he could have said that would have surprised me more. A fraud? Mr. Overly Confident, who had landed on bestseller lists?

"And it was embarrassing," he added.

"It's embarrassing to be a bestselling author?"

He averted his gaze, looking toward the trees. He put both of his hands in his pockets and leaned back against the railing. "It is if your dad is your only customer."

"What does that mean?"

"It means my father, in an attempt to make up for years of neglect, decided to hire the services of an organization that guarantees getting on the *New York Times* bestseller list. I thought that I had landed on it through some combination of luck, talent, and maybe even having a senator for a dad, but it turned out that he just bought my way on."

I should have felt triumphant over this news. He had just handed me a very serious weapon that I could wield to hurt him if I wanted to. I could hold it against him and mock him for it. Instead I just felt . . . bad for him.

I didn't like that.

So I did something unexpected. I was nice. "I'm sure your dad just thought he was trying to help."

"Well, he helped me into tanking my writing career. My second book was a huge failure and didn't make the list and didn't move any copies, and my publisher ordered too many, and despite them doing their best to advertise it, it flopped. So now I'm back home, licking my wounds and trying to do freelance reporting jobs until I get my third book finished and can start submitting again. And I won't even be starting over at zero. I'll be in the negative. Publishers will see me as a bad risk. My agent might drop me if this new book isn't something special. He suggested I use a pen name so that the taint of my failure won't ruin my future prospects." He let out a deep breath and said, "Wow. Sorry for dropping all of that on you."

It had been our shared dream to be published. I had been wildly jealous that he had succeeded, and succeeded beyond anyone's wildest dreams by landing on that list with his first book.

I had stopped wanting that dream for myself a long time ago, when I realized I wasn't good enough and it wasn't really where my passion lay. I still loved reading, but that was as far as it went.

I'd spent all that time being envious of something I hadn't even really wanted for myself. What a waste of time.

And it must have been really hard for him to see his dream come true and then have it yanked away. I felt awkward, unsure of what to say. I settled on, "I didn't even know you published a second book."

"Most people didn't," he said with a wry smile. "I don't normally share that story. Did you inject me with some kind of truth serum today?"

"If I was going to inject you with something, it wouldn't be a truth serum."

He chuckled, but he still sounded sad, and I couldn't help myself. My completely uncharacteristic actions continued. I reached over and rested my hand on his forearm, wanting to comfort him.

His intense gaze went right to where my hand was touching him and then up to my face, as if he were asking a question that he didn't speak aloud.

I could almost hear it. *Are we allowed to touch each other now?*

I yanked my hand away like I'd been scalded. He stood there, not moving, not speaking, just watching me. I didn't know what I had been thinking. That was the thing—I wasn't thinking. I was reacting.

With my heart and not with my head.

I didn't know what to make of that.

"You wouldn't have to inject me with a serum," he said softly. "Anything you want to know, ask it. Ask, and I'll explain and be completely honest with you. I've never lied to you, Sinclair, and I never will."

My heart was thudding low and hard, crowding out my lungs so that I couldn't breathe. I didn't want to believe him, but I did.

If that was true . . .

"Mason! Savannah!"

I turned to see Bridget waving and making her way toward us.

And I realized I was disappointed that Mason and I were no longer alone together.

CHAPTER TEN

I had hoped to look nice tonight, but Bridget? She was stunning. Like a goddess coming down from Mount Olympus to frolic with a mortal man.

Mason didn't stand a chance.

I didn't want to compare myself to her, but I couldn't help it. She was so beautiful, and it made me feel completely inadequate.

"Savannah! I'm so glad you made it!" I could tell she genuinely meant that, which confused me. Why would she want me to be here, possibly interfering with her chance to hook up with Mason?

She hugged me hello, and I felt guilty. Here I was being jealous of her and she was happy just to see me.

Bridget turned toward Mason. "Hello to you as well!" He said hi as she stood up on her tiptoes to kiss him on the cheek, and that jealous feeling was back, but I decided to fight it off by refusing to acknowledge it.

"This is a cool little wooden bridge!" she declared.

Even though he was responding to her statement, he looked at me as he said, "It is. It reminds me a lot of this dock I hung out on once."

His words pierced me, and I felt a hit of fear. Or adrenaline. I couldn't tell the difference right now. "I thought you said you didn't remember anything from earlier."

"Oh, it's all coming back to me."

Was this going to make things even more weird and horrible between us? If he was remembering what we both had said, how was he going to feel when he realized what he had revealed to me?

His worst enemy?

My mind started rushing with thoughts of what he might choose to do. Would he get angry that I had that information? Would he write a mean article about me? Leave some terrible reviews online? I really was in the weaker position here. I was the one in danger of losing my job, and a bad word from him could hurt me.

"Should we go inside?" Bridget asked, apparently ignoring the undercurrent of whatever was happening between Mason and me.

"Let's." He nodded. He went to the restaurant door and opened it for Bridget.

"Such a gentleman," she cooed at him. "I've heard good things about this place."

"I have to admit that it's the first time I've been on a date with reptiles."

"Not me," she said as she went inside. "I've dated plenty of them."

Mason laughed, and that jealous feeling intensified tenfold and slammed into me, making my chest go concave.

I still didn't understand my apparent ability to hold multiple emotions at once. How I could want to touch him, be envious that Bridget made him laugh, freaked out that Mason had the power to potentially hurt me, and still really hate him. A lot.

He held the door open for me, and I debated whether or not to tell him I didn't want him to open my door, as I didn't need any help from him. But then I would never hear the end of it from my mom for being rude, so I decided to settle on the path of least resistance and went into the building. He brushed past me to go to the hostess's stand, and I had to fight off a wave of wanting him.

Had I done this? Opened Pandora's box by trying to comfort him? Had I doomed myself to hating him while also craving his touch?

It didn't matter. I was going to keep him safe tonight, get his word that he wouldn't do anything stupid in the morning, and then send him on his way. I wouldn't be seeing him again.

Apparently Mason had made a reservation, and after he gave his name, the hostess asked, "For three?"

"Yes, for three." That jerk turned to wink at me, letting me know that he'd accurately guessed I was going to show up and had made a reservation sure that I would come.

Part of me wanted to spin on my heel and walk out, just to spite him, but I didn't. Instead I followed behind Mason and Bridget as the hostess led us to our table.

It was on a balcony completely enclosed in glass so that we had a good view of the alligators without all the humidity and bugs ruining our dinner. There were three place settings, and the fourth side of the table was pushed up against the balcony wall. Mason pulled out Bridget's chair on the left side of the table, and as she sat down, I debated where I should sit. Next to her, to be a buffer? Putting me in the center between them? That seemed like the best bet. But then Mason would be across from her and would be captivated by her eyes and her, uh, other assets.

Keeping him a bit farther away seemed like the better option, and as I went to sit down in the middle seat, he said, "Wait."

Then he pulled my chair out, and I was worried he might try to yank it out from underneath me. I kept both of my hands on it as I sat, and he made an exasperated sound.

"I'm not going to drop you on the floor, Sinclair."

Bridget pretended not to notice, and I ignored him. I didn't trust him. When my rear end had made full contact with the chair, he helped me scoot it in a bit, more strongly than was probably necessary.

He sat across from Bridget, on my right side. And it was then that I remembered he was left-handed, which meant he was probably going to be bumping into me all night as we tried to eat.

I sighed. None of this was going how I'd planned.

Bridget set her purse on the table, and Lulabelle stuck her face out, her tongue lolling out of her mouth like usual.

Mason startled. "What is that thing? A rat?"

"She is a Chihuahua, and watch what you say. My Lulabelle is very sensitive."

"Is it sick?"

"She always looks like that," I told him.

For the first time since he'd been back, Mason seemed to be at a total loss for words.

I picked up the menu. "So do they serve alligator here? Because that would be horrible, and I definitely don't want to order that by mistake."

"I looked it up online, and they don't. They're just here for the ambience," Bridget said. "I'm in the mood for some ribs, but they only do a full rack, and there's no way I could finish that off. Savannah, do you want to split it with me?"

I was glad to have someone else making decisions for me at that moment, given that the words on the menu were kind of swimming in front of me because this entire thing was so surreal.

I was a third wheel on my best friend's date with Mason Beckett.

If somebody had told me a week ago that this was going to happen, I would have bet my entire life savings against it.

"Sure," I said as I set down my menu.

"That sounds good," Mason said. "I'll get the same thing."

I wondered if either one of them had considered how much of a mess their choice was going to make, and I found myself saying, "Ribs aren't really a first-date kind of food."

"I guess if you can be messy in front of someone and they don't run away screaming, you'll know if they really like you," Bridget said with a coy smile.

Mason smiled back and said, "Is that why you bring your sickly rat-dog? To weed out the first-date guys who aren't serious?"

"I can weed out unsuitable men all by myself. I bring Lulabelle because she has anxiety if she's left alone, and I don't much care what men think about it, first date or not."

If this was flirting, they were bad at it. And I knew Mason wasn't bad at it, as he'd been making me feel like my ovaries were on fire, and Bridget had the long groove in her bedpost to prove she was basically an expert, and this was all just confusing.

But instead of staying quiet, I decided to add to the overall weirdness by saying, "I think we should decide as a society to combine first dates with running errands. That way, if things don't work out, at least you got some groceries and picked up your dog from the vet."

There was an entirely awkward silence after I spoke, and I wanted to bury my face in my hands. Well, mission accomplished. I had totally pooped this particular party. I hid behind the menu and stayed quiet.

The problem was, nobody else was talking, either. I kind of thought Bridget might ask Mason a question about himself, to show some interest in him, but she didn't.

If this was how she got guys to fall head over heels in love with her, I was impressed. Because one, I couldn't figure out how it worked, and two, if it did work, I wouldn't be able to stand the silence and would never be able to copy her method.

Thankfully, as I was just on the verge of making another inane comment, the waiter approached and introduced himself. Bridget placed her order. "I'd like to get the ribs, but please ask the chef not to put barbecue sauce on half of the ribs. I can't eat gluten. And can you bring an extra plate so that I can share with my friend? Thank you so much."

Mason said, "I'll have the same thing but with lots of barbecue sauce."

The waiter said he'd put the order in right away, and I found myself wanting to grab him by the tie and make him stay. I was extremely uncomfortable right now and wished I at least had the menu so that I could continue pretending to study it. Would it be rude to take my phone out?

I didn't know third-wheel etiquette.

Mason cleared his throat and then asked, "So, Bridget, what brought you back to Playa Placida after college?"

"I attended a trade school for cosmetology and was working up near Orlando after I graduated." There was a bit of an accusatory tone in her voice, as if it annoyed her that he assumed she'd gone to college. I knew that he was just trying to make conversation, but I wasn't going to insert myself into this again.

Then she added, "I came back to Playa Placida to run my mom's flower shop when she got sick."

"I'm sorry to hear that," Mason said, and I wondered if he really didn't know about Bridget's mom. The way that Heather streamed information through her mouth made it hard to imagine that she hadn't mentioned it at some point.

Bridget picked up her phone, as if she were done talking to Mason. I kind of expected him to ask about her mom, but he didn't. He shot me a weird look, and I didn't know how to respond.

Silence.

Then I thought that maybe Bridget would ask him something about himself, which would make sense, given that it was how conversations usually worked, but nothing.

I had wanted to be a wet blanket on their date, but it looked like I had seriously underestimated my abilities. I was the wettest, most blanketest killjoy who had ever lived, apparently. My very presence was ruining the night.

Lulabelle wheezed loudly, and Mason again looked concerned. "Are you sure she's okay?"

"She's fine," Bridget said as she set down her phone and then straightened her cutlery. "So, Mason, did you know that Savannah volunteered to help with this year's summer PTA fundraiser? The silent auction was her idea, and she's in charge of gathering up all the donors."

"I've heard something about that. But I'm wondering why they're having a PTA fundraiser in the summer?"

I started to answer, but Bridget cut me off. "It was an initiative started by the president last year—she wanted them fundraising year-round, and since the school district cut the arts program budget in half, Savannah and your mothers are trying to make sure that there's enough money to replace what was cut. Isn't Savannah the sweetest? She really cares about others. You probably didn't know this, either, but during the school year, she goes in once a week to her mom's classroom and volunteers to help the kids who are a bit behind on their reading."

"I didn't know that," Mason said, but he looked as weirded out as I felt.

What was Bridget doing?

"She really is so kindhearted and compassionate. And the most loyal friend you'll ever have."

"I did know that," he said in a sad way that made my insides twist.

I hated Mason Beckett. Why did I have to keep reminding myself of that fact?

"And, Savannah, did you know that Mason is involved with several different charities in New York that focus on childhood literacy? He's been quietly fundraising for them and getting his dad to make big financial contributions for years."

It probably shouldn't have surprised me, given that he was a writer and how devoted both of our mothers were to the cause of childhood reading, but it did. I was a bit shocked that he would do something selfless.

"How do you know that?" Mason asked, looking as surprised as I felt.

"Oh, I do my research."

"Nobody knows about that besides my parents."

Bridget made an apologetic face. "Your mother came into the flower shop today after the false alarm and was very chatty. She also mentioned that Mason takes his little half brothers on boys-only trips to New York, and they go to the zoo and FAO Schwarz, and they both adore him."

If I'd been surprised before, I was stunned now. He had been really angry with his father after the divorce, and I figured he couldn't have been happy when his dad remarried a woman only a few years older than Mason and then had two more kids.

But it sounded like he was a good big brother, and it was endearingly, confusingly sweet, and it melted away another part of my defenses, even though I was trying desperately to hold on to my anger.

"And, Mason, you probably didn't know this either," Bridget went on, like she was reading from cue cards or something, "but Savannah goes by Mrs. Rosner's house every Sunday to visit and have lunch with her."

"Our old English teacher?" he asked.

Bridget nodded. "She's retired and doesn't have any family."

What was happening? Bridget sounded like a deranged game-show host introducing us to an invisible audience.

I stood up suddenly and announced, "I'm going to the bathroom, and you're coming with me."

"I am?" Mason asked, and I glared at him.

"She meant me," Bridget said with a self-satisfied smile. "Could you keep an eye on Lulabelle until we get back?"

"Are you sure she won't die while you're gone? Or go into cardiac arrest?"

"She's fine," Bridget said as I grabbed her by the wrist and pulled her away from the table and into the bathroom.

We were alone, and I was glad. I slammed my purse down on the counter and asked, "What are you doing? It sounds like you're writing dating-app profiles for us but out loud."

She slowly opened her clutch, pulled out a lipstick tube, and faced the mirror, leaning forward while she carefully added another layer. She smacked her lips together and then announced, "I think I'm being your wingwoman."

CHAPTER ELEVEN

"My what?" I asked.

"Your wingwoman." Bridget dropped her lipstick back into her clutch. "I've never done it before, so I don't know if I'm doing it right, but that's what I was aiming for."

My mouth hung open for a moment because I couldn't process what she was telling me. "Why?"

"I just think the two of you should know nice things about each other because you are both nice people."

That made the rage fire in my gut flare to life. "I'm a nice person. He's Mason Beckett."

"And he's a nice person. I think you should remember that and talk things out with him."

I couldn't keep having this conversation. It was making me bonkers. Like he'd cast a spell over the entire town and I was the only one who could see through it.

Correction, the spell was working on me, too. Because I was finding myself being more interested in how attractive he was than actively calling up my hatred for him.

I didn't know how or why that had changed, and I didn't like it. Bridget certainly wasn't helping with her

Mason-secretly-volunteers-for-charity-and-hangs-out-with-his-younger-brothers-and-isn't-he-the-cutest-for-it? thing she was doing. It went completely against the kind of life I imagined him having in New York, one that involved a lot of wanton and selfish behavior.

"I'm really confused," I told her. "I thought you came tonight because you're trying to hook up with him." Which I was actively trying to stop, but I left that part out because I wouldn't have been able to answer without breaking Mason's confidentiality.

But keeping him safe from potential predators of both the animal and human varieties wasn't the only reason, though.

I wasn't able to tell myself the real reason why, let alone anyone else.

She grabbed a tissue and blotted, then threw the tissue into the trash. "Sweetie, I know a lost cause when I see one."

"Meaning?"

Bridget put a hand on her hip and turned to face me. "Meaning there's no point in trying to land a man who is so obviously into someone else and always has been."

Mason liked somebody? For a split second that conversation with Sierra flashed in my head, the one that had made me wonder if she liked Mason. What if she actually was interested in him? And he was interested in her? Was he being nice to me because he had feelings for my sister? "Who?"

She rolled her eyes so hard I felt a slight breeze, and then she looked at me like I'd said something incredibly stupid. "You."

The alarm, shock, and total disbelief I felt in that moment were off the scale, and now it was my turn to shoot her the same expression. "You can't be serious."

"But I am. You two have always had so much in common, and he obviously likes you."

I couldn't prove that he hated me, but I could refute her other statement. "The only thing Mason Beckett and I have in common is how he tried to ruin my life."

Bewilderment settled onto her face. "Because he ghosted you for that dance? Sierra told me about it."

Sierra knew that wasn't the reason why, but I guessed that Bridget had probably hounded her about what was going on with me and Mason, and that was as good an explanation as any. I realized that I hadn't ever shared the real story with Bridget since we'd renewed our friendship as adults. We hadn't been close in high school and had hung out with different groups. I was sure she'd heard the rumor, like everybody else, but she probably had no idea that Mason was the one who had started it.

Her phone buzzed with a text. "Hang on a second," she said as she typed a reply.

When she finished, I said, "You are my friend and I love you and would do anything for you, but please don't try to set me up with men that I have actively fantasized about stabbing."

She pursed her lips together as if she were trying not to smile. "He's not all bad. That's all I was trying to show you."

"Even if that's true, does it matter? It's not like he's doing enough good stuff now for it to cancel out the bad. I can't just say, 'Hey, great, you're a decent person now and everything's cool and don't worry about the past and let's just move on.' You don't get to spread a rumor like that and then move on."

"What rumor?"

"The one about me and Mr. Landry."

Her eyebrows flew up her forehead. "You're still mad about that rumor?"

"I know it's petty that I can't let go of things. Other people would have moved past it. I'm sure you would have. I just can't, and it makes me hate Mason for doing that to me."

Bridget looked so sympathetic. "I know exactly how you feel. I know what it's like to feel scared that people will gossip about you." She paused for a bit and then added, "That changes things, though.

I wish I'd known. Which makes my timing terrible, but that text was from my mom, and she is feeling a bit worse, so I said I'd go home and take care of her."

She was leaving?

And I was going to be alone with Mason?

"You can't go," I said and instantly felt bad. "I mean, yes, please go, and say hi to your mom for me, and let me know if there's anything I can do to help out. I can bring by some breakfast in the morning after my first appointment if you'd like." But I still wanted to beg her to stay.

"That would be great. I'm going to go out and say goodbye to Mason, and I'll see you later!"

Then she was gone, and I went into a bathroom stall, closed the door, and hid for a while. My mind was too muddled to think clearly, but once I calmed down, it suddenly dawned on me that there was no conflict now. Bridget had gone home, and Mason was no longer in danger, so I could just go.

I washed my hands and went back to the table. Mason wasn't seated, and for a second I wondered if he'd ditched me, since Bridget had left. The waiter came over with our ribs and set them down.

"Can I get the check and some boxes?" I asked him.

The waiter looked a bit surprised, but he just smiled and said, "Of course. Let me box this up for you."

"Thank you." I couldn't believe Mason had stuck me with the check. To be honest, it didn't seem like something he would do. He had to be around here somewhere.

Maybe he was hiding out in the bathroom, too.

I wondered if I should go looking for him.

The lights in the enclosure just beyond the balcony went on, and I shielded my eyes for a second. It was bright.

Several people went over to the windows, crowding around my table. I wondered what they were looking at and saw a couple of men, one of whom was carrying a bucket, as they walked toward the alligators.

Mason. Mason was carrying the bucket.

What was he doing?

It dawned me on that they were going to feed the alligators. There was no fence, no way for them to be safe if the alligators decided they wanted a Mason-size snack for dinner.

That fear / adrenaline / heart-in-my-mouth feeling was back.

He was going to die.

He was going to walk over to them and those alligators would sense his fear and he'd be eaten alive and I'd have to watch it happen. There would obviously be some small degree of satisfaction that karma was real, but then the rest of it would be terrible. Not just the carnage but having to tell his mom about it.

I stood up and pushed through the other people so that I could press my face against the glass, my heart constricting in my chest.

Mason and the other man came to a stop, still quite a bit away from the alligators. But I knew how fast those suckers could sprint. They were deceptively slow moving, but they could run four times faster than a human. Mason reached into the bucket, grabbed something pink looking, and threw it toward the alligators.

A bigger one caught the meat while other alligators snapped and growled. The winning alligator quickly turned and took his spoils into the water, steering clear of would-be poachers.

The other man said something to Mason, and they shook hands. To my great relief, Mason headed back to the building while the man reached into the bucket to throw hunks of meat to the patient and waiting alligators.

The other diners continued to watch the show, but I went to sit in my chair, feeling a bit wobbly. I needed a second to collect myself, and then I turned to see the moment Mason entered the room.

When he walked in, he was wearing the biggest smile. I was struck by the desire to run over and hug him, glad that he hadn't died.

He rushed over to me and sat down in his seat. "Did you see? I fed an alligator!" His voice was full of triumph, like he'd just won a state championship.

"You did," I said, still in shock at what I'd witnessed. I still remembered the field trip to the zoo in middle school where he'd refused to even walk into the reptile house because of the alligators, which had been behind a thick glass window.

"For the rest of my life, this is something I can say I did. I fed an alligator."

There was this zing inside me that took me a moment to identify, but it felt a little like I was proud of him, so I had no choice but to push down that feeling until it went away. Instead I took note of the way he seemed to be trembling. "Are you okay?"

A big grin. "Were you worried about me, Sinclair?"

"You want to know if I was worried when you approached the man-eating death lizards with no sense of self-preservation?" The answer seemed obvious to me. I would have worried about anyone who had just done what he did. "Your hands are shaking," I pointed out.

"Adrenaline," he said. "Right now I feel like I could conquer the world."

"Which is why I came here in the first place. So that you wouldn't do your best gladiator impression and try to fight a beast for the crowd's entertainment."

He laughed and said, "There's this rush—I feel terrified and excited and amazed that I've done something I've always wanted to do."

"Is it out of your system?" Was it safe to leave him alone?

"Who knows?" He sat down in his seat and glanced around him. "Where's Bridget?"

I wondered why she hadn't said goodbye to Mason. "She got a text from her mom and had to go home to take care of her."

"That's too bad. I hope her mom's doing okay. But on the other hand . . . and then there were two," he said, leaning forward.

I ignored what he'd said. "Why did you go out into that death trap without saying anything?" I probably would have tried to stop him.

But maybe it was a good thing that he'd done it without me knowing. He seemed so proud of himself, and I might have talked him out of that.

Much as I loathed him, I wouldn't want to take away that sense of accomplishment he was feeling.

In answer to my question, he said, "I'd made arrangements earlier today, and the manager came over to grab me while you two were in the bathroom. I texted Bridget to let her know, but I don't have your number."

"It's the same as in high school," I said, distracted by how much danger he'd put himself in. "But if you did this to impress your date, shouldn't you have made sure she was here to witness it?"

"If you're impressed, that's on you. I didn't do this for anyone but me. I fed an alligator."

I wasn't his date. I meant Bridget. It was like he was deliberately misunderstanding, and it irritated me.

He took his phone out and typed something, then looked at me expectantly. "Did you get my text?"

I'd been planning on giving him an earful about making untrue statements, but I was thrown by the fact that Mason still had my number memorized. What did that mean? "No," I said. "I have you blocked." Without thinking, I undid the block and said, "Try again."

His text came through that time, saying:

Greetings from the Conqueror of Crocodiles.

The waiter returned then, and he handed me a bag with the boxes. Then he put the leather folder with the check on the table and said he'd take care of it whenever we were ready.

"You packed up the food?" Mason asked while he reached into his pocket to get his wallet. He put a credit card into the holder, and our waiter stopped by to grab it and said he'd be right back.

"I thought you'd left," I told him.

"Did you really think I'd ditch you?"

The thought had occurred to me, but I had also dismissed it as something he wouldn't do. I couldn't tell him that, though. I didn't want to have charitable thoughts about him. "With Bridget being gone and your alligator adventure over, I don't have to stay here and try to prevent you from saying yes to things you shouldn't, so I had him pack things up."

The waiter returned with Mason's card and thanked us for coming in. I briefly wondered how much Mason would tip him. For all I knew, he might be a secret cheapskate, which would work out well for me, because after I'd waited tables in college, guys who didn't tip well were an automatic deal-breaker.

It'd be nice to have another reason to hate him.

Unfortunately, now that Bridget had told me all these good things about him, I was willing to entertain the possibility that Mason probably wasn't like that, and I didn't want to keep thinking kind thoughts where he was concerned.

"Well, this was something," I told him as he slid his credit card back into his wallet. "Get home safely and try not to do anything else that might potentially make you lose a limb."

I stood up and he said, "Wait. Can I get a ride home with you?"

The idea of being trapped in a small, enclosed space with him for the next half hour didn't sound like a good one. Not with my body waging war on my mind, urging me to forget the past. "Didn't you drive here?"

"I've been using my mom's car while I'm home, but she had a sewing class tonight, so I took a rideshare."

"You can take a rideshare back home."

He cocked his head to one side, like I was being ridiculous. "We are going to the same place, and I'll give you gas money."

It wasn't about gas money. It was about not spending any more time with Mason so that he could exit my life and be nothing but a bad, distant memory.

Then he added, "You want to make sure I get home safely, don't you? That I don't take any other outrageous risks? I'm not sure you should leave me to my own devices. Who knows what dangerous thing I might do?"

I narrowed my eyes at him. "Why do I feel like I'm being blackmailed?"

He shrugged innocently, but we had enough of a history that he knew I'd lose sleep if he got hurt doing something dumb and I could have prevented it.

"Come on, Sinclair. I promise I'll behave."

I did not believe him.

And when he looked at me with those pleading, gorgeous eyes of his, I wasn't a hundred percent sure that I'd be able to behave, either.

CHAPTER TWELVE

As if he sensed me weakening, he said, "You can be my fill-in Uber driver. I'll even tip you and leave you a five-star review, if that helps."

At his mention of a star rating, my mind went immediately to all the bad reviews Timothy had left me online, and I wondered if Mason's suggestion was a thinly veiled jab, but he wasn't wearing a sneaky or underhanded expression.

Although I supposed that was how the devil got you—by showing up looking like an angel.

"I'll be waiting forever for a rideshare to show up out here," he said. "That adrenaline is wearing off, and I kind of just want to go home and crash."

He was right. We weren't near any major cities, it would take a long time for a car to get here, and we were going to the exact same place. It made logical sense, even if I wasn't in the mood to be logical. I sighed loudly. I could give him a lift.

It was very big of me. Somebody should have given me an award. "Okay. I'll give you a ride. But you have to sit in the back seat."

He looked like he wanted to ask me if I was serious, but he must have seen in my expression that I was. If I was going to be stuck in a car with him, I would make sure that there was some kind of barrier between us. I didn't need him sitting next to me, taking up the entire front seat and looking the way he did and smelling good and my body figuring out a way to touch him somehow and . . .

"Sounds great. Thank you," he said.

I nodded and grabbed the bag of food. I felt him standing right behind me, dogging my steps as I went out to my car. The hostess told us to have a good evening, and I smiled at her while Mason thanked her. I opened the front door and hurried across the wooden bridge, unwilling to think about those moments that he and I had shared on it.

Better to put that behind me.

I unlocked my car with my key fob, and as I opened the driver's-side door, I expected him to make a play for the front seat. To my surprise, he didn't and slid into the back on the passenger side without complaint.

It was probably a bit cramped for him back there, but that was not my problem. I started the car up and headed out of the parking lot.

"I never thought our first date would involve a third person," he announced, startling me, and I nearly slammed my brakes in response.

"That was not a date," I said, glancing at him in the rearview mirror.

"You say not a date, I say most definitely a date. We went out, I paid."

"I didn't order anything!" I protested.

"I still paid. And now you're taking me home with you."

He was not as charming as he thought he was. "I am driving you to your mother's house and leaving you there."

"It's a long trip home. The night's still young. Things can change."

I grit my teeth in anger. The night was still young? Things could change? Like I was going to have some kind of epiphany on the freeway that I couldn't possibly miss out on the chance to be with Mason Beckett and insist we drive to the nearest hotel. As if I were going to just take Bridget's place and try to hook up with him tonight. Why was he always pushing my buttons? It was like he knew exactly what to say to infuriate me.

"How about some music?" I said, reaching for my console.

"No thanks."

"I wasn't actually asking." I turned the music on loudly, determined to drown him out.

I looked in the rearview mirror again, and he was grinning to himself, like he had some kind of private insight and thought this was hilarious.

He actually managed to stay quiet, though. I couldn't really hear what was playing—the only thing running through my mind was my desire to drop him off and get as far away from him as possible. I might have driven just a tad over the speed limit to hurry up and get us home.

I got all the way to the outskirts of our town before he slid forward and used his long arms to turn the music off.

I had just come to a stop at a red light and was about to yell at him to leave my music alone, but then he asked the one thing that would distract me.

"How is Sierra doing?"

"Fine."

"No, I mean with everything."

What *everything* was he talking about? "Such as?"

He rested his arms against the front passenger seat, leaning forward so he could talk to me. "With the hospitalization and her recovery."

I shifted my car into park so that I could turn my whole body toward him. "How do you know about that?"

He didn't immediately answer, and I ran through possibilities in my head. Sierra had been hospitalized four years ago because she became so weak and so ill my parents were afraid she was going to die. She finally told us the truth—that her ballet instructor had been telling her she was too fat and would never make it professionally with "all that extra weight" and that was why she had been struggling with disordered eating for so many years.

That had completely infuriated me—my sister was perfect just the way she was.

I had flown home from college and spent three days sitting by her bedside, not able to imagine a world without my twin in it.

Fortunately, that had been a turning point for her. My parents and I weren't the only ones scared. She'd gone to therapy and programs in the past at my parents' insistence but had always been resistant. She quit ballet, which I knew had been hard for her. She took her recovery seriously, did the work, and focused on the healing she needed. I knew it was something she still struggled with every day, and I was so proud of her for the choices she made on a daily basis.

But it was information that Sierra didn't want shared around. So I knew my parents hadn't told Mason. Heather most likely knew, and while she was a chatterbox, she would never let a secret like that slip.

And I hadn't told him.

Which meant . . . "Sierra told you?"

He didn't confirm or deny it, but I knew I was right.

"You and Sierra have been talking," I figured out. "Since when?"

Mason finally seemed to realize his mistake and scooted back. "We keep in touch here and there. No big deal."

It felt like the biggest of deals. Like my twin had betrayed me. I was right back in that headspace where I was freaking out at the possibility that my sister and Mason Beckett liked each other. Why else would she not tell me that they'd been talking? Sierra had some serious explaining to do.

"Uh, the light turned green," he said, gesturing toward the windshield.

"I don't care if that light turns into Kermit the Frog and starts singing that it's not easy being green. Are you . . . friends with my sister?"

I had to say *friends* because the idea that they wanted to date or might already be dating was overriding my ability to use the correct word.

He didn't answer.

I couldn't watch this happen. I couldn't. I wouldn't be able to be happy for her or support this monstrosity of a relationship. "Are you trying to win me over for her?"

"In what way?"

"In the way that you want to date Sierra and so you need to get on my good side because you know she won't date you unless I'm okay with it."

His expression shifted, changing into a knowing, smug smile. "Would it bother you, Sinclair?"

Bother me? *Bother me?*

I gripped the steering wheel so tightly that my knuckles turned white. I would pull this car over to the side of the road and throw a Molotov cocktail in it and let the whole world burn down in a fiery inferno if it meant I could prevent him from dating my sister.

"It would bother you," he observed.

He didn't get points for stating the obvious.

"You don't have to freak out, Sinclair. Sierra and I are just friends. Nothing more."

I let out a deep sigh that I was unaware I'd been holding in.

"The light's still green," he added.

I put the car back into drive and headed toward his mom's house.

"You jump to some pretty bizarre conclusions," he informed me, and I gripped the steering wheel tighter.

"It isn't really paranoia when it's confirmed," I told him. "Things are making sense now. You have some secret friendship with my sister, and that's why she's pushing me so hard to talk to you."

"What did she say?"

I was still all hopped up on rage and fear, so I wasn't thinking clearly. If I had been, I never would have responded to his question, because it wasn't his business. "She said we should talk so the next forty Christmases aren't awkward."

"We've been doing a pretty good job with that so far without even discussing it."

Mason was right about that. We'd never talked about it, but the first Christmas after our friendship ended, he went to his dad's house. The year after that, my mom had said he was coming back to Florida, and I told her that my roommate had invited me over to her family's house for Christmas. Two years after that, I sat alone in my apartment with a frozen meal, as I was determined to avoid him. Nobody knew that I had spent it by myself, and I blamed him for that. Yet another reason I was angry at him—for costing me time with my loved ones.

I supposed technically it wasn't his fault—I still could have gone home and just given him the silent treatment, but I knew it would have made everyone uncomfortable and both of our moms really unhappy.

The last couple of years, he'd spent Christmas exclusively at his father's house. Maybe he'd come to the same conclusion as me.

"Kind of like a dance," I remarked.

"A dance?"

"Yes. We were in a weird dance with each other, doing the same steps without communicating."

He stayed quiet for a moment and then said, "There's always communication when you dance. The way that you touch, how your body moves, the way you look at each other. You speak without words."

His declaration sent sparkling, warm tingles through me, and I drew in a shaky breath. He was creating images I did not need. I'd never danced with Mason, not once.

And I'd always wanted it. To have him hold me like that, swaying to music; it was the epitome of romance to my teenage heart.

I didn't say anything back, willing my heart rate to return to normal, and was relieved when I finally pulled into the driveway at his mom's house. "We're here. Have fun in your basement."

He undid his seat belt and scooted forward again. "You know we don't have a basement. I'm actually staying in the guesthouse." The Beckett home was one of the nicest in the area—they had a pool and a small guesthouse, too. I'd spent many hours at that pool, enjoying watching Mason swim.

I expected him to say thanks and leave, but he just sat there.

Turning around to face him, I said, "Okay, get out now."

"Let's take Sierra's advice and talk."

"No thanks. I want to go home and sleep." This had been a very emotionally draining day. I needed to hydrate and recharge.

"Not tonight. Like tomorrow. Let's go to Flavio's. Dinner's on me. Again. Or I could call Bridget to see if she wants to hang out. Do you think nighttime skydiving is a thing? She can even bring that poor thing that looks like it escaped from a defunct Taco Bell ad campaign."

What part of Bridget had seemed fun tonight? The part where she left suddenly or when she spent the whole time chatting us up to each other?

"You can't go nighttime skydiving." I didn't know if that was a thing, but if it was, it sounded dangerous.

"Well, if I can't jump out of a plane . . . I've always wanted to jump off the roof into the swimming pool. Do you think I can make it?"

He got out of the car and began walking toward the main house, which was two stories. He really was going to jump off a roof.

I took off my seat belt and chased after him. "Jumping off a two-story house is dumb. I thought you said you were worn out!"

He grabbed an extremely tall ladder and set it against the side of his home. "Second wind. It's time to say yes to life!"

"Say yes to life by not risking yours." I saw the look in his eyes, the one that told me he might very well do something nuts, and again wondered how much of this was my fault and how responsible I'd be when he wound up in a full-body cast.

It felt like I only had one bargaining chip here to use. I just had to run the clock down until he was serious, responsible Mason again and this YOLO fool was gone.

He started climbing the ladder, and my sense of urgency forced me to say, "I will go with you to Flavio's to hang out but only if you promise to stay safe until tomorrow afternoon. No jumping off anything."

That made him pause, and the smile he gave me could only be described as triumphant. "Deal."

As he climbed back down, I said, "You have to promise me that you will go inside and stay put and not respond to any phishing emails or phone calls about your car warranty."

"I don't own a car." He was finally back on solid ground.

"I know. That's the point. Don't get scammed by anybody, don't call Bridget, don't go looking for alligators . . . Just don't do anything that might potentially endanger your life."

"Only if you promise that you'll be this delightful at dinner," he teased back. "Tomorrow night?"

"No, I have clients tomorrow night. I can do it the night after."

"At seven?" he pressed. "I'll pick you up."

"You will not," I said. "I'll meet you at the restaurant."

"It's not like I don't already know where you live."

"That's not the point. This is not a date, so I'll meet you there. And I'm agreeing to hang out with you, and that's it. You're not going to force me to talk about anything that I don't want to talk about."

"I'd never do that," he said. "If you don't want to talk about anything serious or about what happened between us, I could always interview you for the article."

I had kind of forgotten about that, what with the whole trying-to-keep-him-alive thing. "Fine. We can talk about my job, and that's it."

"I'll take it. And we can work from there."

"We will not work from there," I protested, realizing that he was again baiting me. I just shook my head and started walking back to my car.

I had opened the driver's-side door when he yelled so loudly that the entire county could have heard him, "What? No good-night kiss?"

As I drove off, I considered the fact that in the space of a day, I had gone from resolving to never see Mason again to hypnotizing him, having him convince me to have dinner with him and Bridget, drive him home, and have dinner with him again.

Much as I wanted to deny it, I wasn't doing this just because I didn't want him to smash his skull in. I was also doing it because some part of me desperately wanted to spend time with him.

Which had me worrying what else he might easily "convince" me to do.

CHAPTER THIRTEEN

Sierra was asleep when I got home. I considered waking her up, but her schedule was so chaotic I didn't want to interrupt what sleep she got. I figured I could talk to her in the morning.

But when I woke up, she was already gone. I texted her and asked if there was a time we could chat. She usually responded instantly, but it took a bit before she answered. She told me she would be working a double and could have breakfast with me tomorrow morning.

As I moved through my day, I found myself thinking about Mason way too often. Like, a disconcerting amount. I was tempted to call and interrupt my sister at her job just so that I could ask what was going on with her and him, but I could wait until we were face-to-face.

I did text Bridget to see how she and her mom were doing, and she didn't reply, either. I texted again to remind her of my offer to bring them breakfast, and she did respond to that message. She told me not to worry about it, that they were doing okay.

Then I invited her to breakfast with me and Sierra the next morning, and she sent me back a thumbs-up emoji.

That seemed unlike her. Her texts were usually more like novels.

Frowning, I made myself a note to stop by their house and check on them. Maybe I'd grab some gluten-free cookies from the bakery and bring them over. This would happen sometimes—the chemo would wear Bridget's mom out, and Bridget would devote herself entirely to her mom's care.

The least I could do was bring by a treat to try to make things a bit easier.

Thinking of Bridget reminded me of what she'd said. How convinced she seemed that Mason was into me. It was patently ridiculous, but it was still there, lurking at the fringes of my mind, wanting me to pick it up and examine it more closely. I had a job to do and food to eat and water to drink—I had no time to consider whether or not Mason was interested in me.

Despite both of their reassurances to the contrary, a part of me still worried that this was all a big, secret setup and that Mason and Sierra were going to blindside me with their engagement.

Which I never would have thought my sister capable of, but the fact that she'd been friends with him for years and I never knew? I thought Sierra and I didn't keep secrets from each other, but it turned out we very much did.

So I didn't know if his niceness and flirtatiousness were due to a bigger plot or if Bridget had it right—that Mason wanted to go out with me.

If he had a crush on me, well, it gratified my ego more than it should have, because the shoe was finally on the other foot, but it didn't matter in the long run, because nothing would ever, ever happen between us.

And despite the fact that I'd been making a lot of declarations where Mason was concerned, I was pretty sure I'd have no problem keeping that one.

I decided to do my evening sessions at home, which turned out to be a mistake because the house wasn't empty. I had thought my mom had her quilting circle, which she always dragged my dad to, over at Heather's house. Instead she was in the kitchen, washing up dishes.

"There's leftovers in the fridge," she said when she noticed me. Whenever I saw my mom, I was struck by how different we looked from her. People used to joke that they must have accidentally switched us with another set of twins. Where Sierra and I had dark hair and were tall, my mom was a short blonde. If anything, she looked like she could be Bridget's mother.

When my mom pivoted toward the dishwasher, I noticed that she had quite a bit of gray hair that I'd never seen before. I wondered how many of those I was personally responsible for.

"Thanks," I said. "I thought you had your quilting thing tonight."

"Tomorrow night. Do you want me to heat something up for you?"

"No. I've got an online appointment in about ten minutes, so I'm going to go up to my room."

"Do you want to sit and have ice cream with me after?" Eating ice cream was our family's go-to activity. Going to the ice cream parlor down the street was always a major treat, and my mom would stock our freezer with pints of their bestsellers for when we were sad or needed a pick-me-up.

Or when she wanted to have a serious conversation with us.

I sensed the latter was the reason for the offer. "I can't. I have studying I need to get done after that," I said.

Time to make a quick escape.

I'd just put my foot on the first step when she said, "I heard you hypnotized Mason."

Trying not to sigh, I walked back over to the kitchen doorway so that I could see her more clearly. This conversation was going to happen sooner or later—I might as well get it out of the way. "I did."

"And Heather says he's been acting differently ever since. Do you think he's going to stay that way?"

"It's not a movie, Mom. Hypnosis doesn't work like that."

She put another plate into the dishwasher. "But you have told me that sometimes people only need one session."

"I . . ." That made me hesitate. That was true. I had said that. And I had witnessed it. There were clients who would find their anxiety gone or their physical pain cleared up after just one session. It was pretty rare, but it could happen.

Despite my assuring everyone, including myself, that Mason was going to snap out of it soon, what if he didn't? Shell-less turtle or not, I couldn't follow him around indefinitely to make sure he wasn't making life-threatening decisions.

"He'll be fine," I said, and I wasn't sure whether I was trying to convince myself or my mom.

She closed the dishwasher door and pushed the start button. "I appreciate you doing it. I know it meant a lot to Heather that you were willing to spend time with him."

That ouched. I hated that my anger toward Mason made his mom sad. Heather had always been like a second mother to me. "I'm glad."

And I was. At least one good thing had come out of this.

"I heard you're going to dinner with him tomorrow night."

News spread fast in Playa Placida, and even faster between my mom and Heather. Our houses were only a few minutes apart. Mason must have told his mom right away, and she had immediately called my mother.

It felt like that meant something, but I didn't know what.

"Yes," I said hesitantly, worried about what she might be getting at.

"Like a date?" she said brightly.

There it was. "Not a date. We're hanging out."

"Are you going to work things out with him?"

"Mom," I said in exasperation, "I don't know what's going to happen. I understand that you'd like things to go back to the way they were, and I know I haven't shared much about it with you, but there's a lot of hurt and mistrust there." And hatred. Seething, vibrant hatred, but she didn't need to be reminded about that.

"I hope you give him a chance."

"Yeah, yeah, you and everybody else," I muttered as I walked upstairs.

Maybe there was something in the water that made everyone take Mason's side instead of mine, including my own family.

And I was the only person not drinking it.

~

The next morning, Sierra left me a text saying she'd meet me at Starbucks because she had an errand she had to run. My sister was not the kind of person who did things early. She had a tendency to show up late to everything. I had fully expected that we would drive over together, giving me the chance to grill her. It was odd that she had left.

Was she up to something?

I hated that this Mason stuff had made me suspicious of my twin. Another reason to be mad at him.

Not that I needed a new one.

Sierra was on her phone when I arrived. I didn't see Bridget. I went over to the table, and my twin set her phone down quickly, her expression a bit wary.

"It's so early," she said, stifling a yawn. "Why did we let morning people create the world's operating schedule?"

"They did it while we were asleep," I said. Part of me wanted to jump down her throat, but the other part didn't like being angry with my twin, so I waited.

"Nana always says the early bird gets the worm, but as far as I can tell, the late bird gets a slightly smaller worm. There's plenty of worms everywhere. Nobody needs to wake up early to get one." Our grandmother often spoke to us in platitudes, as if they would solve all of our problems.

I wondered if she would have one for the situation I currently found myself in.

"I was hoping to skip the small talk today," I said, trying to open up our conversation to more important matters.

"What did you want me to say? 'Hey, Savannah, good to see you, and what do you think the meaning of life is'?"

No point in beating around the bush. "You've been talking to Mason behind my back. For years."

"Yes."

I was glad she didn't try to deny it. "Why?"

"It's a long story."

"So tell it to me," I said, sitting down in the chair across from her.

She leaned forward and reached for my hand. "I want to explain it all to you. I do. I just don't think you're ready to hear it yet. And before you freak out on me again, no, I don't want to date him. We are just friends. Like siblings. Nothing more."

I let out a sigh of frustration. I wanted to tell her that wasn't good enough, that she was my sister and owed me an explanation, but that all sounded really selfish. Most likely because it was selfish. "It's like you had a choice between what was clearly right and what was clearly Mason, and you chose him."

"That's not it. I promise that I will tell you. And soon," she said. "When things calm down a bit."

What did she think was going to calm down? Me? That wasn't going to happen. Hurricane-force winds of hatred were still whirling inside me. "I can't stand the idea that you're keeping secrets from me."

"It's not a secret so much as not sharing certain information with you that I know will make you have a nervous breakdown." She was teasing, but I heard the concern in her voice.

This was making me wish I hadn't gone back to school to get my master's degree in counseling, because now I knew that the right thing to do was to let her tell me in her own time. Even if I was impatient and waiting was the last thing I wanted to do.

"Okay."

"Am I still your favorite sister?"

"Genetics dictate that I have to love you. But I am very upset with you."

"It's okay. You'll get over it," she said as she hugged me. I hugged her back because she was right—I would get over it. I couldn't ever stay mad at Sierra.

"Speaking of getting over things, have you broken up with Joseph yet?" I asked.

She released me and sank back into her chair. "Can I just not talk to him for a long time and hope he figures it out? As a society, haven't we decided that when someone ghosts you, you should respect the dead and move on?"

"I've had it done to me, and it feels really good when a guy just stops talking to you." I laid my sarcasm on a bit thick.

"You did it to Mason."

"That's different and you know it."

As if realizing that she'd overstepped, she backpedaled like she was an acrobat in the Cirque du Soleil. "Let's not talk about him. Back to Joseph. If I try to break up with him, I'm going to have to tell him why, and I don't want to explain. It'll be a whole ordeal."

"You don't need to justify why you want to break up with him. It's not like you have to convince a jury of twelve impartial peers that your reasoning is fair."

It was frustrating that Sierra didn't see that she deserved better. That she had the right to be with someone who would make her really, really happy. I could only tell her so many times, though. At the back of my mind, I felt like I always had to take her mental state into account. When she felt too much pressure or like she had to be perfect, that was when she would backslide.

It had been years, but the fear that she would relapse was always right there on the edge, for all of us.

I decided to not bug her about Joseph anymore. She was an adult. She could make her own choices. "You do whatever you think is right. I support you. But please know you deserve a good guy."

"So do you," she said.

"You're right. I should be better about having a good romantic relationship. These days it feels like my healthiest and longest relationship has been with my DVR."

She smiled at that and then, as if she couldn't help herself, said, "There's a decent man out there who's right for you. And maybe that good guy's name might rhyme with Jason Meckett."

"Sierra," I groaned. "This is so pointless. He and I hate each other."

"Why do you think he hates you?"

"You were here the other morning. You saw how he scowled at me and said my name all rude."

She blinked at me once, then twice, and said, "Are you for real?"

"Yes?" I said it as a question because of her tone.

"He smiled at you, and his eyes lit up when he said your name. You are so caught up in your own hatred of him that it's coloring your vision. You have on hate-filled goggles. You're an unreliable narrator."

"I am a very reliable narrator," I said with a frown.

"Fine, Ms. Reliable Narrator. Then please explain to me why he wants to keep hanging out with you."

"Because he's writing an article about hypnosis and is on a quest to annoy me to death."

She muttered something under her breath and shook her head. "You don't think there's a chance you could just let things go?"

"I think we both know the answer to that question."

Bridget arrived then, setting down the purse that held Lulabelle.

"You're here!" Sierra said. "What did you do last night?"

"No one," she sighed dramatically as she sat on the stool next to me. She looked at me appraisingly and said, "Savannah, why is it that every time I see you lately, you look like someone just told you the test came back positive?"

"I don't know? Mason Beckett, mostly."

"But he seems so nice," she said.

"Great. Now I have a new trigger phrase to avoid," I replied. "'Calm down.' 'You're overreacting.' 'Mason seems nice.'"

"Bridget, I have a question for you," my sister said. "When Mason saw Savannah the other morning, how did he look at her?"

"Like he'd been fasting for a month and she was a life-size porterhouse steak."

I tried to protest that they were both wrong, but I knew when I was being ganged up on, and that I wasn't going to be able to change their minds.

They were free to hold on to their delusions.

A barista put out a sign indicating that they were out of egg bites, and Bridget grumbled. "Just great. Now what am I going to have for breakfast?" She longingly eyed Sierra's blueberry muffin. "Maybe I could have one of those."

"Don't do that. You'll get sick," I said. She was already looking a little run-down and tired. She didn't need to add stomach troubles on top of that.

"I know. It's my toxic trait—seeing food that I know will upset my stomach and wondering whether it will still hurt this time. I'm basically in a civil war with my intestines."

Sierra said, "My toxic trait is that I think people will have common sense and then I get mad when they don't."

They both looked at me expectantly, and I said, "My toxic trait is—"

Then, as if on cue, Mason walked in.

And headed straight for us.

CHAPTER FOURTEEN

"Good morning!" he said, sounding far too chipper. "Lovely to see you all. Sinclair, you're looking particularly beautiful today."

I felt both thrilled and angered. Being around him was like getting on a roller coaster that had no exit. I always felt a bit off kilter, like I was going to puke, and the tiniest bit exhilarated.

Sierra and Bridget greeted him, but I stayed quiet. Bridget asked what he was up to today, and he said, "I'm grabbing coffee for my mom, and she doesn't like to be kept waiting. I'll see you all later. And, Sinclair, I'll see you tonight for our date."

"It's not a date!" I yelled after him, and half the patrons around us turned to stare at me. "It's not a date," I repeated quietly.

Mason's order was waiting for him, and he grabbed it and headed for the door. He waved goodbye to me.

"Porterhouse steak," Bridget observed with satisfaction. Meanwhile, Sierra's eyes were so big she looked like an anime character.

"Not one word," I said to her.

"But I have so many words! First, what, and how, and what, and when and huh? Basically, all the questions!"

Bridget clapped her hands together. "Okay, tell me every single little detail about what happened on your date the other night after I left. Most especially the parts that are inappropriate, explicit, and totally objectifying."

"Wait," Sierra interjected, "Savannah was on a date alone with Mason? I'm confused. I thought you wanted to date him, Bridget, and Savannah was just crashing it. How did Savannah wind up on a date with him?"

I again tried to say it wasn't a date, but no one was listening to me.

"Oh," Bridget said with a wave of her hand, "wanting to go out with him was about my pride and his hotness. I'm over it."

"What about girl code?" Sierra insisted. "You like him, and so Savannah can't date him."

That sounded like a good point to me.

Bridget shot it down like a rear gunner. "Neither one of you would be able to date a single man in a hundred-mile radius if we abided by that code."

That made my sister laugh, and even I had to smile a little, but my smile faded when Bridget turned to me and said, "You didn't tell her about my game plan?"

Sierra spoke before I could. "I have not heard about a game plan. This is the first time I've seen her since the night you all went out on the world's weirdest date."

"Well, I was trying to get them together and talking to each other. I pointed out some of their more noble qualities and the kind things they do so that they'd see each other in a new light."

"Good for you for thinking outside the box," Sierra said.

"You shouldn't be admiring her," I told her.

"Why not? She was clever."

Bridget turned Lulabelle's bag so that the dog could wheeze toward us. "I understand that this is not my business, but I literally want to know a hundred and fourteen percent of what is going on right now with you and Mason."

Despite her bubbly statement, there was something off about Bridget. I couldn't quite put my finger on it, though. She was smiling and making her jokes and quips, but underneath the surface, something else was going on.

Her mom really must not be doing well. I wanted to ask her about it, but I knew that if she wanted to talk about it, she would tell me. So instead of asking, I caught them up as quickly as I could, including why I'd agreed to have dinner with him tonight.

Sierra pursed her lips slightly and then said, "He's taking you to your favorite restaurant and you said yes?"

"He basically blackmailed me," I protested.

Bridget gestured at the space between her and my sister. "If Sierra and I were detectives on an episode of *Law & Order*, this would be when we exchanged knowing glances."

"Right." Sierra nodded. "I'm sorry, but your story doesn't add up. Nobody could blackmail you into anything." She left the rest of her implication unspoken—that I was going because I wanted to. I heard it, anyway.

"See? This is why I didn't pursue him," Bridget said. "It's obvious to everyone that he's into Sinclair here and no one else stood a chance. And I don't know if his feelings are completely one sided."

Her using Mason's nickname for me caused a twisting sensation in the middle of my chest, which rendered me a little speechless.

Which was probably a good thing because if I told her that the notion I could have feelings for Mason was so totally off base, someone would have made a joke about me protesting too much.

It was probably better to remain silent than to give them more encouragement.

"Ooh, maybe we could tag along tonight and watch from a distance," Sierra suggested, like me being forced to spend time with Mason was some kind of spectator sport.

"I'd be willing to lay odds on whether or not the night ends in a kiss," Bridget said.

"I'll take that bet," I said, finally finding my voice. "A million to one against because that is not happening."

~

And hours later, as I sat alone at Flavio's, there was no chance I was going to lose that bet.

In large part because Mason hadn't bothered to show up.

He'd gone to all this trouble to ask me to join him on this outing, had made me get dressed up in one of my cutest outfits, had repeatedly called it a date, and then he was a no-show.

It shouldn't have surprised me, given that he'd done it to me before. Maybe he'd call me seven years from now to tell me how scared he'd been to go out with me tonight and how he'd thought it was too much of a commitment and it freaked him out. Make it a real full-circle moment.

Flavio's had always been my favorite place to eat growing up. It was brightly lit, with twinkling lights running along the wooden beams overhead. The burnt-orange walls were covered with multicolored art and tchotchkes. A man playing the acoustic guitar sang love songs on the small stage in the corner.

This was where I'd come to celebrate all the big events of my life— and also where I'd come to drown my sorrows.

Only now, since I was finally old enough, I could drown them in actual liquor instead of fried ice cream. There was a top-shelf bottle of tequila that I'd always wanted to try, and I told the bartender to pour me a shot.

I'd take a rideshare home and come back tomorrow to pick up my car. Tonight I was going to drink to my own stupidity and enjoy myself without worrying what anybody else might think about it. I hadn't done this in years, and it felt a little overdue.

Plus, it would make sure that I wouldn't be fixating on the fact that Mason Beckett had stood me up.

Again.

My phone rang a few times, but I didn't check it. After all the stress of the last couple of days, I deserved a night out. I briefly considered inviting my sister and Bridget to join me, but I remembered that Sierra was working the late shift tonight, and I didn't particularly want Bridget to come and try to sell me on why Mason "Mr. I'm Too Good to Show Up for Dates I Arrange" Beckett was a good guy.

I was on my second shot when the bartender, named Romeo, came over to ask if I wanted something to eat.

That was probably a good idea. I asked him to get me nachos. Because nachos got me. They were basically just tacos that didn't have their life together.

And, at the moment, I felt like I didn't have anything together at all.

When Romeo came back with my tacos—er, nachos—I asked him if he wanted to join me. I'd gotten all dressed up for nothing and felt like I should have some company.

"And your name is Romeo, which is basically a sign from the universe," I told him. "It's romantic. I might be your Juliet."

He gave me a quick smile, like he'd heard that one before, and then went over to serve somebody else.

Which was probably a good thing. I knew that I got a bit too friendly when I overindulged slightly.

And just after shot number four, I heard an unwelcome sound.

"Sinclair?"

There stood Mason, holding something in his hand.

"Mason!" I declared loudly, throwing my hands up in the air. "You're here!"

"Have you been drinking?" He looked confused. Which made sense. I had never partied in high school and was a glass-of-wine-once-or-twice-a-week kind of girl now. Not that he would know anything about my current consumption.

Just that he'd never seen me slightly tipsy before.

"Only liquor, promise."

"And how drunk are you?" he asked.

"A lot to very," I reassured him.

"Tequila, huh?" He nodded at the bottle. "How much have you had to drink?"

"Tonight? Or in my whole life?"

"Tonight."

"It's hard to say."

I waved my empty shot glass in Romeo's direction. "Romeo! I need another one! Pour favor!" I smiled back at Mason. "I was using the English 'pour,' with the *u* in it, not 'por,' the Spanish word. A multilingual pun. It was funny."

He smiled at me. "And why are you drinking like someone strapped you to a World War I operating table?"

"Hmm, let me drink about it," I said, drumming my fingers on the bar. "For fun?" There was this nagging voice at the back of my brain telling me that I was supposed to be upset about something, but for the life of me, I couldn't remember what that was.

"Whatever the reason is for this, I don't think tequila's the answer."

"Maybe not, but it's worth a shot!"

That got me a laugh, and it was a glorious sound that made me feel warm all over. Or maybe that was the tequila. Either way, I was feeling good. I should make him laugh more often.

He gestured Romeo over and asked for a taste of what I was having. I wanted another shot, but Romeo left before I got it.

Huh. He must not have heard me.

"I've never been into shots," Mason said. "I prefer to savor my drink."

I wouldn't mind being savored, I thought, but out loud said, "I never understood that. Taking a drink and saying you get, like, notes of bog and sea foam. Just drink the thing and enjoy it."

Romeo had poured barely any into a shot glass, and Mason took a small sip and grimaced a little when he put the glass back down. "That is potent. I picked up the taste of indifference mixed with subtle notes of disdain."

"Subtle is overrated. Palpable disdain is much better."

"I've come to find that I agree," he said with a wink.

"You're not going to have a full shot? It's much more fun," I said.

"I get the feeling I should keep my wits about me tonight." He looked at my empty nacho platter. "Did you have some nachos?"

"I'm pretty sure I ate the restaurant's entire nightly supply of nachos," I said conspiratorially. "I'm a strong woman who is capable in so many areas, but restraining myself around chips and melted cheese is not one of them."

He laughed again. "I'm hungry. I'm going to get a menu." He called Romeo over, and the bartender pointed to a piece of paper that Mason could scan to get the menu.

"Pfft," I said. "I'm with the boomers on this one. I'm not scanning a QR code to retrieve some menu."

"I need to know what they're serving because I'm starving. I got caught up in something I was working on and forgot to eat."

"That would never happen to me. If I missed one meal, I would turn into the Tasmanian devil from *Looney Tunes*, and two meals? That would be total organ failure."

"You've never done a cleanse?"

"I'm more into clogs," I said.

"No intermittent fasting?"

"Nope, just intermittent feasting for me. That's where you eat a huge breakfast, way too much lunch, overindulge at dinner, and then go to bed early."

He laughed for a third time, and again I couldn't quite remember why I didn't spend all my time making him laugh. "You used to be really into fitness," he pointed out.

"It takes sixteen muscles to throw back a shot. Does that count?" I got a big smile from him, and then I said, "I kind of stopped when Sierra got sick. It was hard for her when I went for a run or to the gym because she used to exercise for hours. I could probably go now, but I just don't ever feel up to it. I know it would give me energy, but I need energy to go. Which feels like some kind of massive pyramid scheme."

"You could work out with me."

My brain was flooded with images of all the kinds of ways I would like to work out with him. While I was enjoying my mind candy, that nagging voice returned, and it reminded me that I was mad at him and why.

"You stood me up," I said, poking his chest with my finger.

"I didn't stand you up. I'm here."

I narrowed my eyes at him. "But you were late. I should make you leave."

"Yes, I was late. And I can explain. And I brought you a peace offering if you'll let me stay."

CHAPTER FIFTEEN

I liked presents far too much to say no, and well he knew it. "Fine. You can stay." I held out my hands, and he picked up the object he'd laid on the bar when he first arrived.

It was something wrapped in brown paper, and it took me a second to figure it out. It was a "bouquet," but instead of using flowers, he had taped bags of M&M's to long sticks.

Mason had created something that he knew I would love. My stomach started doing little flips of excitement. "Okay, this is super cute, but I am still mad at you."

"My mom had a flat tire, and I had to take a rideshare to get to her because she didn't know how to fix it. Then I had to call a tow truck because she didn't have a spare."

"Ah, yes, the old my-dog-ate-my-mom's-tire excuse."

"I didn't say . . ." He peered at me closely, in that way where it was like he was trying to uncover all of my secrets. "It wasn't an excuse. It happened. I tried calling you, but you didn't answer. I even tried calling you from my mom's phone in case you'd blocked me again."

"You're not blocked, even though you probably should be," I said, studying his expression. "You're probably not lying, because I could easily find out whether or not you're telling the truth."

"Yep, it'd be dumb of me to lie about it."

That was true, and he had brought me a handmade present. "You're right. I sort of have trust issues," I told him.

"Can I ask why?"

"I mean, there's you, but I was thinking about it the other day. This one year in middle school I went to summer camp by myself because Sierra was in treatment, and I'd never been apart from her before. I was so scared and so lonely, and I met this girl—Monica Lake. We bonded and became besties. I told her secrets about myself, about my family, things I'd never shared with anyone else. And the next day I walked in on her telling our whole cabin everything I'd said while they all laughed. Totally violating my trust. I felt so completely betrayed. Like it broke something fundamental in me at an important developmental stage. There's probably a part of me that always keeps a wall up with everyone for that reason."

"Wow. I didn't know that," he said.

"I never even told Sierra about it." I hadn't wanted her to worry about me. "Enough about me. We were talking about your mom and her tire and how you brought me candy. It's sweet how you take care of your mother. It's one of your many fine qualities."

His eyes twinkled. "I have fine qualities? You're being very nice."

"No, I'm saying something I don't mean. That's not nice; that's called being polite."

That scored me another laugh.

Romeo came back to see if he could grab us some food. Mason asked him to bring out two of the enchilada dinners and some water.

"I don't need water," I protested as Romeo left to put our order in.

"You do," he said.

"Disagree to agree."

He smiled and then said, "Maybe I'll actually get to eat this time."

"The ribs were very good," I told him.

"So you ate the food I bought for you? Isn't there some Greek myth about belonging to someone after you eat their food?"

"My dad ate most of the leftovers, so if you want him to stay in Hades with you six months out of the year, I guess you'd have a good case. Hey, maybe you could get Romeo to bring us a shot so we can make this a night *not* to remember."

"I think I'm good. Like I said, I'm planning on staying sober tonight."

"Spoilsport," I muttered, but my mood instantly lifted when Romeo returned with some chips and salsa. "I don't know what the secret to happiness is, but I do know that I've never been sad at Flavio's."

"I'd forgotten how important food is to you, and how much you love this place," he said, watching me dip my chip in the freshly made salsa.

"Yep. Some women want to be wined and dined; I want to be tequila-ed and taco-ed."

"Noted."

We ate in companionable silence for a couple of minutes, and I became aware of the fact that the couple sitting next to me had just met, and the man was nervous and obviously working up his courage to ask the woman out.

I listened in, fascinated. She was giving him all the signals to move forward, both verbally and physically, by doing things like touching his arm.

Mason figured out what I was doing, and he cocked his head to the side to listen, too.

The woman checked her phone and said that she had to be going to meet up with her friends. She had just started to stand up when the man finally blurted out, "Before you leave . . . do you want to go eat a movie sometime?"

She quickly replied, "Sure. I always watch what I eat."

As they exchanged numbers, I turned to Mason and said, "She's much quicker than me. I probably would have said, 'Thanks, you too.'"

Romeo came over with our enchiladas and told us to enjoy. I, surprisingly, was no longer hungry.

Mason did not have the same issue. "I'm sure you have game, Sinclair. Give me one of your best pickup lines."

I tossed my hair to one side and then leaned forward and asked, "Is this chair taken? How about you?"

"Okay, okay." He nodded. "Not too bad."

"What about you?"

"The main thing is to make them laugh. So I might approach someone and say, 'Titanic.'"

"Titanic?" I repeated, confused.

"Yeah, that's my icebreaker."

I laughed so loudly that several people turned to look at me.

"Then," he said, "I might tell them that I'm a writer and researching important dates in history and ask if they'd like to be mine."

That earned him a slight giggle from me.

"After that second laugh, I'd say, 'When I text you good night later, what number should I use?' Works every time."

"It wouldn't work on me," I said, although I was fairly certain it would. I was ready to give him my number and he hadn't even been trying to get it.

Also, he already had it.

He nodded, like he was carefully considering the sort of lie I'd just told. "The best kind of line is one that is really specific to the person."

"You're right," I agreed. "Like if I was trying to get you to come home with me . . ."

I let my words trail off, and I reached out to lightly touch him on his forearm, letting my fingers softly trail along his warm skin. I heard him suck in a breath, and I smiled, glad that I could have that kind of effect on him.

Tequila had apparently removed my hate-filled goggles. There was no mistaking the way his eyes darkened, the hunger and lust I saw there. It made me ache in a way I didn't know was possible.

What would he do if I leaned forward and asked him if he wanted to get out of there? Offer to let him hypnotize me a little bit into saying yes. I'd even quack like a duck if he wanted me to.

I knew what would happen. Without my other stuff getting in the way, I clearly saw that he would leave with me in a heartbeat. That was a problem, even though I couldn't remember why.

"Did it hurt?" I asked in a low, soft voice.

"Did what hurt?" he said after a moment, with a smile so sexy it stole my breath.

I pulled my hand away from him and sat up straight to say, "When you broke through the earth's crust, ascending from hell."

He was shocked for a split second and then laughed so hard that this time everybody in the restaurant turned to stare.

They were going to kick us out of here.

"Shh," I told him. "You're being very loud."

"We've got a little bit of a pot/kettle situation going on in that regard," he told me and started eating his enchilada.

I didn't have much of an appetite, given that I'd already eaten enough chips to feed an entire military regiment, and I pushed the beans and rice around my plate. "Do you think they'll have fun?"

"Who?"

"That couple that was next to us earlier."

"I hope so. Bad dates can really mess with your head. What's the worst date you've been on?" he asked.

There were oh so many for me to choose from. "There was this guy I went out with who had to parallel park in front of the restaurant. He had me get out so that I could help guide him in. He tried to park four times, and then when he couldn't manage it, he just drove off and left me standing on the curb."

"Ouch."

"Yeah, pretty bad. What about you?"

"I went out with a girl who tried to text her friend that I was so boring and she wished she hadn't gone out with me, only she accidentally sent it to me instead. That was an awkward car ride."

Who would say Mason was boring? He was the total opposite. "Her loss."

He raised both eyebrows at me but didn't comment on my response. Instead he said, "With my keen powers of observation, I've noticed that you are a bit less . . . inhibited than normal. Should we talk about my article?"

"Go for it. I'm a free newsletter!"

"An open book?" he suggested.

"Yes, that sounds more right. What do you want to know?"

"First, how did you get into it? Why hypnosis?"

"I'm not sure I want to go down memory lane with you, because our memory lane is paved with broken glass and . . . other bad, pointy sharp things, but I seem to remember that I told you I would, so here we go."

He shot me an expectant look, but I had been distracted by his hair and the way the light hit it, and I wondered if it was soft or felt more textured. I'd never noticed when we were younger.

"Sinclair?"

I straightened. Right. I'd been saying something to him. How I got into hypnosis. "Do you remember junior year, when I got injured at that game against Nova?"

"I do. You killed your shoulder. You were out the rest of the season."

"Yeah. And that pain never went away, but I managed it. I did everything I could to fix it: physical therapy, corticosteroid injections—you name it, I tried it. After I graduated from college, I started working as an English teacher."

"Mom mentioned that you were a teacher. Just like our mothers."

"Well, I figured out pretty quickly after graduation that I didn't have the talent to be a bestselling author." The five hundred rejection letters I still had in my closet were a testament to that. "What else could I do with an English degree but teach? It didn't take long for me to see that it wasn't a good fit, and the pain in my shoulder got worse, probably due to stress."

Mason pushed his empty plate away and looked at mine, both of his eyebrows raised in a question. I moved my food over to him so he could eat it.

"Anyway, the pain got to the point where I literally couldn't lift my shoulder any longer. I was desperate and willing to try anything, and a colleague of mine suggested hypnosis. That was when I met my mentor, Camila, and by the end of our sessions, the pain was completely gone, and it hasn't bothered me since. I wanted to be able to help other people the way she had helped me, and so now here I am."

"How many sessions did you have to go to?"

"Um . . ." I tried to remember. "I think about six."

"Is that typical?"

"Definitely. The point of hypnosis is to address the underlying issue and move on. Most clients see me for three months or less, depending on why they've come in."

"Hmm." He took another bite and after swallowing said, "That's not what I would have expected."

"Things aren't always what you expect."

He nodded, studying me. That consuming gaze of his was back, the one where he seemed to take me in, where it almost felt like he was touching me just by looking at me. It made my heartbeat pick up and caused a knot in my throat that I couldn't swallow down.

"I am learning that things are nothing like what I expected," he said in a low voice that made shivers dance along my skin. "I have so many things I want to ask you. Is it okay if I do?"

There was some underlying subtext there that I couldn't quite make out. He was asking for something beyond just permission to interview me, but my brain was too scrambled from his nearness to figure it out.

Did it matter, though? I was having a good time.

I knew I might regret it later, but I said, "Ask me your questions, pretty boy."

CHAPTER SIXTEEN

Of course he couldn't pretend like he hadn't just heard my drunken slip. "Pretty boy?"

"It's your fault I'm drunk," I pointed out.

"But you're so delightful this way. You remind me of the old Sinclair."

His words caused a painful pressure in my chest. "You mean back before I had enough baggage to fill an airport?"

His smile dropped. "Everybody has baggage and issues. Even me."

I was about to ask him what kind when he said, "So why Playa Placida? What brought you back?"

"I am getting my master's degree in mental health counseling and it's expensive, so I thought maybe I should move back home and do it all online. Sierra had already moved home to save up money to get her own place, so it seemed like a good idea."

"But I thought you were happy doing hypnosis. Why would you go back to school to become a therapist?"

"Oh, I don't know, probably because when people find out what I do, they accuse me of being a fraud or in a cult."

"Defensive walls reengaged," he noted. "What causes that?"

"Where do my defensive walls come from with regard to my job? A lot of places, probably. I know that part of it is from getting labeled in school. That when they say you're 'gifted and talented,' there's these expectations of the kind of life you'll lead, the sort of job you'll have. That if you're not out in the world curing cancer, then you're just wasting your life, even if what you're doing makes you happy. How even when you are actually doing well, you still feel like a failure."

"I know how that goes."

Huh. He had been in all those advanced academic classes with me and Sierra. He probably did know exactly how I felt—how I became a teacher because I thought I had to live up to my potential or whatever. "Plus, if you were in a job that's always portrayed as some kind of joke, you'd be defensive, too."

"Yes, journalists have no idea what that's like," he said with a note of sarcasm, and I realized he was right.

"Then you will understand why I decided to go that extra mile. My mentor is a licensed therapist who does traditional therapy and uses hypnosis as an extra tool, and people tend to take her more seriously."

"So . . . it's because of what other people might think of you? You can't live your life caring what other people think. You should become a therapist because you want to be one, not because of someone else's expectations, or to get other people to take you more seriously."

But I had spent so much of my life doing just that. Caring about what everyone thought and living in pain when I wasn't rising to their expectations. My eyes went a little blurry with unshed tears, but he didn't seem to notice.

He said, "I'm sorry I said what I did about your job being like a cult or fake. I was actually teasing you, and I guess it didn't come off that way."

I remembered Sierra declaring that I was an unreliable narrator and didn't see things as they actually were but rather as I imagined them to be. I wondered if that was the case here.

What if I had perceived other things in my life incorrectly? Viewing them through a distorted gaze so that I didn't have the whole picture?

What if that had happened with Mason?

And I must have spent a long time mulling over what Sierra had said and whether or not it was true because Mason waved one of his hands at me. "Earth to Sinclair! Want to share your deep thoughts?"

I cleared my throat. "They're not that deep. I was just thinking about the fact that chocolate is a flavor of milk, but milk is also a flavor of chocolate."

He smiled slightly, as if he didn't believe me, but he just nodded. I could tell my joke hadn't deterred him, which he proved by saying, "Tell me a bit more about this deep stage of hypnosis you accidentally put me in. I know you said there was heightened awareness and responsiveness, and that some people undergo surgeries without anesthesia in that state."

"It's big in some childbirth circles, too. They use hypnosis instead of drugs."

His eyes widened. "Would you do that?"

"Oh, no thank you. I'm not a fan of pain, and when I give birth, my happy place will be an IV bag full of drugs."

He laughed and then said, "So you want kids?"

What a weird question. "Do you?"

"I do."

An image flashed in my mind of a laughing toddler-age boy, with Mason's light brown hair and light eyes, and I forcibly shoved it out.

"Me too," I found myself saying. I had always thought that I'd be a mother someday. That seemed to make him strangely satisfied, so I added, "Not with you, though."

Just in case he was getting any funny ideas.

I didn't like the way things felt at the moment. Like we'd decided on something.

My face had been feeling flushed all night, but my internal temperature seemed to be increasing even more. Even though things were weird, I liked his smile and his annoyingly handsome face, so I found myself leaning over toward him and saying, "Mason, can I tell you a secret?"

"Anything."

"I don't actually think that you're the devil." It felt like a huge moment to admit that. "You can quote me and put that in your article. Which I think is big of me, considering how much you hate me."

"Can I tell you a secret?" he said.

"It depends on whether or not you want me to remember it. You should know that my superpower is total drunken recall. I never forget anything I did or said while drunk."

"As far as superpowers go, it's not a great one."

"Yep, I got screwed over that day!" I agreed. Especially since the average person very much wanted to forget everything they did while drunk. "What's your superpower?"

Mason shot me a sexy grin that made my pulse jackhammer. "My boyish good looks."

He wasn't wrong.

He didn't need to know that, though.

"So what's your secret?" I prompted.

"My secret is that I don't hate you, Sinclair. I never have."

My lungs seemed to compress, and I had a hard time filling them back up with oxygen. He didn't hate me? Then why else had he done what he did? I was very confused, and I was finding it harder and harder to focus. It didn't help matters that we had apparently reached the losing-my-balance portion of the evening, which Mason seemed to notice.

"Are you doing okay?"

"I'm just feeling like I'm about to humpty-dumpty off of this barstool," I confessed.

"Maybe don't do that, because I hear horses are not good at putting people back together again."

I laughed at that, even though it didn't really make much sense. This felt like me and Mason again—telling each other silly things just to get a reaction. The way we'd been when we were younger.

It hurt my heart to remember it and how he'd ruined it.

"I think I should drive you home because I'm afraid if I leave you to your own devices, you're going to end up on the news," he said.

"Unlike your taste in women, that idea's not half-bad," I announced before taking a drink of water. He had been right about hydrating with a liquid that wasn't amber colored.

It occurred to me that my tequila had been the same shade as Mason's eyes. If I were sober, I wouldn't have been taking that as some sort of ominous warning from the universe.

But it was concerning me now.

"What do you know about my taste in women?" Mason asked, and it made me pause. All of my friends in high school had harbored a crush on him, but he hadn't dated any of them seriously. He had taken a girl out here and there—no girlfriends, though.

I knew nothing about what he looked for in a woman now.

It bothered me that I didn't know something so fundamental about him.

He flagged Romeo down and asked him for the check. When he returned, I reached for it, but Mason kept it out of my grasp.

Which wasn't hard, considering how bad my fine motor skills currently were.

"For the record, that's two dates," he said as he left some twenty-dollar bills with the check.

"Who carries cash?" I asked him.

"People in a hurry," he said. "Let's get you home."

I tried to stand up, but my legs weren't cooperating. I wobbled dangerously, and Mason was there, grabbing me by the elbows to keep me upright.

"Whoa. I got you, Sinclair."

Electricity zinged along my nervous system, lighting up every nerve ending that I possessed just because he was holding me. My skin felt flushed and prickly, oversensitized. If he moved his hands at all along my heated skin, I was probably going to spontaneously combust.

Instead he gripped my elbows tightly. I heard his breath hitch, saw his jaw clench.

"Hold on a second," I told him, putting my hands against his chest. Was it my drunken imagination, or was his heart beating faster?

"I'll hold whatever you like," he murmured, his gaze settling on my lips.

If I was this excited by him barely touching me, what would it be like if we kissed? Blood pulsed in my ears, blocking out the sounds of the restaurant.

His good looks really were his superpower, and I felt helpless to resist. "You and your tequila eyes," I said with a shake of my head.

"My what?" he asked.

No time to explain when there were better things we could be doing with our mouths than using them to make words.

"I think at the end of our second date, I would do this," I said softly. He looked adorably confused for a second, not registering what I was about to do.

I moved closer to him so that my chest pressed against his and slid my hands up to his neck. He made a sound at the back of his throat that turned my knees to jelly. My lips tingled in anticipation, wanting nothing more than to feel his mouth on mine. I saw the want in his eyes, felt the pull of desire low in my stomach. I pushed myself forward with the intention of kissing him.

"What are you doing?" he asked, and his voice sounded strained but excited.

"You know what I'm doing." I breathed the words against his lips as I moved closer.

Everything seemed to be happening in slow motion, my heart thudding slowly in my chest, the anticipation ratcheting up with each shared breath between us.

And just as I was about to make contact . . .

He moved his head out of the way.

CHAPTER SEVENTEEN

His rejection was sharp and fierce, and I hadn't ever felt more stupid. I immediately pulled my hands away and stepped back, leaning against the bar. This was what happened when you had a twin sister and a best friend who constantly lied to you. You believed the fairy tales they tried to sell you.

Mason Beckett was not interested in me, as he'd just proved by rejecting me.

Not able to leave well enough alone, I had to make the situation worse by asking a question he'd already answered. "You don't want to kiss me?"

"There is nothing I want more," he said, his voice rough and shaking, like he could barely contain himself. His hands were still at my elbows, still gripping me tightly. "Right now you can't consent to it."

"I too can!" I protested.

"You *toucan*? Like the bird?"

That wasn't right. "I can, too!" Obviously I could consent, which was why I had tried to kiss him.

"I think you just proved my point, and your judgment might be a tad impaired."

That mollified me slightly. It was true—I wasn't quite myself. But I could tell whether or not I wanted to kiss someone.

That nagging feeling had returned, like I was forgetting something very important. Something that was going to make me angry when I remembered. But nothing was coming to the forefront of my mind. I was still revved up, with no way to ease this ache.

Well, whatever this nagging feeling was, it could just wait until tomorrow.

"Where are your keys?" he asked me, and I handed him my purse, still feeling pretty unsteady.

Mason took the purse from me and began to rummage through it. "Why are there so many candy wrappers in here? It's like a chocolate cemetery." He grumbled for a bit longer and then finally located my keys.

"Come on, Dory," he said, pointing me toward the door as he wrapped an arm around my waist to help me walk.

Him being pressed against me felt delicious.

"Dory?" I asked.

"Because you drink like a fish?"

I smiled. "I thought it was because I was forgetful."

"What are you forgetting?" he asked as we walked through the front door and out into the parking lot, the humid air wrapping around me like a thick blanket, making me sweat.

"I don't know, but I get the feeling that when I remember, I'm going to be mad."

"I'd agree with that," he said.

He pushed the button on my key fob and unlocked the doors. He opened the passenger door to help me get in, and I stopped to grin at him. "You just told me you wanted to kiss me. That's embarrassing for you."

"You wanted the same thing," he reminded me.

"Yes, but I'm drunk. What's your excuse?" I asked as I slid into the car. He closed the door behind me, and I struggled with my seat belt because I lacked the coordination to clip it into the buckle.

"Here." He had entered the driver's side, and his long fingers brushed against mine as he helped click it into place.

"Thank you," I said, enjoying being this close to him. His gaze darted up to mine, as if he realized what position we were in, and he scooted back and started up the car.

Even though it was muggy outside, I rolled down my window so that I could feel the rush of fresh air against my skin. Despite my most recent humiliation, everything felt shiny and happy, as if it were surrounded by a golden haze, and like I didn't have any worries or concerns at all. I could just be free.

Time seemed to both stop and fly by at the same time.

Probably because I had fallen asleep.

I woke up to Mason gently shaking my shoulder. "Sinclair, we're here."

"Oh!" I sat up and rubbed my mouth, hoping I hadn't accidentally drooled, but I was good. "Thanks."

We sat in the car awkwardly for a moment. My instinct was to run away, but I felt trapped by his gaze and stayed put.

Why was he so handsome? And chiseled and broad and well built and ridiculously attractive?

"If it's okay with you, I'll drive myself home and bring the car back tomorrow," he offered.

"Yes, sure, whatever." I wanted to kiss him again, so I definitely needed to go. It was much easier to release the belt than it had been to buckle it, so I was up and out of the car quickly.

I heard Mason following along behind me.

"What are you doing?" I asked.

"I'm going to walk you to the door. The last thing I need is for you to fall and knock yourself out and for your mom to come out and find you that way in the morning. I'll never hear the end of it."

I completely understood that sentiment, as wanting to keep him safe from physical harm had been driving my actions for the last couple of days.

He walked with me up to the front porch.

"Good night," I told him, ready to make my escape and go to bed. My hazy happiness had started to wear off, and instead my brain was uncomfortably reminding me that I had tried to kiss him and he'd rejected me.

"Night," he said.

Again there was that moment where I felt like we both wanted more, but he'd already said no, and I wasn't in the mood for further humiliation.

I put my hand on the doorknob and twisted it, but it was locked.

"Oh no! Locked." My parents didn't lock the door until they went to bed. They must have turned in early tonight.

"Don't you have a key?"

"No, I haven't needed one. Usually somebody is always up when I come home." I registered how sad that was—that my middle-aged parents were typically wide awake when I came back from a night out because I tended not to stay out very late.

I walked away from the door, headed for my backyard. It took a second for Mason to follow me, as he was obviously confused by my actions.

"Where are you going?" he asked as I let myself through the gate.

"To the back door."

"Why don't you just ring the doorbell? Or call somebody to open the door?"

"Because I'm not going to let my parents see me drunk!" I said as we walked along the path toward the back of the house.

"You're twenty-four years old. I'm pretty sure they know you drink," he said.

"But I'm the one who has to be perfect," I responded. The one who didn't worry them. The one who did everything right and always succeeded so that I wouldn't add any stress to their lives.

I didn't say that part, but from the look Mason was giving me, it was like he understood.

Worried that he might ask me to explain myself, I added, "My mom knows I was with you, and my current state would just be grist for the mill, and I do not need her input tonight. Plus, my dad would come out here and grill you about your intentions."

He put his hand over his heart. "I could assure your father that my intentions toward you are purely sexual."

Molten heat exploded in my abdomen, and I had to focus on breathing because my lungs had stopped cooperating. He'd obviously meant it as a joke, and I felt like I needed to let out a forced laugh so that he wouldn't guess at the reaction I was having to his words.

"You don't have to pretend to laugh just to humor me," he said with a smile, as if he hadn't said something so provocative that I was still trembling from it. He walked over to the biggest tree in the backyard and peered up at our treehouse. "I remember when we used to play up here."

"I had plans in high school to lure you up there." I didn't know why I'd said it but regretted it the second I did.

"What were you going to do with me if you'd succeeded?" he asked with interest.

There was no way I was going to elaborate. I'd had enough rejection for one night. My reply was to keep walking to the back door. Mason followed closely behind, and the warmth from him, his scent . . . I was feeling intoxicated all over again.

The back door was locked as well, just as I'd suspected—my dad was always thorough in his nighttime routine—and I took off my shoes.

"What's the plan?" Mason asked.

"I'm going through the doggy door," I told him. He looked like he was about to bust out laughing.

"Shut up," I told him.

He held up both of his hands, like he was being arrested. "I didn't say anything."

"You said it with your face," I said. "Sierra and I used to sneak in this way all the time in high school."

"Speaking of dogs, where is Bosco?"

Our family dog, Bosco, had adored Mason. "He died a few years ago, and Mom hasn't had it in her to adopt a new dog. I think my dad will just show up with a puppy one day, if I know him."

I knelt down on the porch and waved Mason over to the side because I didn't want to flash him as I crawled through the door. "Stand over there, please."

He did it without asking why. But he did say, "I'm not sure this is a good idea. I don't think you currently have the right amount of coordination to get through that door."

"I can crawl," I said dismissively. I put my arm and one shoulder through the door. It was a bit narrower than I remembered. I put my other arm and shoulder through so that my top half was in the house and my bottom half was still outside, then tried to move forward.

But I couldn't.

I was caught.

Despite tugging hard, I could feel that my dress was stuck on something, holding me fast.

"Trouble?" Mason asked.

"I'm clearly stuck," I said, exasperated.

"I guess this is what happens when you still live at home and have to sneak in like you're a teenager," he said in a smug way that made me want to kick him.

"You live at home with your mom!"

"I live in the guesthouse."

"That's not any different," I protested.

"It is."

"I am stuck like Winnie the Pooh here. Could you just help me and feel superior to me later?"

"Seeing as how I'm not stuck in a dog door, I'm kind of feeling superior to you now. You always thought you were smarter than me."

"Only empirically," I retorted.

He laughed, and I worried that we might wake up my parents if we weren't quieter.

"Are you going to help me, or are you going to keep making fun of me?" I asked.

"There's no joy in mocking you right now. It's too easy. I wouldn't even get any pleasure out of it. Hang on."

I could feel his hands near my waist, tugging on me as he looked for what was holding me captive. I wanted to disappear. This was what happened when you thought you had reached your maximum capacity for embarrassment; the universe found a way to show you that it wasn't true. I thought I'd reached rock bottom, but it turned out there was a basement subfloor for me to crash through.

"I got you. Hang on."

He started pulling me backward, and I heard the sound of my dress ripping. I supposed that couldn't be helped, but he tugged me back into the yard when he could have just as easily pushed me forward.

Although he probably would have had to put both of his hands on my butt to push, and that would have made everything even more humiliating. It seemed he'd picked the least miserable option for both of us.

"I'm sorry about your dress," he said after he'd helped me clear the door. "Did you want to give the dog door another shot?"

For as long as I lived, I was never crawling through that doggy door again. I wondered if my face was all red. I got to my feet. "That's okay. I'm just going to climb my trellis."

"Sinclair, don't climb the trellis."

I shrugged him off and headed over to it. Finding some footholds, I started climbing. "I used to have this fantasy that you would sneak into my bedroom at night and we'd make out." I didn't really have any experience beyond that, so I never mentally took it further, but it was something I'd fervently hoped might happen.

"You used to have a lot of fantasies about me."

Now my face definitely felt hot, and I was glad I was facing the house and not him. I climbed up a bit farther. "There was this one time Kenny Hoffmeyer climbed into my bedroom and I screamed. He thought it was Sierra's room, and she was waiting for him, and it was a whole thing. Very disappointing for everyone involved."

Mason moved beneath me, over to the right.

"What are you doing?" I asked.

"I was standing there so I could catch you, but I'm moving over here now so that I can be a gentleman and not look up your skirt."

I had forgotten about that. "It's a dress," I said. "And thank you."

My foot slipped, and my adrenaline spiked as I lost my hold, going straight down to the ground and landing hard on my left foot.

He rushed over. "Are you okay?"

Pain radiated from my ankle, and I felt nausea at the back of my throat. "I think I broke my foot. Can you take me to the hospital?"

CHAPTER EIGHTEEN

"Let me get your parents," he said.

"Nope." If I didn't want them to know that I had been drinking, I most definitely did not need them to know that I had been stuck in the doggy door and had fallen off the trellis. This was one of those things that I planned on taking to the grave. "Sierra's working tonight at the ER. She can help."

He tried to help me to stand, but as soon as I put pressure on my left foot, I yelped in pain.

Without hesitation, Mason swung me up into his arms and carried me across the backyard and back to my car like it was easy. Like I was weightless.

In between bursts of throbbing pain, I was super impressed.

And I liked how it felt to have him hold me in his arms. As if he could keep me safe.

This is where you belong.

And this time I didn't tell my inner teenager to be quiet. Instead I let my head rest against his shoulder and felt the brush of his lips across the top of my scalp, making it tingle as he put me gently into the car.

The drive to the hospital seemed to take forever, and Mason had to carry me from the parking lot into the lobby of the ER. He set me down in a chair and went over to tell the registration nurse why we'd come in.

"We're not too busy tonight. Let me grab a wheelchair, and she can come on back."

I was actually disappointed that Mason wasn't going to be able to carry me any longer. When the nurse came out, she stopped short and said, "Sierra?"

"I'm Savannah. Her identical twin."

"Wow, do you two look the same! I'm Cynthia, by the way."

I held back my retort that, yes, we looked the same because that was the literal definition of *identical*, but I stayed quiet. Since Cynthia might be the one responsible for giving me painkillers, I wasn't going to be snarky.

The grin on Mason's face told me he knew exactly what I'd been thinking.

Cynthia and Mason helped me into the wheelchair, and then she rolled me back into an examination room. They both had to help me get into the bed, and I tried to ignore how awkward I felt.

"Tell me what brings you in tonight," Cynthia said.

"She fell off a trellis," Mason answered. "After she got stuck going through a dog door."

He was making me sound terrible. "In my defense, I was drunk, and that's why I got stuck and then fell off a trellis."

"That's not a defense. It's just a description of what happened," he said.

"So yes to alcohol consumption tonight . . . Let me get some of your vitals." Cynthia took my blood pressure, then checked my pulse, oxygen saturation, and temperature. She told me what she was doing with each device and then recorded all of her findings on a tablet she had with her.

She asked for my height, my weight, and the date of my last menstrual cycle, and I didn't make eye contact with Mason as I gave those to her.

"There might be some other tests that we need to perform later, like a urine test," she said. "The doctor might also want to order an X-ray. Is there any chance that you could be pregnant?"

I wanted to laugh. "No. No chance at all."

Cynthia glanced up from her tablet at me. She shifted her gaze over to Mason, appraising him, and then turned it back to me.

"Are you sure?" she asked in disbelief.

That made Mason grin.

This was going to get back to my sister, and she would enjoy it far too much that her colleague had jumped to this conclusion. "Yes. Very sure," I said.

"Dr. Otterson is here tonight, and he'll be in to see you shortly," she said, then left us alone.

I frowned at him. "Why are you grinning like you just told Alice how to find the Queen of Hearts?"

"She thought we were dating," he said.

Yes, I had picked up on her oh-so-subtle insinuation. "Which was ridiculous, because I don't date men like you."

"Smart, charming, attractive, ambitious, with an incredible sense of humor and the ability to forgive?"

The last one stung a little. "My type tends more toward the modest kind who aren't full of themselves."

He shrugged. "Facts are facts."

"I think you mean opinions are opinions."

"Opinions we both share are facts."

While I wanted to protest that I didn't share in his overinflated opinion of himself, I knew there was a part of me that did, so instead I said, "That's not how that works!"

"One of the things I like best about you is how you always tell me what you're thinking."

Oh no, had I said that overinflated / I-agreed-with-his-opinion part out loud? I couldn't remember. "It's not always a good thing. It's why I only have two friends."

"Three."

"Three what?" I asked.

"Three friends. I'm your friend."

"We're not friends."

Sierra came into the room, looking panicked. "Savannah! Are you okay?"

"I'm good," I told her. I yawned. It had been a long night, and I was getting really tired.

"Can I get you anything?" she asked.

"Some water and all of the hospital's acetaminophen."

"Given what Cynthia just told me, you still have a bunch of alcohol in your system, and it doesn't interact well with acetaminophen. We don't want your liver to explode, because from a medical standpoint, that would be bad. Dr. Otterson will have a recommendation for pain management when he gets here."

"Buck up, Sinclair," Mason interjected. "Take Coach Dailey's advice and just walk it off."

That made me smile. My volleyball coach had been notorious for telling her players to walk injuries off. Including when Alyssa Sharpton had broken her arm.

"Can I talk to you?" Sierra addressed this to Mason, and then she took him by the arm and out into the hallway. Her voice was raised slightly, but whatever he said seemed to calm her down, and she nodded. Then he hugged her. He turned to wave to me, and then he was gone.

I was a bit surprised. I'd thought he might stick around.

And I was strangely disappointed.

When my sister came back into the room, she said, "I told him to go home, that I'd take care of you. I'll get you hydrated and your ankle checked out, and then I'll drive you home in the morning."

"I didn't get to thank him."

Sierra had come over to check my pulse manually, but that made her pause. "Do you know what your problem is?"

"Oh, no thank you." I did not need more of this right now.

"You don't say the important things you need to say to other people because you're afraid of what they will think."

That wasn't at all what was going on here. I wasn't afraid of Mason's opinion. However, she was the second person tonight to tell me that this was a problem of mine. That might mean there was some merit to it. I also didn't want to consider whether or not it meant something that Mason liked that I was so open with him, even though I apparently wasn't with other people. "That has nothing to do with Mason."

"I think it does. I think you've been mad at him for so long that you're worried what people will think if you confess that you have feelings for him and have always had feelings for him."

I tried to sit up, but she put her hand on my shoulder. "You need to rest. Also, to back up what I am saying here, Cynthia sent me a text about how much you were flirting with Mason and how he was flirting right back."

"He was?" I asked. I couldn't think of anything that had happened since we got to the hospital that might be construed as flirting. "Why would he do that?"

She was looking at her watch while holding my wrist and said, "My guess? Because he would like to make out with your face forthwith. Posthaste, even." At my expression, she added, "Sorry, I was watching a Jane Austen movie earlier today."

I didn't argue with her, nor did I mention the fact that I had l literally thrown myself at him and he had said no. The sting of that particular memory was still pretty fresh. It wasn't something I was ready to discuss, and I didn't think it was going to fade anytime soon.

"You're sort of right," I told her. "I did have feelings for Mason growing up. A pretty intense crush. And I wanted so badly to go on a date with him. To get that chance to see if we could be something more. What we might be like as a romantic couple and not just friends. But everything is too complicated now. Even if he appears to be a nice guy, that doesn't erase the past and what he did to me. Not to mention that he's a client, and the absolute last thing that I need to be doing right now is dating a client, because then I will definitely lose my certification."

And I didn't know what that might mean for becoming licensed as a therapist. Would this follow me? Would it prevent that from happening?

"You wish you could date him without the baggage."

"Don't quote me on this, because I am still very drunk, but yes." It was like a Mason-size boulder had been lifted off my shoulders. It was a relief to admit to it.

"In vino veritas, my sister." At my blank expression, she added, "Booze makes you tell the truth."

"I guess."

Sierra reached for a chair and pulled it up next to my bed. "I think I'm ready to tell you about Mason and me."

My heart seized up in a panic, and I reminded myself to relax. I took some deep breaths. She had already assured me that nothing was going on between them romantically, and I chose to believe her.

"Mason and I are friends."

"I knew that part, traitor," I teased her.

She smiled briefly and went on. "What you don't know is how much I've relied on him. Especially when I was going through treatment."

This time I did sit straight up in my hospital bed. "What?"

"Lie down," she instructed me, and wouldn't say anything else until I did as she said. "He was someone I could talk to whose feelings I didn't have to worry about. I could say anything I wanted to him, and it didn't matter. I spent so much time stressing out about your feelings and Mom's and Dad's, but Mason was able to care about me without being invested the same way a family member would. I could unload on him and he took it and just listened, and it was exactly what I needed."

"Why didn't you ever tell me that?" I whispered. Because it felt like this might change everything. That he had been there for my twin when she needed him most—had helped her get through the hardest time in her life.

How was I supposed to be angry at a man like that?

"I knew how mad you'd be," she said. "It's why I didn't tell you. And my friendship with him is why I don't think he spread that rumor about you. That's just not who he is. He's the kind of guy who wouldn't go out with his frat brothers on a Saturday night because I needed someone to talk to."

This still felt slightly surreal, but she sounded so honest that I knew it had to be true. "You could have called me."

She reached over to take my hand. "I know I could have. But you would have worried. You would have thought I was going to relapse. You would have gotten on a plane and come to be with me. Mason was a good listener, and I wasn't his whole life the way I am for our family."

"I can't believe he did that." That wasn't true—I could believe it. Even in high school, he wasn't like the other immature slimeballs with zero hygiene skills. He had always been compassionate and caring.

But despite that, I knew what had happened and what he'd done to me, even if it seemed out of character for him.

"He was the only one who saw us," I told her. "The rumor had to come from him."

"I know that's what you think, and I hope you'll let him explain."

"Why didn't he try explaining himself in high school?" I asked. "If it's so important to him for things to be better between us, he's had years. Why now?"

"That's mostly my fault, too," she admitted. "He wasn't sure how to talk to you, and he asked my advice, and I know how you are and told him to give you time to process and get over it. I just didn't know you'd hold out for six years. He wanted to reach out, and I stopped him. I was worried he was going to hurt you again, and I didn't want that."

I couldn't even be mad at Sierra for meddling in my life because I had done it so many times to her. It was what we did—we looked out for each other and had one another's backs.

But part of me wished she hadn't warned Mason away.

And another part wished that he hadn't listened to her.

She leaned over and kissed me on the forehead. "It's a lot, but I hope you'll be able to get some sleep. Push the call button if you need me."

This was so much to process, and I wasn't even sure where to start. Maybe I should take Sierra's advice and ask him.

Weariness overtook me, and as my eyes drifted shut, I wondered what he would say to explain everything.

And whether or not I would believe him.

CHAPTER NINETEEN

I became vaguely aware of sunlight filtering in as I woke up, and for a brief moment, I didn't know where I was.

"Good morning, sleepyhead," Sierra said as she came into the room and opened the blinds so that even more light flooded in. Oh yeah. I was in the hospital.

I groaned and covered my eyes with my hands. "Too bright."

She came over to my bedside. "Look at you. All sweaty and gross. It reminds me of that one morning when you tried to give up sugar."

"Too loud. And ha ha."

"Do you feel as bad as you look?"

"Yes. I need a shower and to brush my teeth for three years straight and I need something for a killer headache." I was glad Mason had left. I wouldn't want him to see me like this.

Although I got the feeling that he probably wouldn't care if I was a mess.

I started to sit up, and every single memory from last night came rushing back to me. Just like I'd told Mason, my superpower kicked in, and I had total drunken recall.

Every embarrassing thing I'd said, the way I'd been open and vulnerable with him, told him things I didn't want him to know, and worst of all . . .

I groaned and buried my face in my hands.

"What's wrong?" she asked.

Nope. If she could hide the fact that she and Mason had been secret friends for years, I could conceal that I'd tried to kiss him and he'd said no.

My twin did not need the encouragement, and I wasn't particularly anxious to relive that moment. Although that was all I was doing right now—running it through my head over and over. Me attempting to kiss him and him moving his face as far away from me as he could.

"Are you feeling anxious? Because that's actually pretty common," she said. "They call it hangxiety. It's because alcohol mimics GABA, which is a brain chemical that makes you feel relaxed and happy. And then when it's out of your system, it increases glutamate, another brain chemical, which has the opposite effect and makes you feel restless, anxious, and worried."

"Thank you for the science lesson," I mumbled. This was just plain old embarrassment, though. "But I don't think I have that."

"Either way, I'm here to take your IV out."

I lifted my right arm for her. I had the vague recollection of being woken up when a nurse I didn't know put in an IV line for fluids. That was after they had taken me in for an X-ray, which showed that my ankle wasn't broken. It was only a sprain.

Just after Sierra had removed the IV, a man walked into our room. A man I knew.

"Mr. Franklin?" Frederick Franklin was one of the Board members who had censured me.

"Ms. Sinclair? My apologies, I'm looking for my niece. I must have the wrong room."

Next thing I knew, I heard a voice I recognized.

"Room eleven, not room ten, Freddie." Vivian walked through the doorway. The same Vivian who worked on the floor above me and had seen me with Mason during the fake fire, when she'd assumed he was my client. "Savannah! Sierra! How are you? Are you okay?"

My heart was beating so hard. It might have been a delayed chemical reaction from the alcohol, but regardless, my fight-or-flight reflex kicked in, and I wanted to run. "I accidentally fell while doing some gardening. I have a slight sprain. Sierra's been looking after me. How do you two know each other?"

"Freddie is my brother. My daughter had an eardrum burst, and he's always been overprotective, so he rushed down here to help out."

I knew that Vivian was a single mom who struggled with taking care of her daughter alone, and while I was glad that she had family close by to help out, it had never once occurred to me that Frederick Franklin and Vivian Franklin might be related.

"How do you know Freddie?" Vivian asked, a perfectly reasonable question.

"Professionally," Mr. Franklin said quickly, and thankfully didn't go into any more detail.

"Right." She nodded, looking like she felt silly. "I know you're both hypnotists. I should have made that connection. I've just been up all night, and I'm a little out of it."

With them standing there together, I could see the resemblance. I had been so upset at my meeting that I hadn't noticed it.

"I hope Taylor is doing okay," I said, finally finding my voice.

"She is. I'm actually about to take her home. Come with me, Freddie. Heal up quickly, Savannah!"

They left, and I did my best to not hyperventilate. If Mason had been in here when Mr. Franklin had accidentally walked in, with Vivian knowing what she did . . .

"That was so close," I said.

"What's wrong?"

"Frederick Franklin is on the Florida Board of Professional Hypnotists. He was one of the people who voted to censure me. Vivian saw me and Mason together the day of the false alarm and knows he's my client. What if Mason had stuck around?"

Oh, it would have been so bad.

Sierra looked concerned. "He was here until about half an hour ago."

"What? Why?"

"He stayed in the waiting room all night."

That didn't make any sense. "I don't understand."

"I know you don't. That's part of the problem."

I grasped at the only thing that made sense. "Out of guilt?"

"You got yourself drunk and fell off the trellis all by your lonesome," she scoffed. "What does he have to feel guilty for?"

"I have an actual list."

"He was worried about you."

"You know, he showed up really late to our prearranged hang last night. You don't get to do that and then not feel guilty about it when the other person who was waiting for you gets drunk and maims themselves."

"You're not maimed. You're fine. Elevation and ice, and I'll make sure that you're doing it, so don't think you're getting out of healing up properly."

My heart was still racing from the casual news she'd just shared with me and from how close I'd come to being caught in a potentially compromising situation.

What right did Mason have to be all kind and caring and stay up all night in a waiting room? He wasn't my boyfriend. He wasn't even a friend, despite his assertion to the contrary.

What if he'd come in to say goodbye and had stuck around? There were so many ways this could have blown up in my face.

All Vivian had to do was see me and Mason together and my career, which I'd fought really hard for, would be over.

I couldn't allow that to happen.

No matter what.

My mentor had told me to avoid giving the Board any further ammunition. Mason Beckett wasn't just ammunition. He was a full-blown nuclear warhead who could detonate my entire life.

~

For the last few days, I'd done as Sierra had asked and rested. I spent my time reading and doing my online appointments and my schoolwork. It was actually nice to be able to escape the real world for a little while.

I had thought that Mason would have at least reached out to me, but he hadn't.

On Sunday evening Sierra came into my room. "My ankle's elevated!" I told her. She'd been checking up on me constantly. I actually felt fine and had been walking around with absolutely no issues, but I didn't tell her that part. "I'm feeling better, you know."

"Good. I'm sure you'll be okay to go back into the office tomorrow."

"That's the plan," I said.

"Hey, guess who's coming to dinner?"

"Sidney Poitier?"

She gave me a blank look. "I don't understand your reference."

"Do a Google search, Sierra. That was funny."

"If your joke involves me having to look something up online, then it's not actually funny."

"So I'm guessing the answer to your riddle is Nana?" She came over every Sunday night, and she was one of my favorite people in the whole world.

"Nope. Try again."

"Who?" I asked suspiciously, because she sounded strange.

"Heather and Mason."

That made me stand up in alarm. "Tell Mom I'm not feeling well."

"I'm not going to lie to our mother. Especially as you stand there on your healed ankle."

I coughed. "Maybe I'm coming down with something."

"I'm an actual nurse. You think I don't know a fake cough when I hear it? You know Mom will come up here and drag you downstairs if she has to. I just wanted to give you a heads-up so that you could mentally prepare or whatever. You can't fight with him in front of Mom and Heather. It will make them upset."

She was right—it would.

"I have to get changed," I said, running over to my closet. I'd been lounging around in pajamas because I was resting, and my casual attire had made it so that my dad had called me Sierra no less than three times already.

"Why would you need to get changed?" she asked as she flopped onto my bed and picked up the fantasy book I had been reading. "You don't like him."

"I need . . . to look nice." I didn't know how to explain it, but I wasn't going to let him see me looking like this. I started pushing hangers aside, trying to find something that would work.

"Gotta get that armor on, right?" she asked.

I quickly changed, as I didn't know how much time I had. I had gone over to my mirror and pulled my hair up, intending to do a French twist, when I heard Mason's voice.

"Knock, knock." He stood in my doorway holding a bunch of flowers. Heat started to prickle along the back of my neck.

"Who's there?" Sierra responded playfully.

He shook his head. "I don't have anything prepared for that."

"Even that's funnier than Savannah's joke. I said, 'Guess who's coming to dinner?' and her response was 'Sidney Poitier.'"

Mason started laughing.

I put a hand over my stomach. We used to watch old movies together all the time, especially ones that he had watched with his grandfather before he passed away. Of course Mason would get it.

Sierra shot me a you're-so-made-for-each-other look before she stood up. "I'm going to go see if Mom needs help."

I wanted to tell her to stay because I didn't want to be alone with Mason Beckett in my bedroom.

She smiled at him as she left, and he walked into my room, uninvited. "Fall off any good trellises lately, Sinclair?"

Despite what my sister had told him, he wasn't funny. I glared at him, but he didn't get the message. Instead he looked around, taking everything in. "Just like I remember."

I didn't respond, because him being so close was making it a bit hard to breathe. All I could think about was how much I'd embarrassed myself the last time we were alone together. Then I reminded myself that if the wrong person saw us together, I could kiss my job goodbye, and I summoned up all the hate I had for him.

It was necessary to keep him away.

Mostly to remind me to behave.

Because as much as I had wanted to dismiss it as a drunken impulse, I still really wanted to kiss him.

I was clearly deranged.

"It looks pretty down," he said, and it took me a second to realize he was talking about my hair, which I hadn't finished styling. So I put it up into a ponytail, using the scrunchie on my wrist.

Not how I would normally do it, but it was better than him thinking I was leaving it down for him.

"Who are those for?" I asked, pointing at the flowers he was carrying.

"Maybe they're for you. Maybe I'm wooing you."

That set off internal sirens just as loud as the fire alarm in my office had been. "Woo somewhere else. You're not allowed to woo. Your woo is being cut off."

He laughed and then said, "They're for your grandma."

Nana hated pretty much everybody in the world besides our family and Mason. She always talked about him.

I adored her, but it was annoying.

"Can you not?" I asked. "You've already won Nana over. You don't need to be so overkill."

"I can turn the charm down, but I can't turn it off completely."

And I knew that from firsthand experience.

"Look," I said. "We can get through this. You stay on your end of the table and I'll stay on mine and—"

"Never the twain shall meet?" he offered as he moved closer to me. The flowers were almost squished between us.

"You're going to flatten those," I said, my breath catching at the fire in his eyes, my abdomen swirling with want and liquid heat.

"It'd be worth it."

My lips parted at his words, and that intensity in his eyes increased.

"Savannah?" My mom had come into my room, breaking whatever spell he had managed to cast over me, and I jumped back, as if she'd caught us doing something we shouldn't. "Oh, there you are, Mason. Would you mind helping Sierra set the table? I need to have a word with my daughter."

"Sure thing, Jodi. I've got some flowers to deliver."

He walked backward for a few steps, keeping his eyes on me. Like he was promising something.

When he was gone, I put my fingers over my lips. They were still tingling from anticipation.

"Sit down," my mom said, patting a spot on my bed next to her. "We need to have a chat."

CHAPTER TWENTY

There was nothing that made you feel more like a teenager again than your mother telling you that she needed to have a chat with you. If she lectured me about finding Mason in my room, I was going to run amok, arms flailing about wildly.

I sat down next to her.

"Please be nice today," she said. "Heather has been having a bit of a hard time lately, and I want her to enjoy dinner."

Concerned, I asked, "What happened?"

"It's nothing you need to worry about," she said, and I bet Mason knew and would probably tell me.

"I'll behave," I said, feeling guilty that so many different people had to tell me to keep my emotions in check.

"Thank you. And I need you to come be a part of the dinner. That means no running off to your room to read."

"I promise."

"Or Sierra's room!" she added, foiling the loophole I had already planned on using.

"I won't."

"Thank you. Your dad just got back with Nana, so we're going to eat in a few minutes. Come down and say hello."

I was hoping I'd get the chance to fix my hair and put on some makeup, but she waited for me by my bedroom door. So I followed along behind her, trying to do what Sierra had suggested and mentally preparing myself. By showing up in my room, Mason had already thrown me off my game. Why did I physically respond like that to him when I was still angry?

And the more I thought about it, the angrier I got. If he was attracted to me and did like me, then why didn't he apologize for what he'd done? Didn't he think it was important to clear the air? There was no way anything could happen between us while that still hung over our heads.

As Mom and I went down the stairs, I reminded myself that it didn't matter. Even if in some alternate timeline Mason and I wanted to be together, he was a client, and the last thing I needed was for gossip that we were dating to get around town and for Vivian to mention it the next time she talked to her brother.

Mason might be hot, but I wasn't willing to risk my career for him. Anger was my weapon of choice, a feeling I understood all too well. I had to keep it close by, use it, so that I could control myself around him.

We went into the family room, and everybody was sitting on the couch. Nana was in her favorite armchair, which my dad usually occupied when he watched sports. She smelled the flowers that Mason had given her and then told my mom to put them in some water.

Heather came over to hug me hello. I hugged her tightly and said, "Is everything okay?"

"Just a bit of a health scare," she said. "I think I'll be fine, though."

No one else was paying attention to us, as they were all talking, but I still looked at Sierra to see if she'd overheard. I wondered if she knew what was going on.

Heather took her seat again, and I went over and kissed my grandma on the forehead. "How are you, Nana?"

"No news is good news," she said. "How are you, one of my favorite granddaughters?"

Sierra and I were her only grandchildren, but it still made me smile.

"I'm good," I told her, lying through my teeth. Nana would definitely be on Mason's side. Especially after the flowers.

"Have a seat," she said, and it was then that I noted that Sierra must have engineered the seating arrangements, as the only empty spot was next to Mason.

I wasn't going to fall for that trap. I sat down on the couch in between my sister and my father, even though there really wasn't any room. Sierra protested, but this was her fault. She could go sit by Mason.

"Did you see my flowers?" Nana asked, and I nodded.

"They are pretty," I said.

She reached over to pat Mason on the knee. "Such a good boy. One of you should marry him and give me some great-grandbabies."

"Sierra's not dating anyone," I offered, and my sister frowned at me. She didn't like being thrown into the lion's den any more than I did. Nana, who'd only had one baby, my father, later in life, had always wanted a large family. We fed that need for her for a little while, but once we'd turned twenty-one, she had basically decided we were old enough to start popping out great-grandchildren for her, and she talked about it every Sunday.

She turned back toward Mason. "You should really be passing on those genes of yours."

"Well, if I find the right girl, I'll do just that."

Of course he was staring at me when he said it, and I felt like everyone in the room noticed.

"I didn't bring my readers. Can you go outside and grab the newspaper and tell me what the headlines are? Then I can tell you if I want you to read the article," Nana said to Mason.

Newspaper? We hadn't had one of those delivered since I was in elementary school. Nana usually brought her own—why did she think we had one here?

"You forgot your paper, Mom," my dad reminded her.

Mason grabbed his phone. "I could read you some of the headlines that Google recommends."

"That would be fine," she said.

"Okay. The first one is an article about how to wake up every day at five o'clock in the morning. I'm guessing it involves an alarm clock."

I twisted my lips together so that I wouldn't laugh.

"Not that one. Next."

He scrolled a bit. "Here's one about seven ways to not die from a rattlesnake bite. I would bet the first recommendation will be to not get bit."

I couldn't help it. A short laugh escaped, and his eyes lit up when he heard it.

Mad. I was mad at him. Why couldn't I remember that? Why was it so hard to conjure up those feelings?

To be fair, he had warned me that he couldn't turn the charm off, and he was true to his word.

Thankfully, my mom announced that dinner was ready, and we all filed into the dining room.

I sat in my regular seat, and when Sierra went to sit next to me, my mom said, "Sierra, you sit over here, next to Heather."

Which meant the only seat left open for Mason was next to me.

Could my family be any more obvious?

Sierra reached down and grabbed the sharp knives from both of our place settings. "Just going to remove these potential murder weapons," she said, quietly enough that only I heard her.

She probably had a point.

That urge to run had returned, but I had promised my mom I wouldn't go up to the bedrooms and hide out. I would get through this dinner with Mason sitting right next to me and his arm bumping up against mine the whole time, and I would be calm and polite and make sure that Heather and my grandma had a good time.

And I managed to do it for a good twenty minutes, until I became worried I was going to burst out of my own skin.

At first Mason and I didn't speak to each other, but his elbow kept brushing against my arm as we ate. Of course they had seated Mason not on my left but on my right, which pretty much guaranteed that we would bump into each other because of our dominant hands.

It was like my mom had orchestrated this entire evening just to frustrate me.

The longer it went on, the madder I got.

Part of that anger was because of how much I liked touching him, even accidentally. I was stupid and pathetic, and the longer I felt that way, the worse it got.

Tingles kept running up and down my arm, and I was having a hard time eating and breathing. It was like my brain wasn't functioning properly, because all I could think about was how strong his arm felt and how warm his skin was and how good he smelled.

"Make sure you get your vegetables, Savannah," Nana said, handing them to Mason to give to me. "You are what you eat."

"I don't remember eating stress and a sore ankle," I said softly, and I saw the way his face lit up, as he'd clearly heard me, and I hated how much I liked it.

I also didn't like the reminder that he and I had spent years making little inside jokes about my grandma's platitudes and that I had just done it again, by accident.

I couldn't even pay attention to the conversation. All of my energy was focused solely on him. Everyone else seemed to be enjoying themselves, and I would have tried to contribute if I'd been able to put two words together, but I was tongue tied and worked up and mad all at the same time.

It was so confusing.

My family were all sitting around talking to Mason like he hadn't hurt me and everything was awesome, and I felt like the outsider, while he was the prodigal son who had finally come home.

Maybe I was the reason for that. Like, I was isolating myself. I should stop letting him distract me and pay more attention. Nana was telling a story about how she'd joined a knitting club but realized it wasn't for her, and so she'd tried to give all of her yarn to one of her friends, but they'd had a falling-out because her friend didn't want "used yarn."

"I told her not to look a gift horse in the mouth," Nana said.

Mason leaned over to whisper to me, "To be fair, lots of people died because no one took the time to look in the most famous gift horse's mouth in history."

Only Mason would make a Trojan horse joke at dinner. I was amused against my will, and the back of my neck was breaking out in goose bumps from him whispering in my ear, his breath hot against my skin.

While caught up in my bewildering responses, I had to bear witness as Mason charmed Nana. Which caused my grandmother to make several comments to Sierra about Mason being single, which Sierra agreed was, in fact, a crying shame while sending pointed looks my way.

A conspiracy. This was an absolute plot to wear me down.

As soon as dinner was mostly over, I immediately stood up. "Please excuse me."

My mom probably expected me to help clear the table, but I couldn't do it right now. It was like my drunken night out with Mason had flipped some switch and I couldn't turn it off again.

I wanted him despite all my best judgment, despite all my anger and resentment.

Then I had to remind myself that he hadn't wanted me. That he'd turned me down. Even though he'd said he wanted to kiss me, too, he hadn't done anything about it when he had the chance.

That's not fair, an inner voice said. *You were drunk, and he told you he didn't want to take advantage of that.* But I was in no mood for logic.

I rushed out of the dining room and for a moment wasn't sure where to go. It just had to be away from everyone else. I headed into my dad's office. It was at the back of the house. When he got overwhelmed by living with three women, this was where he went to escape. I closed the door behind me, leaning against it for a moment, and let out a deep sigh.

My father loved all types of books and had a pretty extensive library. Some of my best memories were of sitting in this room with him on rainy days while we both read quietly from our respective books.

Something Mason and I had also done together.

Walking over to the shelves, I let my fingers drift along the spines until I came across one of my childhood favorites, *Ballet Shoes.*

I took it off the shelf and went over to the couch, settling in and tucking my legs underneath me. I smiled as I remembered how this book had made me briefly consider becoming an archaeologist, and how I wanted a name that started with *P.*

Then I got a mental image of how Mason had indulged my whims and gone out to the backyard with me to dig up dinosaur bones. My parents yelled for a long time after they saw the holes we'd made.

No. I wasn't going to think about that. I was going to focus on my book, on calming down and not letting Mason Beckett steal my peace.

I had just finished the first chapter when I heard the door to the study open. My mom had come to scold me.

"I did what you asked," I said without looking up from my book. I had been polite and hadn't made a scene and hadn't escaped to my room. "I'm not in my bedroom."

"I can see that."

Mason. My eyes flew up to lock gazes with him. Him being here in this safe haven, when I was having so many conflicting feelings about him, just infuriated me. I knew I was being irrational but couldn't help myself.

"What are you doing?" he asked.

"I'm reading."

"What are you reading?"

"These newfangled inventions called books. It's where curves and lines are connected into something we call words, and those turn into sentences, and you read them quietly to yourself. So shh."

"I meant, what's it called?"

"It's called go somewhere else and let me read my book in peace because I don't like it when people infringe on my reading time."

"I remember." There was so much unspoken in that two-word sentence, so much subtext and nostalgia and reminding of my unrequited crush that it hurt to think about it.

"You can leave," I said, trying to turn my attention back to my book, but the words were swimming on the page.

He did the opposite of what I'd said and closed the door, coming into the room until he stood close to me.

"Back to being angry with me again," he said, and it made my blood turn carbonated, rage fizzing around inside me. "I thought we were making progress."

I glared at him. "What would make you think that?"

"I don't know. Probably you trying to kiss me. Is that why you're mad?"

Because I was embarrassed? Right now that was probably a big part of it, but there was no way I was going to admit that to him. "No!"

There was no way to miss the moment when his eyes darkened and he got that hungry look of his that turned my insides to liquid and made my breath hitch. "Is it because you've been waiting for me to kiss you and you're angry that I haven't?"

CHAPTER TWENTY-ONE

For a moment I was so struck that I couldn't speak. "That's not . . . I don't . . . You are so . . . I can't . . ."

Now he hovered over me, forcing me to crane my neck to look up at him. "Have you ever noticed how you can't finish a sentence when you're lying? Is that just with me or with everyone? Do you do that in your own mind when you lie to yourself?"

Who was he to tell me anything about myself? To make those kinds of assumptions? Incandescent with rage, I slammed my book shut and threw it on the couch. I stood up so quickly that it surprised him, and he should have taken a step back to give me space, but he didn't.

I started poking his chest with my right index finger. It was childish, but I was so mad I didn't know how else to express it. "You can't be quiet when you're supposed to be doing a hypnosis session, you can't be quiet when I'm trying to read. Why won't you just be quiet?"

"Make me," he challenged in that low, intoxicating voice of his.

So I did the only thing that made sense.

I threw my arms around his neck and kissed him. Anything to get him to shut up.

It was the most glorious feeling in the entire world, his warm and firm lips pressed against mine, being engulfed in that delicious cologne of his, having his body form a long, hard line against me.

Immediately, I realized my mistake and pulled away. "I'm sorry," I said, panting. "I shouldn't have—"

But before I could finish my sentence, he reached out, grabbed the back of my neck with his right hand, and pulled me into the hottest kiss that I had ever been a part of.

His mouth was devouring, demanding, bruising, and I couldn't keep up. He just kept moving his lips against mine, slanting this way and that. Like he was starving for me and had been wanting to kiss me just as desperately as I had wanted to kiss him. There were so many different things happening at once that all I could do was cling to him so that he could keep me anchored.

Mason Beckett kissing me was more incredible than anything I could have imagined. Greater than any teenage fantasy I'd ever conjured up. He knew what he was doing, and he did it better than any other man I'd ever dated.

As if knowing me so well meant he understood instinctively exactly what to do to drive me wild.

He reached up and tugged the scrunchie out and started running his fingers through my hair. If any part of me had wanted to protest his kiss, this one act would have ensured my eternal silence. It felt unbelievable.

I moaned against his mouth, and he made a noise in response that would have flattened me to the ground had he not been holding me upright.

With one hand behind my head, cradling my face to his, and the other at my waist, he started backing me up until I hit some book-shelves. I both heard and felt the jolt but did not care.

"Sorry," he murmured.

"Don't talk," I told him. I didn't want to think—I only wanted to feel. I pulled him back into the kiss because I wanted it more than anything else.

Each movement of his lips sent a deep pulse that throbbed throughout my entire body. My stomach turned into tight coils as fire thrummed inside my veins, reaching my nerve endings and exploding into continual fireworks. Pleasure pulsed from the base of my spine and made me demand more.

Which he was willing to give.

I never would have guessed that this kind of electric, overwhelming passion would have existed between us. It was almost too much. I didn't know how to contain what I was feeling, as if I were going to shatter from sensations.

There was no restraint in him, no holding back. There was just hunger and want and need and an ever-growing flame that threatened to consume us both. I wouldn't have cared if it burned down the whole house around us, just so long as he kept kissing me. Because his kisses smoldered and blazed, and if any part of me had wanted to stop, he quickly incinerated those thoughts.

His taut body was pressed fully against mine, trapping me against the built-in shelves. I loved his hard ridges and planes pushing against me, the way that I could feel his thundering heartbeat in my own chest.

His kisses were deep and greedy, like he was afraid I'd never let him do it again, and that was a valid fear. Some still-rational part of my brain knew that I shouldn't be letting it happen now, that it definitely couldn't ever happen again, but I was going to enjoy every single second of what was going on in this moment.

He leaned his head back, and my lips tingled, feeling bruised in the most delicious way possible, as I waited for him to kiss me again. It wasn't happening. It took me a second to open my eyes because I was still drowning in the sensations he'd created. I felt hazy and unfocused. "What?"

"Do you still hate me?" he asked, his voice teasing and infuriating and sexy all at the same time.

"Yes." I breathed the word out, not sure how much I believed it. "I hate you."

Mason reached out with his left hand and grabbed my wrists and put both of my hands above my head. His large hand clasped my wrists easily, keeping me pinned, and I didn't struggle. I didn't want to.

"I bet you'll hate me doing this," he said and bent down to start running his mouth along the side of my neck.

My knees buckled, and the only thing keeping me in place was the hand holding my wrists and his other one at the small of my back, pressing me against him. "Yes, I hate that," I whispered weakly.

"You say that with so much conviction." His mouth was hot against my throat as he teased me, and I let out a whimper that made him smile against my skin.

I'd imagined kissing him a million different times and a million different ways. But how could my teenage self ever have known that he would make me feel like I was burning from the inside out, as if I were going to combust and turn into a pile of ash on the floor? And I could feel it from him, too, how much he wanted me, how ravenous and searing his mouth was, how he had to get closer to me.

His mouth moved up to my jawline. "Do you hate this?"

I tried to nod, but my head was not cooperating. "I do hate it. And you."

Then he moved his lips over to my earlobe and sucked it gently into his mouth. My eyes rolled into the back of my head, and I arched against him.

"What about that?"

"I hate that the most," I gasped. How could I loathe someone this much and still crave his touch like this?

Then I felt his free hand at the top of my sundress, undoing the first button as he kissed his way down my neck and flicked his tongue across my clavicle. I realized where he was headed, and it was a testament to how desperate we were for each other that he had apparently completely forgotten about all the other people currently in the house.

"Stop," I said, and every cell in my body cried out in protest at my stupidity.

At that, he immediately released me, causing my arms to drop. He stepped back and held both of his hands aloft, like I was trying to arrest him.

"I'm sorry," he said, breathing hard.

My own chest was heaving just as hard as his, and it took me a second to get enough oxygen into my lungs so that I could speak. He had nothing to apologize for. I was the one who had kissed him first.

Even though he had provoked me by being so annoying and irresistible.

"I can't think when you do that," I said, not able to explain why I'd told him to stop any other way.

He lowered his hands. "When I do what? Kiss you?"

I nodded, gulping hard.

The sexy and knowing smile that spread across his face was almost my undoing. "That's a good thing."

It was a very good thing, but that was beside the point. "People saw you. Us. Together. The morning of the false fire alarm. They know that you were my client. And I could get in trouble."

"Why would you get in trouble?"

It was an indication of how much my family and Bridget loved me that this piece of gossip hadn't made the rounds.

But I couldn't give a journalist any ammunition, especially when he planned on doing a story about me. I had to keep it vague.

"I just would. We can't." My body was making a very strong argument about why it was a bad idea to tell him to stop, and I was definitely listening.

He looked from side to side and then said, "Are any of those people here in this room?"

My skin flushed in response, in anticipation. "No. But we shouldn't be doing this." My protest sounded weak even to my own ears.

"I want to kiss you. I've wanted it ever since the moment I laid eyes on you again, glaring at me like you were ready to murder me." He said it like it was endearing.

"I am ready to murder you."

"Then why did you kiss me?"

That was the question of the day. "I don't know."

"Yes, you do," he said with such certainty that it made my spine feel like Jell-O. He came closer and closer to me, and I held my breath, waiting. It was like torture.

Until the moment when his chest made contact with mine and I let out a whimper of relief because this was exactly what I wanted. He rested his right forearm against the bookshelf, above my head. He trailed his left fingers along my jawline until he reached my sensitized lips, and when he rubbed his thumb against them, I had to bite back a moan.

"Say yes, Sinclair. It will feel so good to say yes. Try new things and see how good it makes you feel." He was so seductive and alluring that it took me a second to figure out where I'd heard that before.

It was what I had said to him in our hypnosis session. He was trying to use my own words against me. "That's not going to work. You can't hypnotize me."

"Yes, I can."

He was right. He could. I'd felt mesmerized by him since he'd come back to Playa Placida, as much as I'd wanted to deny it.

He moved his fingers away and held his lips just above mine. "What is it you want?"

That was a loaded question I wasn't ready to answer.

"It's too fast," I told him. "Slow down." I wasn't sure exactly what I was referencing, but I knew for sure that I couldn't hook up with him in my father's study while my nana was out there telling yarn stories.

"Are you sure?" I felt him smile as he asked. "I could take my shirt off."

I wanted that so much I felt almost panicked by it. "You can't."

"Fine. I'll take your shirt off."

That did make me smile. "It's a dress."

"Those come off, too."

"Clothes on."

"Whatever you say." And although it seemed to defy the laws of physics, his mouth got even closer to mine without making actual contact. "Whatever you say, I'll do it."

That sent a shudder through me, causing shivers to break out along my nerves. This was so, so bad.

I really was under his spell, and I would have done just about anything to get him to kiss me again. Even humiliate myself.

He moved his head slightly so that there was this frustrating phantom feel of his lips, so close but not close enough. "Tell me what you want," he said.

Swallowing down every bit of pride and anger I had left, I admitted, "I want you to kiss me."

CHAPTER TWENTY-TWO

Another self-satisfied smile from him before he bent his head slightly to capture my lips, and I immediately put my arms around his neck to prevent him from going anywhere. His response was to deepen the kiss, sending me into a thick spiral of heat and desire.

"Mason," I breathed against his lips, not able to help myself.

"I want to spend the rest of my life listening to you panting my name like that," he growled in a possessive way that made little pinpricks of sweat break out on my temples. "Do you know how many years I've waited to kiss you?"

It was an admission that I couldn't deny or dismiss. I'd told myself that he hated me, didn't want me, but he had just told me that he did.

I chose to ignore it. "You are so good at this." I had been a bit too passive in this exchange, overwhelmed by him, and that wasn't usually our dynamic. I wanted to win. I wanted him on his knees, dying for me.

"Very good?" he asked and then let out a choked sound when I pressed my lips against his throat. His skin was warm and smelled like him. I dragged my lips along his neck, and he said, "In that session, when you said I was doing very good, it took all of the willpower I possessed not to grab you and pull you on top of me and kiss you senseless."

Now it was my turn to smile. I liked the feeling that I had power over him.

I was kissing my way up to his mouth, letting his stubble rub against my lips, my jaw, and I felt a tremble pass through him. Since he'd brought up the shirtless option, I had been intrigued. I kissed him softly and tugged at the back of his shirt, pulling it loose so that I could run my fingers along the strong muscles of his back.

"If you keep doing that, I'm not going to be able to keep my promises to behave," he said, nuzzling his nose against mine.

"What is it you want?" I asked.

He pulled his head back and looked into my eyes.

Only I didn't see desire there. I saw something softer, inexplicable. He reached up and brushed my hair back, tucking it behind my ear. He let his fingers trail down the side of my face.

"You're the one I want, Sinclair."

Something important was happening, but it was like he'd scrambled my brain so much with his kisses that I couldn't figure it out.

"Savannah?"

I heard Sierra calling me. I pushed on his shoulders, suddenly frantic. She was going to find me, and he was so obviously disheveled, and I figured I must look the same. Messy hair—had I been wearing lipstick? I couldn't remember. If I had, it was probably smeared all over my face. I searched the ground for my scrunchie and found it, doing my best to pull my hair back.

Mason just watched me with an amused look as I ran over to the window to see if I could make out my own reflection. No lipstick, but I did notice that my lips looked swollen, my cheeks bright pink. I hoped my sister wouldn't notice.

"Savannah?"

"In here!" I said, running over to the couch and picking up my book.

My sister opened the door and stuck her head into the room. "We're going for ice cream. Do you two want to come?"

"Yes, I do! I've been told it feels good to say yes," Mason announced, and I tried really hard not to flush at his words. "I'd love to get ice cream."

"None for me, thanks." I kept my eyes pointed at the page and hoped they would just leave so that my sister wouldn't figure out what we'd been up to.

"Let's go," she said, and I could feel Mason's gaze on me, but he left without saying another word. Sierra started to follow him, and then she said my name.

I looked up at her.

She pointed at her chest. "Your top button's open, and you're hold-ing your book upside down," she said with a wink, and I collapsed against the couch when she closed the door behind her.

I was never going to hear the end of this from her.

Especially since it shouldn't have happened. I never should have given in to those impulses.

This had to be a onetime thing.

I couldn't ever let it happen again.

~

My solution to this potential problem was to hide out as much as I possibly could. I stopped meeting my sister and Bridget out in public and spent most of my free time at home.

The one issue I currently faced was that the PTA's silent auction / fundraising party was tonight. Technically my part of it was done—I had gotten all the donors, printed out a sheet for each item, and called everyone before the event to make sure they were ready to go.

Except Mason. I hadn't called Mason to see if he was still planning on offering up a writing critique. I did print out a paper for it, though.

Everything was set up and ready to go. They didn't need me tonight.

I worked myself up into a frenzy because I was so worried about seeing him at the fundraiser, to the point that I felt like I might throw up. I curled up in my bed, tucking my blanket around me and wishing it could be my shield so that I could hide out forever.

That roller-coaster feeling was back with a vengeance. I couldn't separate out all these conflicting feelings I was carrying around, and I had gone and made it a thousand times worse by making out with him.

Because now I knew for a fact what I was missing out on—a physical connection like I'd never experienced before.

Not to mention the emotional connection we used to share.

I groaned and turned over. I could not go and face him tonight. Vivian was active in the PTA, so she would be there, and I couldn't risk something happening with Mason out in public, because I'd already shown that I was more than willing to throw caution to the wind when he smoldered at me.

When my mom came in to check on me, I legitimately felt terrible and told her I couldn't go, which she accepted.

My sister, however, did not.

"Are you faking?" she asked, sitting next to me on the bed.

"I'm not. I feel so sick to my stomach."

Her hand reached under my blanket so that she could feel my forehead. "You don't have a fever."

That wasn't true. I did have a fever, and its name was Mason, and he had permanently infected me, and I apparently had zero antibodies to him, and I was never going to get over feeling this way about him.

Sierra pulled her hand away and sat quietly, waiting. I lowered my blanket so that I could look at her. "What?"

"At the risk of my sounding like my therapist, what is wrong with you?"

"Are you trying to have a talk of shame with me right now?"

She shrugged one shoulder. "You are the one who was about to hook up with Mason with our grandma in the next room."

When I didn't answer, she added, "I don't mean to pry . . ."

"Don't you, though?"

"Aren't you dying to tell someone the details?"

It was killing me not to share this with her, but it felt private. Like it wasn't for her ears. "We yelled, then we kissed, and we stopped. There's not really much more to it."

"Oh, I think there's a lot more to it. Math was never my strongest subject, but even I know that one plus one always equals two."

"What do you mean by that?"

"It means, dear sister, that despite how much you try to deny it, you have feelings for Mason."

"About him, not for him!" I protested a bit too vehemently. "Why would you even think that?"

"Because of how much you actively hate him."

Did she not see how twisted her logic was? "Hatred is the opposite of loving someone."

"No, the opposite of love is indifference. Hating means there's emotion involved. Passion."

Sierra did not know the half of it.

"You haven't talked or thought about Timothy since that censure thing happened," she went on. "He's someone you should hate, but you can't be bothered to spend any of your emotion or time on him. You spend loads of both on Mason."

While that made a certain kind of sense, she didn't get it. "I don't like him."

"I believe you," she said, patting my hand. "Do *you* believe you?"

No.

Which was the problem.

"There's nothing there," I insisted.

"You are my sister and I love you, but you look at him like he's a human-size bag of M&M's."

"I do not!"

"To quote Socrates, yuh-huh."

While I wanted to snap back with a *nuh-uh*, it would have kept us going in circles. Instead I just sighed loudly to show my displeasure with this entire conversation.

She didn't get the hint. Or else she just ignored it.

"Look," she said, "when I told you that him asking me out would be the next best thing to asking you out, you misinterpreted that as meaning that I wanted to date him. I was trying to imply that he's so into you that someone who looks exactly like you would be a good runner-up. Because this situation is not one sided. He's head over heels for you."

My heart clenched at that statement. "That's not true." It couldn't be.

"Why do you think he kissed you? For funsies?"

Sierra did not understand this situation at all. "Being physically attracted to someone is not the same thing as having feelings. Obviously you can hate someone and still kiss them."

"*You* can't," she said. "I mean, I understand why you keep him at arm's length, but he's always been it for you. No one else has even come close."

"I've dated!"

"Not all that much."

Again, she was discounting history to make her point. "Matt was a serious boyfriend."

"You dated Matt for three months and then dumped him because he didn't like that TV show you were obsessed with. The one you used to watch with Mason, I'd like to point out."

I had no good rebuttal to that, so I settled on, "So?"

"Let's be honest. The only serious long-term relationship you've ever had is with sugar."

I made a sound of disgust. "Dating in your twenties is mostly stupid anyways. You never know if you're going to marry someone or if they're going to turn out to be the reason you spend so much money on therapy."

Mason was a therapy bill waiting to happen.

"I feel a little like a broken record here, but you should talk to him."

Deep down, very deep down, I knew my sister was right. That I was being petty and ridiculous. Mason might have a perfectly reasonable explanation as to why things had happened the way they did.

But if he could explain things away . . . what did that mean for me? I'd kissed him once, a mistake I absolutely could not make again. It would take so little for him to make me entirely vulnerable to him, completely defenseless, which would make it easy for him to destroy my heart again.

I wasn't going to let that happen, but Sierra didn't need to know about my inner turmoil. "He doesn't get a pass for bad behavior or to not have to feel shame about what he did. Talking to him doesn't change anything."

She seemed to consider my words and then said, "We all make mistakes, and part of being human is forgiving and moving past them if we can. If he continued to be toxic and hurt you, that would be one thing, but if he's changed? It would be nice if we could erase the past, but hanging on to this anger? The person it's hurting is you. Not him."

Again, she was right. "It isn't my job to absolve his guilty conscience."

My sister nodded. "I get that. But forgiveness, moving on, it's not for him, it's for you."

I squeezed her hand. I knew she had my best interests at heart. Clinically, I could agree with her sentiment. I knew holding on to anger and not forgiving others was not the best thing for mental health. I was living proof of that fact. It didn't mean that I wanted to risk letting Mason back in.

But I budged a tiny bit, just for her benefit. "Fine. The next time I see him, I'll listen to his stupid excuses."

"That's the spirit!" she said.

"Why are you pushing me so hard toward him?" I asked.

"Well, there's the fact that I think you two blockheads really do like each other, and because, I don't know, I guess I have a hard time taking control in my own life, and it's cathartic to make you do it."

"You could do the same thing."

"I know. I'm trying. In large part because I envy what you have."

"Loathing and a desire for mutual destruction?" I asked.

"No," she said as she shook her head. "You said you were jealous that I'm so even keeled. I'm jealous of the emotions you have. How you feel the things you feel and they're so big. Sometimes you tamp them down and pretend you don't have them, but they're still there."

"It's not always a good thing," I informed her. In fact, it usually sucked. I hated feeling emotionally frayed all the time.

"Probably not, but when you love somebody, Savannah, I can't even begin to imagine what that's going to feel like for you, and I envy it. And I know you won't settle for anything less than a man who loves you as much and as big as you love him."

Tears pricked my eyes, and I blinked them away. "You don't have to settle, either. Your great love is out there."

"Maybe. Lucky for you that Mom's had yours picked out since you were born. Get some rest. I'll see you when we get back."

I put the blanket back over my head, and that sick feeling returned. How much of what she had said was right?

Did I have feelings of not-hate for Mason?

And did he have those same feelings for me?

CHAPTER TWENTY-THREE

I woke up and it felt oppressively dark. I reached over to the lamp on my nightstand, but nothing happened.

My heart skipped a beat. Power outage.

They were not uncommon where I lived, but they always reminded me of a particularly bad hurricane season when I was a little girl and we'd had to shelter in place. I'd never heard such strong winds. I had been terrified our home was going to be caught up and swept away. Even though I was an adult now, this level of darkness continued to scare me.

I got up and went downstairs, calling for my family members, checking light switches as I went. I thought they'd be back from the fundraiser by now, but there was no response. I did a quick lap of the first floor, just to be sure.

When I got to the study, I heard a distinctive crashing noise overhead, coming from my room.

A sick, silvery feeling rose up in my throat, and my pulse ricocheted wildly in my wrist, my lungs constricting with fear.

Maybe I'd imagined it.

My phone was upstairs, though. And we hadn't had a landline in years. If I needed to call for help, I had to get to my phone. I looked around for a weapon and grabbed my dad's bowling trophy, then held it up as if it were a bat.

I crept quietly upstairs and slowly pushed open the door. Adrenaline hit my system hard when I realized that there was definitely a person in my room!

Not thinking, I threw the trophy at them and heard when it made contact because the figure swore and then said, "Sinclair?"

"Mason? What are you doing? Besides giving me a heart attack?"

"You hate power outages. I came over to check on you."

"So your way of making sure I wasn't freaked out in the dark was to sneak into my house like a burglar and freak me out in the dark?"

"Obviously I can see now why it was a bad idea, but the front door was locked."

"For a reason!" I said, and as I got closer to him, I realized that he was bleeding. I reached up to touch his forehead, and he made a hissing sound.

"What did you throw at me?"

"A bowling trophy. Be glad that it wasn't a bowling ball. Come on, you're bleeding." I took him by the hand to lead him into the bathroom I shared with my sister.

"I'm bleeding because you attacked me," he said.

"Don't break into people's houses. Sit here," I said. He sat on the toilet while I grabbed some supplies from the medicine cabinet. Fortunately there was a full moon out, and it made it a bit easier to see.

"It's not really breaking in when you basically invited me."

"When did I do that?" I opened a bottle of hydrogen peroxide and put some on a cotton ball.

"Ow!" he yelped when I made contact with his forehead.

"Why are you being such a baby?" I asked, wiping the blood away and disinfecting where he was cut.

"Because someone threw a bowling trophy at my head and it hurts," he said dryly.

I blew on the wound after I had cleaned it.

"Why are you blowing?" he asked.

"That's what my mom always used to do when I was little."

He grumbled a bit and then said, "It doesn't seem sanitary."

"But it makes the pain go away."

"Or it's spreading more germs into my open wound."

"You don't have an open wound. You're just a little bit cut," I said as I threw away the cotton ball. "Stop complaining. And you still haven't answered my question. When did I invite you to break in?"

"When you were drunk and said you always wanted me to climb your trellis. Which I did not fall off of, by the way."

"So coordinated," I said sarcastically as I got out a Band-Aid and put it on his forehead.

"I thought you would find it romantic."

That made me pause, my fingers holding the Band-Aid in place, and my heart started a slow, hard thudding. "Why would you want to do something romantic for me?"

"You know why, Sinclair."

I suspected that I did. That Sierra knew, my mom, Nana, Bridget, Heather, possibly every person in this town.

But I wasn't willing to admit it. How could I when this couldn't go anywhere?

When I couldn't afford to let him back into my heart?

Clearing my throat, I said, "There. All better."

I threw away the empty wrapper and went back into my room. For some reason, I didn't consider the fact that he would follow me. I rubbed my arms, suddenly feeling chilled by his revelation, and realizing that Sierra was right. There were feelings here. I didn't understand them all yet, but something was going on, and my being freaked out in the dark was getting worse.

"Are we going to talk about that kiss?" he asked.

That made my heart thud even harder. "Wasn't planning on it." I remembered my sister urging me to speak to him about why I was mad, and this seemed as good a time as any. Maybe I should try to ease into it. Do one of those compliment-sandwich things where you start off nice. "I recently found out that you were Sierra's friend when she needed you most."

"I was. I still am." He sat down on my bed cautiously, like he was worried about what I might do next.

"I can't tell you what that means to me. Thank you."

He paused for a beat before saying, "It feels weird, you being nice to me."

"It feels weird to me, too."

"But I still like it."

Which led me to start thinking about things I liked, which very much included his lips on me, and I found myself saying, "And about that kiss? I need you to keep it quiet."

"My lips are yours, Sinclair. I'm happy to keep them sealed or put them any other place you might like." Like he could read my mind.

Fiery darts of pleasure exploded inside me, and it took all of my strength not to run over and throw myself at him. "Can we agree that us kissing was a mistake?"

"Sure, as long as we also agree that it will happen again at some point. Probably soon."

"No, it won't."

"To quote you, 'Disagree to agree.'"

Why did my limbs feel so heavy? "Why aren't you at the fundraiser? Weren't you going to volunteer?"

"I didn't so much volunteer as I was voluntold I would participate. I did my part, though, and everything ran smoothly. Why weren't you there?"

Because I was home in bed panicking about you and now you're here and I have absolutely no idea what to do with you. I wondered what he would do if I said it out loud.

I knew what he'd do. Tell me he knew exactly what to do with me. Just the thought of it had my knees going woozy.

"I'm not feeling well," I said, and it was true. I may not have had a fever before, but I definitely had one now. He made my internal temperature rise to dangerous levels.

"You look great to me," he said, giving me one of those appraising looks that did funny things to my insides. "And why can't you kiss me?"

"For one, you're my client."

"I am not your client."

"You came into my office and had a session. How else would you define that?"

"As a journalist doing a story and needing to experience the process for myself," he responded. "Also, I didn't pay you."

"What?"

"I never paid you," he repeated. "Money would have to change hands for me to technically be your client, right?"

Yes, that was true. He hadn't paid me.

Mason added, "I don't plan on ever having you hypnotize me again, so I'm not a client."

"You're a journalist doing a story," I said. "I'm your source. Don't you have some ethical code about not hooking up with subjects of your articles?"

He stood up and walked over toward me, and it was like it was happening in slow motion.

Oh, I was so screwed.

"It sounds to me," he said, "like you're looking for an excuse."

"I don't need excuses. I have reasons."

"Tell me your reasons."

Here it was—the perfect opportunity to have the talk I'd told my sister I would have.

But my body quickly figured out that if I opened up that particular can of worms, it might not get kissed. It was very much against my brain's plan, and it was winning this particular tug-of-war.

"No," I said. And I didn't know if I was saying no to telling him why I was mad or if I was trying to get my traitorous body to behave.

He put his hands on my waist, and my breath caught. He slowly slid them around to my back, pulling me against him. He did it so carefully, like he was waiting for me to stop him, but I didn't want to.

Then, when I was firmly against him, I let out a sigh that was both relief and happiness.

"No one has to know but me, Sinclair. I can be your dirty little secret."

Why did that sound so exciting?

My brain made a last-ditch effort. "What if my hypnosis hasn't worn off yet? You said yes to ice cream with my family pretty quickly."

He kissed my left cheek softly, then ghosted his lips over my sensitized skin. "I said yes because I needed to cool off. So that I could slow things down, like you said. I'm not under your spell, Sinclair. And I can prove it."

Delighted shivers were racking my body. "How?"

"Ask me to do something and I'll say no."

"Like what?"

"You could ask me to kiss you."

When I'd been learning about the different types of hypnosis, I'd discovered that one of the reasons people responded to stage hypnosis was that the hypnotist gave them the words or actions to follow. When a stage hypnotist said, "Sleep," they did it because the hypnotist suggested it and they had no reason not to.

So when Mason gave me those words, I found myself in that same spot, repeating them. "Will you kiss me?"

"No." Then his mouth was on mine, so quickly I didn't register it at first.

Laughing, I pushed at his shoulders to get him to stop. He didn't let go of me, though. "You can't say no and then do it anyway."

"Can and did."

"You're disproving your point."

"I'm not under hypnosis. I just can't resist you. If you ask me to kiss you, I will, no questions asked."

"Oh, there will be questions. Like, how dare you? And who do you think you are? And why are you doing that? Do I need to call the police?"

"We'll see," he said, kissing the tip of my nose. "I just sustained bodily injury to check on you. I think you owe me."

"I didn't let you burn up in a fire, so maybe it's you who owes me."

"There was no fire," he countered.

"But there could have been a fire, in which case I basically saved your life, so yes, you owe me."

"What do you want?"

The words were there, ready to be spoken. *Go away and leave me alone.*

But I didn't say them.

I couldn't.

"We can't kiss," I offered weakly, but he must have heard how much I didn't mean it.

"But you've been kissing me."

"It was a mistake."

"That's happened twice," he reminded me.

I thought of Bridget saying Mason was the kind of mistake you would make five or six times, and she wasn't wrong, because I very much wanted to screw up again.

He hugged me tightly to him and then spun in a half circle while falling onto my bed so that he took the brunt of the fall and I landed on top of him.

Had it been another guy, I might have worried that I was squishing him. But Mason was so solid and strong that it never even occurred to me.

Not to mention how much I liked being pressed against him like this.

"Whoops," he said.

"That wasn't an accident."

"You're right. But now that we're here . . . any suggestions for what we could be doing?"

"You could leave."

"I could, or I could . . ." His words trailed off as he started pressing soft kisses along my jawline, and I sighed happily.

Sierra's words came back to my mind again, and while he was busy mapping out my face and neck with his lips, I found the strength to say, "I'm supposed to be talking to you."

He paused long enough to look up at me. "Do you want to talk right now?"

"Not particularly."

"Me neither," he agreed.

While I waited for that moment when our lips would make contact, he surprised me by rolling me to his left side. He didn't let me get far—our legs were intertwined, and I was still in his arms.

Our faces were near enough to kiss, and just as I was about to close the distance, he spoke.

"I know I said that I didn't want to talk, and as much as I love kissing you, I want you to see me as trustworthy again. If I earn your trust, I hope that you'll share why you've been so angry with me. What I did to make you stop talking to me and cut me out of your life. Because I miss you, Sinclair. I've missed you every day for the last six years. I miss what we were, and I definitely miss what we could have been. What we could be now if you would talk to me. But I'll respect you and give you whatever space you need. Just know that I'm here waiting and ready to talk to you."

My heart fluttered up into my throat at his words, and there was no way for me to respond. He missed me. He regretted what had happened. He wanted to be with me. He wanted a relationship.

There was no denying any of that.

So instead I kissed him. Maybe I couldn't trust his words yet, but this felt like something I could believe in.

His right hand moved up to my face to cup it, and he immediately gentled the kiss. This was completely different from the last time we'd made out.

It still had all the same fire, heat, and passion, but this kiss conveyed things, emotions. There was longing, sweetness, tenderness, and something else I refused to name.

Maybe those pesky feelings my sister insisted were there.

His whispery kisses were making my legs melt away. There was such a surety and confidence to the way his lips touched mine. Pleasure spread through me like warm honey, leaving me languid in his arms. Our mouths moved in harmony, like a dance. I remembered him talking about the silent communication that happened in a dance through touch, and it was happening here, too.

He was telling me things I wasn't ready to hear.

Instead I focused on what I felt.

Each kiss from him was exquisitely soft, smooth, intoxicating. I sank deeper and deeper into the sensations he was creating—liquid fire slowly moving up and down my veins. He had me dizzyingly floating in darkness and heat, tethered only by his sweet mouth on mine.

If I'd been blown away the last time he kissed me, somehow this was even more. More intense, deeper, meaningful.

We might have stayed like that for seconds or for hours—time had lost all meaning. There was only Mason and him kissing me. The only things that mattered in the entire world.

The front door slammed shut, and I heard my father call my name.

I swore and pushed Mason so hard that he fell off the bed. "You have to go. Now!"

"Can't we just tell them—"

"No!" There was nothing to tell them. "I may be an adult, but if my dad finds you in my bedroom, he's going to make you a eunuch."

"Neither one of us wants that."

I ran over to the window and pulled it all the way open. Mason scooted out backward until his feet made contact with the trellis. Although I was panicking, I did have a quick moment where I felt like Juliet or Rapunzel.

That feeling intensified when he reached through the window and kissed me, quick and hard and not nearly enough.

I had to put a stop to it. The muggy night air was clearing my head of the cobwebs he'd spun. What was I doing? I couldn't kiss Mason. I pulled away.

"Until the next time I kiss you," he said.

"There's not going to be a next time," I hissed. "There shouldn't have been a *this* time."

"You asked."

"You told me to ask you."

He really needed to go, but instead he said, "You didn't have to. You're not being mind controlled, either."

"Go home," I told him and started to close the window. I had just finished shutting it all the way when my dad knocked on my door and said my name.

I ran over to my bed and pulled the covers up. "Come in!"

My dad opened the door and stuck his head in. "Are you doing okay? I know you hate power outages."

This one hadn't been so bad. "I'm fine."

"I thought I heard a loud thud."

When I'd pushed Mason off me. "Oh, I rolled out of bed. But I'm okay, though."

"Good. Well, I'll be in my room if you need me. I'm turning in. Good night."

He closed my door, and I kicked my blanket off, lying like a starfish as I tried to cool my overheated body down.

I thought of what Mason had said when he was leaving. That I wasn't being mind controlled.

That was the problem. I felt like I was. As if I had no free will when he showed up and couldn't keep him at arm's length.

And I had no idea how to move forward.

CHAPTER TWENTY-FOUR

When I got home from work the next day, Sierra was waiting for me in my room.

This couldn't be good. I wondered if she knew—if her best buddy, Mason, had told her that we'd made out in my bed. Although given that I had imagined it so many times as a teenager, part of me had started to wonder if I'd made the whole thing up, like it was some kind of realistic fever dream.

My twin sister announced, "I have solved all of your problems!"

She knew a way to get me to stop kissing Mason?

But that was not her solution. She said, "You're going on a date with Mason."

That didn't solve anything. "What?"

"So last night at the silent auction, I was the top bidder for his writing package. And I made a very big deal about winning, going around and telling everyone that I, Sierra Sinclair, was the winner."

She said this in a way that made it sound like I should know exactly what she meant, but I still wasn't getting it. "And?"

"And you go on the date as me. Nobody can tell us apart, and everybody at that event knows that I was the highest bidder, so you can spend time with him and keep your job."

To be fair, he and I could just continue sneaking around like we had been, and as long as we didn't tell anybody else, I wouldn't get in trouble with the Board. "That's not really enough of a reason to—"

She cut me off. "You can go talk to him without all of the issues that come with being you. No baggage. Give him the info as someone else, and see what he says. He might have a reason to lie to you—I don't think he would lie to me."

"That sounds like a healthy plan." I said it more sarcastically than I'd meant to and immediately apologized. "I'm sorry. The heat and my personality make me rude sometimes. Plus, Mason just puts me on edge."

In more ways than one.

"This is what you said you wanted. In the hospital. To go on a date with him without any of the baggage."

"It's not a date, though. It's him helping out with my—I mean, *your*—writing. But you don't write. Neither do I."

She waved her hand as if that part of it were inconsequential. "If anybody asks, I'll tell them all about the self-help book I want to write and what a great help Mason was to me."

As deranged as her idea had initially sounded, it was starting to appeal to me. I sat down in the chair next to my desk. It would be nice to have the conversation I needed to have without my hang-ups. To be able to relate the story dispassionately and get his honest reaction to it. "Sierra" telling him felt a lot safer than me having to do it.

Plus, he wouldn't be able to distract me with his lips.

"This won't work," I said.

"You know it will. We've done it enough times. I also texted Bridget about it, and she gave me two thumbs-up."

"Our hair is different lengths," I pointed out. She had grown hers out a couple of inches longer than mine.

"Put it up in a messy bun like I would, and nobody will know."

"You just have an answer for everything, don't you?"

"Yep." She nodded. "You should let him explain. Give him the benefit of the doubt."

"I do doubt him."

"You know that's not what I meant. I figured you could have fun, under the right circumstances."

"Sedated?"

She laughed and said, "No, I meant free of pressure and hatred and denial."

"Denial is highly underrated and effective. Plus, it's only denial if you're wrong."

"No, it's only denial if it comes from a specific region in France. Otherwise it's just sparkling delusion."

I did laugh, although I didn't want to.

"Come on, Savannah, you know you like the man. To quote Nana, 'If the shoe fits, lace it up.'"

I didn't think that was how the saying went, but I didn't correct her. Not about that, anyway. "Maybe I used to have feelings for Mason—"

"You still do have feelings for him, and yes, you also used to as well. Do you know that in all these years that he and I have been talking—every single text, every conversation—he's always asked about you?"

I did not know what to do with that information. Mason had spent years asking about me?

Another part of my defensive wall crumbled and shattered to bits. He seemed to be doing that to me a lot lately.

Much as I wanted to stay here and hide out, he'd already shown me that wasn't an option. He'd just sneak into my room again, and I'd be all too eager for that to happen.

It was probably better to take Sierra's advice. She wasn't going to let this go. She was too proud of herself for setting this up, and I didn't want to disappoint her.

Although I suspected the real reason I was going to say yes was because I wanted to see Mason again.

"Okay. I'll do it," I said. She looked positively giddy. "And be quiet."

"I didn't say anything."

"Your face has subtitles." I let out a deep sigh. "When is this magical event supposed to take place?"

"In half an hour."

"Half an hour?" I said, standing up. "That's not enough time for me to get ready!"

"It's enough time for me to get ready," she said.

That was true. And I would be going as Sierra, so . . . "Fine. Go grab me something of yours to wear."

She squealed and jumped off my bed, running to her own room. I slipped my dress off and considered whether I should put on cute underwear but decided against it.

It might have given me a boost of confidence, but I would trust myself more if I remembered the utilitarian stuff I currently had on. That way there would be no temptation to show it off to anyone, either.

Although I suspected Mason wouldn't much care one way or the other.

Sierra came back in with a pair of light blue scrubs. "Scrubs?" I said. "Are you sure you want me to wear those?"

"Their being in my hands implies that, yes, I want you to wear them. If anybody sees you going up to the Beckett guesthouse, they'll see my scrubs and automatically assume it's me."

She was right. I put the scrubs on, but I was not a fan of the way they were a bit bulky on me, and the material wasn't great. I looked at myself in my full-length mirror. "If I get into an accident tonight, I'm sad that this is going to be my last mental image of myself."

"It's fine," she said with a note of annoyance. I reminded myself that she wore them every day to work and decided not to say anything else.

I put my hair up in a messy bun, like she would, and used a makeup remover wipe to clean up my face. At some point, she had slipped out of the room, because she returned with her deodorant and favorite lotion. "Put these on."

If I was going to try to create this illusion, I might as well go whole hog. I put them on.

When I was finished, she said, "There. Perfection."

Standing next to her in the mirror was really freaky. We were always identical, but this felt more intense, as if we really were the same person in that moment.

I was starting to regret my decision. We might have looked exactly the same, but it had been so many years since we'd switched that I wasn't really sure I could act and sound like Sierra.

"This isn't going to work."

"Go test it out on Mom," she said. "She's in the kitchen."

That seemed silly to me—our mother was going to see right through me. But at least it would prove that I was right and Sierra was wrong.

I found my mom making dinner. She glanced up at me. "Hey, sweetie, did you just get home?"

"I've been home for a little while." I didn't know exactly how long, only that Sierra had been home before me. I went over to the fridge to grab a bottle of water.

"How was the ER today?"

My hand was outstretched, about to grab the bottle, and I froze. She really did think I was my sister. "Good. Same old, same old."

That seemed vague enough, although I probably should have launched into some gross story like Sierra always did to really sell it. But my mom said, "I'm making a casserole tonight."

I grabbed the bottle and closed the fridge door. I went over to the island and intentionally stood in her line of sight. Maybe she hadn't gotten a good look at me. "Can I help?"

She stopped what she was doing and gave me her full attention, a small smile on her face. "The last time I let you help in the kitchen, you nearly set it on fire."

Sierra had done that. Wow. This was working.

"Go tell Savannah that we're going to eat in about an hour."

"I will." I hesitated, still waiting to see if she would be able to tell, but nothing. "And I won't be here for dinner. I'm going out tonight. To do that writing thing with Mason."

"Have fun!" she said.

I waited another few seconds for her to figure it out, but she didn't.

When I went back into my room, I found my sister putting on my makeup. She had on one of my dresses. "Can you help me with my hair?" she asked.

I was so used to doing loose French knots that it only took a couple of minutes for me to do one on her.

"Well? Did Mom know it was you?" she asked.

"No. You were right." Our mother hadn't been able to tell who I really was. She hadn't been paying that close of attention, but Mason hadn't been around us in years.

It would be much easier to deceive him.

"So what you're saying is I'm right and you should always listen to me about everything?"

I looked at her reflection in the mirror because I knew exactly what she was talking about and that the "everything" meant Mason.

"You were right about this, at least." I finished with her hair and had that weird feeling again that the whole world was just a bit out of place, slightly skewed off its axis. "Let me grab a purse and I'll get going."

"No purse," she said. "And let's switch phones. Just in case."

"Good idea."

"Take my car, too."

At that I groaned. I couldn't stand Sierra's massive SUV. It felt like I was trying to drive a yacht through the streets. I was always so worried I was going to run something over or smack into a parked car and wouldn't even realize it.

"If somebody drives past, they'll see my SUV outside his house," she reminded me.

We walked downstairs together, and when we got to the front door, she gave me a big hug.

"Have the best time!"

The best time. As if, I mumbled to myself as I walked over to her car. I practically needed a rock-climbing license just to hike myself up into the driver's seat. My sister stood on the front porch, waving to me as I carefully reversed out of the driveway and onto the street.

I still couldn't believe I was doing this. It seemed nuts.

But this was where my life had led. Doing unhinged things because I wanted to see someone I couldn't admit I had feelings for.

It took me a bit longer to drive over than normal because I was being so cautious and it was weird driving from this height, but I still got to his house with a couple of minutes to spare.

I sat outside, calling up my courage. I was tempted to turn around and go, but my desire to see him won out, and I climbed down from the SUV. I went directly to the guesthouse, my heart banging in my chest with each step, telling me how stupid this entire thing was.

Before I could talk myself out of it, I knocked on the door. Mason opened it and smiled. "Good to see you. Come on in."

He stepped aside so that I could enter.

Time to test my sister's theory.

CHAPTER TWENTY-FIVE

Mason was on his phone, texting something. "Give me a second," he said.

I had Sierra's keys and phone in my hands. What did she do with them without a purse? I put them in my pants pockets, but they felt too heavy, and my elastic waistband was a bit too loose, and that could end up being humiliating.

So I set them down on a table in the front hallway.

He looked up from his phone. "I'm glad you're here!"

It was weird to have this pleasant/nice vibe happening between us. "Me too. I haven't been here in a while."

Oh no, I hoped that was true. I didn't know if Sierra had been here recently or not. There was a lot about their friendship that I wasn't aware of, and I suddenly realized just how much that could bite me in the butt.

I promised myself that if it seemed like he suspected I wasn't my sister, I would make my excuses and leave.

Until then, I would just wing it.

"It has been," he agreed. "I hope you don't mind, but I ordered some Chinese food. That's still your favorite, right?"

I nodded, swallowing back the thickness in my throat, blinking away the tears that suddenly formed. Even when Sierra had been at her lowest points, that was one of the few foods we could offer her that she would eat. Not very much, but she always loved it. I was unbelievably touched that he'd remembered.

We went into the tiny kitchen, where he had a little table covered with Chinese food. He had all of Sierra's favorites. "Plates? Or do you want to eat out of the containers?" he asked. "And chopsticks or forks?"

"Plates and chopsticks." I didn't want to share a container with him. It felt too intimate.

He handed me a plate and a pair of chopsticks and sat down next to me. The table was small enough that his leg kept bumping into mine, and it sent spirals of longing and awareness through me each time it happened.

"How was work today?" he asked.

"Good." That seemed neutral enough. "What did you do today?"

It occurred to me that I had no idea how he spent his days in his mom's guesthouse. "I wrote. I actually got an entire chapter done. I'm really excited about this novel."

"What's it about?" I asked, because I wanted to know and was genuinely curious. I hoped Sierra didn't already know.

He described a suspense thriller based on a real-life case he'd read about in which a woman killed her husband using an icicle and the police had no evidence because the murder weapon had melted away. He outlined the twist that he was putting on it to make it original and his own.

It actually sounded pretty good. I wouldn't have minded reading it.

"It doesn't sound very much like your first book," I said. That one had been more of an attempt at "literary fiction." I had always been a genre girl and didn't have a lot of patience for books that were basically about middle-aged professors suffering from ennui and contemplating their navels while sleeping with their graduate students.

"You read my first book?"

Sierra hated to read. Whoops. "Of course I did. You're my friend. Why wouldn't I read it?"

He shrugged. "I'm glad that you read it. I'm sorry that it wasn't better. I'm guessing you didn't read my second because nobody did."

"At least you earned a lot of money from the first one, right?"

"People don't usually understand how publishing works. I got a nice advance, but my agent took fifteen percent, and then the advance is split up into three or four different payments at different points. There's not much of that money left. That's why I'm here—trying to get my career back on track. My agent suggested that I try writing some articles and using that to build up a new track record. That once I have some articles out online, publishers will be more willing to look at my new book."

I popped the last piece of egg roll into my mouth. "You're right. I don't know much about publishing. What's your article about?"

He grabbed the beef and broccoli and put some on his plate. "My mom swears at how effective hypnosis is, so I thought I would write an article about that."

"So it's important that you sell it." I hadn't realized how much he needed it to do well, what he had riding on it.

"It is. And it would be nice to have some cash. Although I guess it could be worse. I could be in medical school right now."

"Oh yeah. I forgot you were going to be premed in college."

"My dad doesn't," he said, and I couldn't help but laugh. It was meant to be a joke, but I also heard the underlying sadness that he hadn't lived up to what his father had expected him to be.

"Speaking of thwarted expectations, how is your dad?"

"The senator is very happy with his new, picture-perfect family and getting ready to run for reelection this fall. Do you know that he's the reason my last relationship fell apart?"

I let out a gasp. "Did he sleep with your girlfriend?" It was so something his father would do.

"Nothing like that. Didn't I tell you about when I went out with Virginia?" he asked.

"You dated a whole state?"

"No," he said with a smile. "She was a girl I met after a book signing. We dated for a long time. I thought things might get more serious, but I discovered that she was only with me because she thought that my dad's fame would somehow trickle down to me. That she would get more social media likes for her 'brand.' We were fine as long as my first novel was doing well, but things fell apart when the second book failed. She was angry that I wouldn't take her to meet my father, because she wanted to take a photo with him. It took me a bit, but I realized that she was using me."

The girl he'd mentioned in our session. "I'm sorry. That sucks."

"It does." He nodded, and then I felt a bit guilty that I had this information. That he had intended to share this part of himself with my sister and not with me. He might not have wanted me to know, but now I did.

Since he was sharing with me, maybe this was the time to say something. To tell him about why "Savannah" was mad and get his reaction. He claimed not to know why I was upset, and given that his poker face was truly terrible, that seemed at least a little bit true. Maybe he didn't understand how bad what he had done was.

But then he leaned back and stretched his arms, giving me a brief glimpse of his taut stomach. I didn't remember him having that many abs in high school. It was like they were multiplying.

"That was amazing. I forgot how good that restaurant is," he announced, and my eyes flew back up to his face. "Fortune cookie time? Pick yours out."

There were four of them, and I took the one on the far left, Mason the one on the far right. I opened mine and read it out loud. "You will be financially comfortable soon."

Mason opened his and said, "You will be financially comfortable soon."

"No way," I said, reaching for his fortune. Sure enough, it matched mine exactly. "Given that we both live at home with our parents, I think the fortune cookie industry might not be entirely accurate at predicting the near future."

"Try again."

I grabbed another cookie and so did he. This time my paper was completely blank.

He handed me his fortune, and it said: *You will soon fall in love.*

My heart froze in my chest, unable to beat.

"I suppose you're right," he said. "Doesn't seem all that accurate. So I was thinking we could watch a movie, if you wanted."

That wasn't quite what I had in mind, but I welcomed the chance to delay the inevitable and to not think about this all-too-accurate fortune cookie. "Sure."

We went into the living room, and I slid the fortune into my pocket. He had movie snacks waiting. "Help yourself!" he said. "I've got popcorn, Junior Mints, Twizzlers—"

"Gross." I couldn't help myself. "Twizzlers taste like cherry-flavored HDMI cables. I'm a Red Vines girl."

Again, my reaction had been immediate, and I wasn't sure which Sierra preferred. If she liked Twizzlers and that was why he had them. But he reached for a package of Red Vines and handed it to me.

We sat on the couch facing the large TV screen. "What movie did you want to watch?" I asked.

"I was thinking of *His Girl Friday.*"

I was about to say that it was one of my favorite screwball comedies, but Sierra hated old movies. While she might protest if I were the one making the suggestion, she would most likely go along with whatever Mason suggested, just to be polite.

"Whatever," I said, grabbing a blanket and putting it over my legs. I opened my Red Vines as he started up the movie from a streaming service.

It was every bit as good as I remembered. At least, it was when I managed to watch it. I spent most of my time sneaking glances at him, wishing I could move closer to him, hold his hand, or rest my head against his shoulder.

When it was over, he used his remote to turn off the TV. "I love that movie," he said, and I just nodded, knowing I couldn't tell him I agreed.

Okay, this was it. Time to tell him. I had my hands in my lap, and I squeezed them together as I got ready.

"Mason, there's something—"

"Wait a second," he said. "I have something else I want to give you."

What? But before I could ask him what he was talking about, he had jumped off the couch and gone into the kitchen.

He came back out with half of a round cake, and on top of it was a candle sliced in half.

"It's your half birthday!" he said. "I'm not going to sing to you, because that would be a terrible gift for you, but I didn't forget."

He set the cake down on the table in front of me and lit the candle.

Celebrating our half birthday was something Sierra and I used to do. We didn't always like having to share our birthday, so every year we would switch off who got to celebrate our half birthday as their own special day.

We hadn't done it since high school.

But Mason had remembered.

"This is really sweet," I told him.

"That's just the kind of guy I am," he said. "Make a wish."

I didn't make just one wish.

I wished for things I couldn't have. To be able to go back in time and stop Mason from doing what he had done. To not let him be a client now so that I wouldn't get in trouble if I was caught spending time with him.

To be able to get over my anger at him and maybe give ourselves that chance he'd said he wanted.

It had been my secret wish to have this night—a date with him with no baggage, and it was exactly what he had given me. He couldn't have known that this was my ideal date—a quiet night at home with takeout and a movie. It felt like the best gift.

I leaned forward and blew out the candle, and he applauded and whooped when I did it, which made me laugh.

Then he reached over on his side of the couch and pulled up a gift bag with tissue paper coming out of the top. "This is for you."

I knew he had done all of this for Sierra, but it was still really thoughtful. Another chunk of my defense wall fell.

At this rate, I wasn't going to have any wall left.

I pulled out the tissue paper and found a large bag of M&M's. The bag had been cut in half and taped shut. "It's half a pound of candy," he said.

That alarmed me. This was my favorite candy, not Sierra's. But maybe he'd chosen it because it was easier to cut a pound of M&M's in half than it was to cut, like, a pound of 3 Musketeers.

"Thank you." I placed the M&M's on the table.

"There's more," he said, looking very pleased with himself. "At the bottom."

I looked into the gift bag and found a black velvet bag. I glanced up at him questioningly and then reached inside to pull it out. I tugged at the drawstrings, and inside was a silver necklace with half of a white heart on the end.

"This is pretty. Is the other half for Savannah?"

"I have the other half," he said. He tugged at the top of his shirt and pulled out a black half heart that was on a leather string instead of a chain.

My heart accelerated so quickly that I felt a little like I might pass out. "What is happening right now?"

"What's happening is I think you should come over here and give me a kiss as a thank-you."

He had confirmed all of my worst suspicions about him and my sister. Red-hot anger flared in front of my eyes, and I reached for the nearest throw pillow, then started hitting him with it. "You lying, cheating snake! I knew you had feelings for Sierra!"

"Sinclair!" he said, reaching for my wrist and holding it gently to prevent me from hitting him. "I knew it was you. I knew from the second I opened the door that it was you."

213

CHAPTER TWENTY-SIX

"You did not."

"I did," he said, using his free hand to reach for his phone. "I sent myself a text as soon as you came over. Look."

He handed me his phone, and his text-messaging app was open. There, at 6:58 p.m., it said: Sinclair is here, pretending to be Sierra.

I let the pillow drop, and he released my wrist. "Sierra told you."

"She didn't."

Not believing him, I went into the front hallway to get Sierra's phone and sent my sister a text telling her that Mason knew who I was.

She immediately sent me back a selfie of her laughing.

Angry, I called.

"Hello, Savannah's phone."

"This is not funny. Did you tell him that I was coming over here tonight?"

"Savannah, on Nana's life, I promise you that I did not tell him about my plan. I wanted you to have the chance to talk to him as me. I thought that would feel safer to you."

She was telling the truth. As kids we'd made an agreement that if either of us promised on our grandma's life, the other one had to take it seriously.

"Fine. I believe you. But I have to go."

"Call me and tell me everything he says and how he knew—" I hung up on her before she could finish her sentence.

I walked back into the family room. "I've just confirmed that Sierra didn't tell you, so how did you know it was me?"

The amused smile fell off his face, and that look was back, the one I didn't understand but that made me feel tingly and floaty. "Savannah Rose Sinclair, I could be robbed of every single one of my senses and I would still know you."

I drew in a sharp breath, my heart flitting around my chest in response to his words. "You can't say—"

Now he was the one cutting me off. "Do you think I don't see you? Don't know you? I see everything, Sinclair. The good and the bad. I know how kind and compassionate you are. How loving. How loyal. How smart and talented and driven and funny you are. But I also know that you can hold a serious grudge and get angry too quickly and jump to conclusions before you have all the facts."

I opened my mouth to respond, but he didn't let me speak.

"I know that you thought you had to be the perfect daughter for your parents. That you needed to be the best at everything so that your mom and dad didn't have to worry about you the way they worried about Sierra. How often you felt alone because they had to give her all of their attention. That some of the anger you have comes from how mad you were at your sister's disorder and how helpless you felt as she struggled. How much harder all of it had to be on you because this was your identical twin going through it."

I nodded, biting my lower lip. "That day I went to see her in the hospital? It felt like part of me was dying. I didn't know how I'd ever feel whole again if she was gone."

He got up and walked over to where I stood. He reached out and rubbed his hands along my upper arms. "I know. I know because that's how I've felt without you in my life. Like half of me has been missing for years, and I didn't feel whole again until I saw you in that Starbucks."

"How do you know me like this?" I asked, not able to stop the tears that started to fall. He reached up to gently wipe my tears away with his thumbs.

"Because I've been in love with you since we were fifteen years old," he told me, and everything in the entire world came to a screeching halt. Blood pounded so hard in my ears that for a moment I couldn't hear anything else.

I was light-headed. "What?"

"I love you, Sinclair. You had to know that."

My mouth opened and shut several times before I finally managed to say, "I did not know that."

We sat there in silence as I digested this information. My instinct was to flee—to run away from what he was feeling, what I was feeling, because my sister was right and I was a coward. I talked a good game, giving her advice on what she should be doing in her love life, but I had always been a scaredy-cat.

Right now? I was the most scared I'd ever felt.

And I also felt like it was time for the truth. "I'm mad at you because you're the one who told the whole school that Mr. Landry and I were having sex."

Now it was his turn to look completely shocked. "I was not. I did not do that."

"It was the night after the district-level debate." Mr. Landry had been our debate coach and had run the club. "He and I were in his classroom, and he was comforting me because I'd lost. He was hugging me, telling me it was okay."

Mason's face was blank, as if he were trying to place the memory.

"He was probably holding me a little too close," I admitted. "Nothing ever happened between us, but looking back as an adult,

I can see that he acted inappropriately with me. Mr. Landry had a small group of favorites, all girls and all a bit naive. He would have me stay after class or after a debate and find innocent ways to touch me, which I wasn't uncomfortable with at the time because I didn't know any better, but when he hugged me like that? Even I knew that it crossed a line. And you walked in and saw us. The next day, the whole school was talking about how he and I were sleeping together. It completely ruined my senior year. Even now I sometimes walk through town and am still that girl who hooked up with a teacher. You utterly destroyed my reputation. And I was so angry with you for that. Still am."

Mr. Landry had been fired, and I had guessed it was due to that rumor. Or maybe he'd been inappropriate with someone else.

Mason reached for my hands, enveloping them with his own. He paused for a moment, as if waiting for me to stop him. When I didn't, he said, "I have never lied to you, Sinclair, and I'm not about to start now. So the truth is that I do remember that night. I remember walking in and seeing you and Landry together and feeling jealous that he was hugging you, but I promise you, that was it. I never breathed a word of it to anyone. I would never, ever hurt you that way."

"But you were the only one who saw us together," I protested. I wanted so badly to believe him, for all of this to be true, but I had been so furious with him for so long that I wasn't sure I could let go of it.

"I wasn't the only one," he said quietly. "I wasn't alone."

"Who was with you?"

He shook his head, like he didn't want to answer, and a giant boulder formed in my chest and slowly sank its way down into the pit of my stomach. "Who, Mason?"

A long pause and then he finally said, "Bridget. Bridget was with me."

I gasped aloud, and my hands flew up to my mouth.

In that moment, everything became clear. Bridget wasn't my friend then. She had wanted Mason for herself. If she'd realized that he had feelings for me, would there have been a better way to get him away from me than to start a rumor that I was hooking up with a teacher?

Was she the one who had started this rumor? I didn't want to think it was possible, but if Mason hadn't done it, the only other person who'd seen us that night was Bridget, and the rumors had started the next day. It had to be her. We had spent so much time together since we'd both moved back home. Why hadn't she said anything? Especially now. She knew how angry I was with Mason, and she knew why. I'd told her the exact reason the night all three of us went out to the restaurant.

I'd thought we were better friends than that.

Then I remembered how she'd immediately left after I told her why I was mad. A guilty conscience? Had she made up a lie about her mom not feeling well just to avoid me?

I had thought I was the one avoiding her and hiding out so that I wouldn't accidentally run into Mason, but what if it was Bridget who had been avoiding me?

"Why didn't you tell me that Bridget saw us, too?" I demanded.

"Sinclair, I never put the two events together. I didn't know the rumor started after we saw you. I was always the last person to hear stuff like that. I thought the rumor had been going around for a while. If I had figured out that connection, I would have said something to you a lot sooner."

"I have to go. Now. I have to talk to her," I said. "I need to know what happened."

"I'll drive you," he said, and I was glad because my hands were shaking so badly that I wasn't sure I could have managed it.

Mason took me by the hand. He grabbed Sierra's keys in the front entryway, and we went out to the SUV. He didn't seem to have any problem driving her boat. He glanced over at me a few times, as if he wanted to say something but kept changing his mind.

He did hold my hand the whole way, rubbing his thumb along my palm in an attempt to comfort me.

I couldn't speak. What could I say? I had to talk to Bridget. Had to hear her side of it.

Had to know if I had wasted years being furious at Mason for something he hadn't even done.

We pulled up to her mom's driveway. Bridget had moved in when she came back to Playa Placida to keep a closer eye on her mother. Suddenly I wasn't sure if confronting Bridget now was the right thing, given that her mom was probably home, so we sat in the driveway for a while as I wrestled with what to do.

I thought of all the breakfasts she and I had shared with Sierra, how we had all laughed together, teased one another, gone out drinking and dancing, how she had become such an important part of my life, and the entire time she had been lying to my face.

"We can leave," Mason offered.

That spurred me to action. "No, I have to know." She might not even be home, and this would be a waste, but I had to try. I needed to figure out if she was the one who had spread the rumor.

I got out of the car. "Stay here," I said to him before I closed the door. I definitely had to do this on my own.

Folding my arms against my chest, I walked to the front of the house. Each step felt a bit like I was wading through mud, and I slowed down the closer I got. I kept wanting to go and get back in the SUV and have Mason drive me somewhere and make me forget all this. I knew he'd do it.

Instead I knocked on the front door. I heard two voices. Her mom was definitely home. Thankfully, Bridget was the one who answered. She had been laughing at something her mom had said, and her face stayed animated and happy when she saw me. "Sierra! This is a nice surprise."

"I'm Savannah."

"Oh! I just saw the scrubs and automatically assumed . . ." Her voice trailed off as she read my expression. Her face fell, turning pale.

"I'll be right back, Mom!" she called and stepped onto the porch, closing the door behind her.

"You know, don't you?" she asked in a soft voice.

CHAPTER TWENTY-SEVEN

"I came over here to find out the truth," I said, my hands still trembling. I hadn't been able to calm down ever since Mason had told me about Bridget.

She didn't meet my eyes and shifted her weight back and forth from one foot to the other. I had never seen her anything but supremely confident in herself, and it was disconcerting. "It was me. I told everyone you were sleeping with Mr. Landry."

I let out a sound of disbelief, not able to stomach that she had done this to me. Part of me had desperately hoped for another explanation. "I don't understand why."

She audibly gulped and then admitted, "I was having an affair with him."

I had not been expecting that. "What?"

"When Mason and I saw the two of you together after that debate, I was so angry and jealous. I knew Greg—I mean, Mr. Landry—flirted with other girls, and it infuriated me when I saw him with you. My friend Olivia found me crying in the bathroom. I was sobbing about it, and she started to put the pieces together, and I realized that I was about to get caught. So I lied. I told her that you and Mr. Landry were hooking up because I knew it would keep people from looking at our relationship too closely."

"I . . ." I was in such shock that I didn't know what to say.

"I did it because I didn't want my mom to find out. I knew how angry she would have been."

"As she should be! You were a child, and he was a grown adult. It was wrong."

She nodded, tears forming in her eyes and falling slowly down her cheeks. "I know. I know it was. At the time I thought I loved him, but you're right—it never should have happened."

While she had been taken advantage of, no one had forced her to throw me under the bus. And it might have been a very good thing for her if adults in her life had known. "So you lied about me so that your mom wouldn't find out?"

"She was a single mom and was so overprotective of me. She worried all the time that bad things would happen to me, and if I had told her about Mr. Landry, it would have destroyed her, and I couldn't do that. She didn't deserve that kind of pain."

"But I did?"

"No, of course not." She reached out like she wanted to hug me, but her arms dropped when I moved away from her. "Then when he got fired, I figured the gossip would eventually die down and there would be some new scandal that would come along to replace it."

"It didn't," I reminded her. "It was traumatizing for me. People judged me for years. They still do. You destroyed my reputation."

"I know! And when you went away to college, I told myself that it would be okay, and I pushed the whole thing out of my mind. When you moved back here, I was going to tell you about it. But then we started spending time together, and I really liked you and Sierra, and I didn't want our friendship to be ruined. I tried so many times to tell you, but I always chickened out. The longer it went on, the worse it got."

While I understood that, she still should have told me. "Were you just hoping I'd never find out?"

"I don't know. I didn't think things through," she said with a shrug. "I am so, so sorry, Savannah. I know there's nothing I can say that will ever make this up to you. I know that it wasn't right or fair, and I should probably apologize to Mason, too. Because I made a bad decision at a terrible time, and part of the reason I didn't tell you after we came back to Playa Placida was because I knew once I told you the truth, I was going to have to tell my mom so that she'd hear it from me first, and I didn't want to break her heart. I didn't know how to tell her. I still don't."

While I had a lot of compassion for how hard that would be for her and her mom, they weren't the only people involved in this. "I've blamed Mason for that rumor for years. You ruined my relationship with him."

Her voice cracked as she said, "I didn't know! I had no idea you blamed Mason for the rumor until you told me that night at the restaurant. I felt so unbelievably guilty that I had messed that up for you, because Sierra told me how in love with him you were in high school, and it was obvious that he feels the same way about you now. I hated myself for being the reason you weren't together."

There was a sharp, aching pain that throbbed at the base of my stomach. Bridget had been lying to me for a very long time. I understood why, though. What had happened to her was wrong, and as a teenager she probably didn't have the maturity or the tools to deal with it. I couldn't blame her for that. She was desperate and had made a stupid decision. I'd certainly done that enough in my own life that I couldn't be mad at somebody else for it.

But then I thought about what she had taken from me. All those years I might have had with Mason, how happy we could have been, the way she'd hurt both of our families by causing the anger I had toward him . . .

I didn't want to be upset with her. I'd spent the last six years furious with Mason, hating him, and Sierra was right. It was a heavy burden I'd been struggling with for a long time, weighing me down. I didn't want that to happen again. I wanted there to be a way to move forward, but in this moment? I didn't have the answers.

I took a step back, standing on the top step of the porch. "This whole thing sucks. I'm sorry that happened to you. A teacher shouldn't have preyed on you, and I'm sorry that you were scared to tell people. I get how hard that must have been for you. But I don't know how to move past what happened. I think I should go."

"Savannah, wait. You have every right to be angry with me—" she said, but I interrupted her.

Despite my not wanting to be mad, fury rose up inside me. "I'm so glad I have your permission to be angry. It wasn't just me and Mason that you hurt. You've hurt my family, too. I sacrificed time with them because of what you did, staying away because I blamed him. It ate away at my soul to be accused of something I knew I hadn't done, and to think a person I cared so much about had done that to me? It made me not trust people. Your actions made me a more negative person than I'd ever been before."

"I did try to fix it. I went to the police and made an anonymous report against Mr. Landry, showing them evidence. I wasn't willing to testify, but it got him fired. When he landed a new job at a different school, he started texting inappropriately with a student, only it was an undercover cop, and he was arrested. He was convicted and is in prison."

That I had not known. "I'm glad that you spoke up so that he didn't have the chance to hurt anyone else."

She seemed to take this as some sign that my anger was relenting. "Tell me how I can make this right," she said. "I'll do anything."

This was so hard. I found myself wanting to tell her that things would be fine. That we would find a way through this.

But this wound was too new, too big. "I don't think you can. You can't undo the pain, the hurt, and the loss that you caused. I was the butt of every joke for an entire year. For someone like me, who always has to be the best, who craves approval, you can't imagine what it did to me to have everyone whispering about me and laughing at me. The kind of cruel and anonymous texts and DMs I got. It nearly broke me," I told her. "I need to go. I can't keep talking about this. You're not the same person to me anymore."

I walked back to the car. I half expected her to follow me, or to call after me, but she just went quietly back inside her house.

When I got into the SUV, I said, "Please take me home."

Mason took me by the hand again and held it the entire way back to my house, and I was glad for that bit of comfort. I cried the whole time, great heaving sobs that shook my entire body. I cried so hard that my eyes actually hurt and my lungs ached.

When he pulled into my driveway, he undid his seat belt and then mine. Then he reached for me, holding me against his chest while I cried. He stroked my hair and said sweet things to me about how it was all going to be okay, pressing kisses against my forehead.

After I'd calmed down, I took in a big gulp of air and then said, "I'm . . . That is to say, I feel like I should, you know, uh, apologize. To you."

I felt his mouth curl up into a smile. "Are you saying you're sorry?"

"You know I'm not very good at saying when I was wrong."

"No," he agreed. "You're much better at throwing things."

I lifted my head from his chest and reached up to kiss his mostly healed cut. "I am sorry."

"I kind of hope it leaves a scar so that I can show it to our—show it to people and tell them you did that to me."

"You are not going to tell people that I did that and—"

His mouth was on mine, swallowing up the rest of that sentence. I let him kiss me for a bit before I smiled against his lips.

Kisses didn't mean that things were better, though. I thought of how much pain I must have caused him by cutting him out of my life, because I knew how much it had hurt me. I pulled back so that I could look him in the eyes and said, "I blamed you for something you didn't do for so long. Do you think you could ever forgive me?"

"I could forgive you for anything, Sinclair," he said, and despite being wrecked emotionally, his words made my soul feel lighter than it had in a long time. "I only wish I'd known sooner."

"Me too."

Mason reached into the seat behind us and handed me the gift bag. Through all of this, I had kind of forgotten about our evening together. "There's something I don't understand. If Sierra didn't tell you that I was the one coming over, how did you know to get me presents?"

"Your sister was making such a big deal about winning that I knew she was up to something. I guessed it might be you coming over, although I wasn't sure. I did order Chinese food in case she was the one who showed up."

"You really knew it was me?"

"The second I opened the door. I always know you, and I always will," he said in that sappy tone of his that made my stomach flutter. "But you tipped your hand by showing up on time."

Sierra was always late. Why hadn't I thought about that? More to the point, why hadn't she? It was probably because she was so excited and proud of her plan that it hadn't occurred to her, and she just wanted to get me out the door before I changed my mind.

"You're right. The only cardio my sister gets these days is running late."

He smiled at that and then said, "What I don't get is why Sierra wanted to make sure that everyone at the PTA meeting knew she had won."

"There's more to that story." I filled him in on Timothy and the censuring and on the Vivian / Mr. Franklin connection. "I'm just worried that if anyone here in town thinks you're my client and someone sees us together, if there's any kind of gossip about us, there's an actual direct pipeline for the Board to find out, and I might lose my certification."

He took my hand and brought it up to his lips so that he could kiss the back. "Thank you for trusting me with your story. I know how important your job is to you, and how much it matters to you what other people think. That's why you said we couldn't kiss or date."

"Yes. That, and how much I hated you."

"Hated?" he echoed. "Past tense?"

"If I'm being totally honest with you, it's hard to just shift gears. I've been angry with you for so long that I don't know how to be normal around you. Especially after you told me that you love me." Might as well go for broke and put all my cards on the table. "And some paranoid and totally irrational part of me is afraid that you're only saying those things so that you can lull me into a false sense of security in order to ruin my career."

"Well, I'm not going to do that, given that I'm not a supervillain or a sociopath. As for the shifting-gears part, may I suggest sublimation?"

I'd studied that at school but didn't know what his interpretation of the word was. "Meaning?"

"It's where you express unhealthy emotions through healthy ways. So if you're angry at me, you can just kiss me instead."

"That's very clever of you," I said, and he just grinned at me, obviously pleased with himself.

"I do understand that this is hard, Sinclair. Like I told you last night, I want you to trust me, and I'm willing to earn that trust and be patient. We should take things slow until you feel like you can trust me."

His words were perfect, utterly romantic, and just what I needed to hear.

"Why do you say those kinds of things to me?" Because when he did, the last thing I wanted was to take things slow. "You're kind of making me want to pull you into that back seat and sublimate a little."

Another grin. "As fun as that sounds, I'd have to say no. For now. Because it's all part of my master plan to win over your heart and all your other good parts."

"Good parts?" I demanded, hitting him in the shoulder.

He laughed hard and then said, "I was talking about your brain and your soul! What did you think I meant?"

That was not what he'd meant. But he was so delighted with his joke that I let it slide. "Yeah, okay."

His expression grew tender and he reached out to stroke the side of my face, then said, "Do you know what it's like to be in love with someone who actively wishes you physical harm?"

Not where I thought that sentence was going to end up. "I don't actively wish it."

"And yet it still happens."

"That was accidental, and it was your fault for committing a felony."

"Sneaking into an open window isn't a felony," he said.

"I'm pretty sure it is, Smooth Criminal." And as much as I found myself wanting to stay out here with him, I knew I physically and emotionally wasn't up for it. "I should go. Do you want me to get Sierra to drive you back to your place?"

"I'll just get a rideshare," he said.

And I was relieved that that was his choice. My sister would have grilled him, and I wasn't ready to tell her yet. It was going to break her heart that Bridget had done this and lied, and Sierra had been in such a good mood tonight, so thrilled for all of her scheming to come to fruition.

"Okay. I'm emotionally drained and exhausted, and I'm going to go crash in bed."

"Are you sure you don't want me to come tuck you in?" he offered hopefully.

"I think that would negate your whole 'take it slow' plan."

"You're probably right." He grinned. "So I'll call you tomorrow."

"Tomorrow," I agreed and got out of the car. As I walked toward my house, I realized that I was looking forward to hearing from and seeing Mason again.

And it had been a long time since I'd felt that way.

CHAPTER TWENTY-EIGHT

My first client of the day had canceled late the night before, so I had turned off my alarm and looked forward to the opportunity to sleep in. My body needed the rest.

But I didn't get that chance. I'd woken up early in the morning to use the bathroom and intended to get some more sleep. Instead I found Sierra lying on my bed when I returned. "I heard you get up, and I came in to get all the details!"

"I'm going back to sleep," I told her as I climbed into my bed.

She yanked my covers off me. "You are not. You're going to tell me what happened last night."

Sighing, I sat up because Sierra could be very persistent. "So he immediately knew it was me when he saw me. He suspected that we might switch places because of how obvious you were being about winning the auction. We had Chinese food and watched an old movie and then we had the talk."

"*The* talk?" she asked, crossing her legs and tucking them underneath her.

"He told me he loved me?" I didn't mean for it to sound like a question, but it did. I kind of braced for impact, waiting for a big reaction from her.

After a couple of seconds, she said, "I'm sorry, did you want me to look for my surprised face? I'm pretty sure I left it around here somewhere."

"Okay, okay."

"No, really. Did you want me to say 'I told you so' now, or do you want me to wait until I've really had the chance to rehearse it?"

I lightly smacked her with one of my pillows while she laughed. "You were right," I said as I put the pillow behind my back. "Is that what you want to hear?"

"It is. How did things end? Did you ask him about the rumor?"

Last night I had thought that Bridget might try to reach out to Sierra, but given the hopeful and excited look my sister was sporting, it was obvious that hadn't happened.

"I did ask him, and there's bad news. Not about Mason but someone else."

She knit her eyebrows together. "Who?"

"There's not really a way to cushion this, so I'm just going to tell you. Bridget was the one who started the rumor. She was with Mason the night that he saw Mr. Landry and me hugging, and she told me that she was the one who was actually hooking up with him. She created the rumor so that nobody would suspect her."

All the color drained from Sierra's face. "Bridget?"

"She confessed the whole thing to me. She apologized. She didn't want her mom to find out because of how much it would hurt her. Which I get."

"This whole time?" my sister said. "Bridget did that to you and just didn't tell us?"

"Yes."

"I need to lie down," she said and lay on her side. "I mean, I get that people make mistakes and we all do stupid stuff when we're young, but that rumor was so hard on you. My ballet teacher's criticisms led to my disordered eating, so I'm living proof of how the comment of one person can wreck your whole life, and you had hundreds of people being so mean to you on a daily basis."

"Honestly? This betrayal doesn't feel the same as when I thought it was Mason."

"Really?" That seemed to surprise her. "But you love Bridget."

"I do." I nodded. But I had never been in love with Bridget.

I had been in love with Mason.

And I still was.

It was something I had realized last night when I was trying to fall asleep. Him saying he loved me hadn't scared me like it would have had it been any other man. No, coming from Mason, it felt right.

The more I thought about how I felt in return, the more I realized that the things I had told him were true. It was very strange to go from hating him to loving him, only I suspected Sierra had been right about my feelings—that my hate had been so intense because of the love I'd always had for him. Even in my anger I couldn't let go of him and hadn't wanted to.

I'd called it a crush, but I was pretty sure that my feelings for Mason in high school were a lot stronger than that.

I wasn't sure I was ready to tell him that, though. It felt too big to share. Even with my twin. I wanted more time to ruminate on it and wrestle all these whirling emotions of mine into place so that I could express them better.

Despite all of my clarity and consideration, there was still a part of me that was afraid to give him that much power over me. If I told him I loved him . . .

What would happen if he broke my heart again?

I did consider the fact that he had handed me that kind of power over him by openly confessing his love and being vulnerable.

But I was still scared.

"What are you going to do about Bridget?" Sierra asked.

"I don't know."

"Do you mind if I talk to her?"

"Why would I mind? She's your friend, too."

She pointed out, "You minded that I was friends with Mason."

True. But, again, those two situations were very different, as I'd discovered. "Your friendship with Bridget is your business."

"Wow, look at you. Do you see that?" she asked. "That's what we like to call growth. And speaking of growth, how do you feel about Mason?"

Those two things were not related, but I said, "I'm still figuring that out."

"It puts you in kind of a weird position with him, doesn't it? You were so mad about something he didn't even do."

"I should have listened to you and talked to him a long time ago," I said.

She considered this information. "I don't know if that's necessarily correct. I'm a big believer in things working out when they're supposed to."

"Like how?"

"Let's say you knew it was Bridget who spread the rumor in high school. You would have hated her, and we never would have gotten to know her and her mom and what an amazing person she is."

She had a point, and I nodded.

"And if you and Mason had started dating, you two went to colleges on opposite sides of the country. What are the odds that your relationship would have worked? He was pursuing literary fame, and you were figuring out who you were and what you wanted to do. You might have broken up. But now you're in the right place at the right time for both of you, when things can work out and last."

"Maybe," I agreed. "Or he and I might be married by now and giving Nana those great-grandchildren she wants so badly."

Again, this thought didn't terrify me as it had in my previous relationships. In the past, the second things looked like they were getting even remotely serious, I ended it.

At least now I could admit that it was because of the feelings I'd always had for Mason. Despite how furious I had been with him, deep down I didn't want to be with anyone but him.

Sierra said, "Well, if you'd talked to him about this situation, like, at that first hypnosis session, you wouldn't have believed him when he denied it."

"That's true." I wouldn't have. I had to be in the right frame of mind to hear it and believe him. I had already decided that he was the one who'd started the gossip, and I would have taken his denials as further evidence that he'd been responsible.

Those hate-filled goggles of mine really would have skewed my perspective. I hadn't been emotionally ready to hear the truth.

"So, if you can picture yourself married to Mason in some alternate timeline . . . you do love him, too, right?" It shouldn't have surprised me that Sierra was going to hone in on this point, even though I'd just told her I was still figuring things out.

Probably because she knew me too well.

"What makes you say that?" It wasn't an outright denial.

"Mason is a great guy. He's caring and kind, smart, fun, protective, loyal, and he makes you a better person."

"He makes me a better person?" I repeated. "How?" Because I had not been my best self since he'd come back home.

"You like that he's competitive with you. You couldn't stand guys who didn't challenge you constantly."

"That . . ." Was that right?

"You like that Mason keeps you on your toes. That he doesn't act the way you expect him to. And the banter. Even while you were mad at him—I overheard the banter! You two are the cutest."

When had she overheard us? "Have you been eavesdropping?"

"What else are twin sisters for?"

My mom heard us talking and stuck her head in my room. "You two are up early! Come downstairs and have breakfast with me."

There was a buzz from my phone, alerting me that I had a text.

"Coming," Sierra said with a wink. "I think Savannah has a text she needs to check first."

I wanted to tell her that it might not be from Mason, but it was.

Thinking about you.

Sierra gave me a knowing smile, and I just shook my head at her. When my sister and mom left, I responded:

I've been thinking about you, too. Can you come over today at 3:00? Meet me in the treehouse.

Can't wait.

Neither could I.

~

I had an online appointment in about an hour, but I figured it was a good thing to have a hard out so that I didn't get too carried away with Mason. I got the treehouse all set up—a blanket on the floor and a picnic basket with some treats that I was pretty sure were melting in this heat. I should have waited until nighttime, but I was too eager to see him again.

How had I forgotten that the treehouse basically had no ventilation? It was so hot in here that a layer of sweat was covering my body before he even arrived.

Mason showed up right on time, and my heart flipped with happiness at seeing him. The trapdoor rose as he climbed up the ladder, and he let it shut behind him when he was fully inside the treehouse.

He couldn't stand up completely straight, though.

"It's a hundred and ten degrees today," he told me. "But I think it's a hundred and fifty degrees in here, and looking at you I can see why."

Another adjustment. Now when he said cute, flirty things to me, I didn't immediately suspect him of being out to ruin me in some way. "It's me, right?"

"Yes," he said with a lusty, playful grin. "You're hot."

I pointed at the basket. "Speaking of hot, I brought up treats, but I think they're all melted."

He got down on the floor next to me. "That's okay. There's only one treat I'm interested in."

Then he kissed me hello, and it should have been uncomfortable. We were both a bit damp with sweat, our bodies giving off far too much heat, but his lips were so welcome. He kissed me in that perfect way of his—as if he knew exactly what I wanted and needed from one moment to the next, gentle and sweet here, passionate and demanding there, flipping back and forth, keeping me off balance.

Another thing Sierra was right about. I did like that I never knew what to expect from him, despite knowing him so well.

Just as things were starting to get interesting, he pulled back. "Why are we having a secret rendezvous in a treehouse?"

"Do you have a better idea? Where else can we meet that we'd have privacy? That people wouldn't see us?"

"We could have gone to a nice hotel with air-conditioning so that we wouldn't have to be here in your terrarium," he said.

"But if we went to a hotel . . ." I let my voice trail off.

"You're right," he said as he kissed the inside of my wrist, right at my pulse point, which jumped when his mouth made contact. "We're taking things slow, so terrarium it is."

"It is really hot. I think it's destroying what's left of my soul."

"Bah, nice weather makes you soft." He ran his fingers along my bare shoulder, stopping when he reached the strap of my sundress. He bent his head to kiss everywhere that he had been touching. "You're soft."

"I am soft," I agreed in a breathy voice, enjoying what he was doing but feeling as if I needed to apologize for my current state. "Sorry I'm so sweaty. It's been a long time since I've had a workout that made me sweat this hard."

"Do you know what else is a good workout?"

"Swimming?" I said and then immediately realized that he'd been hitting on me. "Oh."

"Yes, oh." He smiled and went back to running his lips along my exposed skin. I leaned my head back to give him better access and because it was becoming increasingly harder to keep my head upright, given what he was doing to my throat with his mouth.

"Sinclair, there's something I need to confess." He said the words against my skin, and they brought me right back to reality as I broke out in an absolute chilly panic.

I thought we had cleared the air. What else could he possibly have to tell me?

Then he made everything worse when he said, "I lied to you before."

CHAPTER TWENTY-NINE

"What did you lie about?" I asked in a whisper, terrified that he was about to shatter this newfound peace we'd discovered.

"When I told you that I wouldn't let you hypnotize me again, that was a lie. I'm mesmerized by you. You've been hypnotizing me since the day I came back. You have this hold over me that I can't shake, and I don't want to. And it's no surprise that you were able to hypnotize me in that session, because just looking at you makes me forget my own name."

My instinct was to punch him for scaring me, but as relief flooded my nervous system, I decided to do some sublimation. I leaned in to kiss him, and he immediately responded, his mouth warm and firm.

"I love you," he said in a possessive but sweet way that made me melt.

"Why do you love me?" I asked him, not quite able to believe that this was real.

"Sinclair," he murmured, smiling at me, "you've always been my best friend. And then one day I looked over at you and all I wanted to do was kiss you and I couldn't. I didn't want to risk our friendship. Until that night at the dock, when it got to the point that being near you was driving me insane, and I had to touch you and be with you. That's why I asked you to the dance."

"And then ghosted me," I reminded him.

"Yes, I was stupid."

"You were stupid," I agreed.

"I'm just sorry for the time we lost."

"Sierra has a theory about that. She thinks this is happening at the time that was right for us, when we could be together and weren't living in different states."

And it occurred to me how much I wanted him to stay here in Florida. I didn't want him to go back to New York, but I didn't want to interfere with what he wanted for himself and his career. It wasn't something we'd discussed yet. "Although I don't know how long you're staying."

He took his phone out of his back pocket, opened up an app, and handed the phone to me. "Here."

It was a picture of a bunch of boxes. "What's this?" I asked.

"That's my mom's garage, full of my stuff. I broke my lease in New York and had everything shipped here. I'm not going anywhere. I want to be wherever you are."

I was both overwhelmed and moved by his statement, so much so that I couldn't speak at first. He misinterpreted what I was feeling.

"I'm not trying to scare you," he said. "But I hired movers after that hypnosis session. Being with you again reminded me of what I was missing out on and how much I wanted you back in my life. I've dated other people, had other relationships. I kept thinking that my memories of you were exaggerated, that you couldn't have possibly been that incredible, but, Sinclair? You're even better than I remember. So I want to put it all out there, cards on the table. I want to be here. I want to be with you."

How could I have ever thought that he hated me? And how could his voice sound so steady and calm when I felt like he'd caused hurricane gales of glee inside me? Happy tears formed in my eyes, blurring my vision. "Living in New York as a writer is your dream."

"You're my dream, Sinclair."

"You'd give up New York for me?"

"I'd give up the world for you," he said.

The love that I felt for him in that moment made me feel like I was floating and drowning at the same time. Little effervescent bubbles of joy fizzed inside me. I didn't know this kind of happiness was possible. "Okay, just promise you're not going to ghost me again."

He smirked at me. "You're going to keep bringing that up, aren't you?"

"I might."

"Does that mean I get to remind you that you falsely accused me of spreading a rumor about you?"

Putting my too-warm arms around his neck, I said, "I think it would be in your best interests to forget about it."

"Really?" He looked very intrigued by what I was saying. "What are you offering to placate me?"

"How about this?" I asked, and then pressed my lips against his. The very second we made contact, my entire body revved into high gear. *Yes, this. Do this all the time,* it said.

He let out a cross between a sigh and a groan.

I asked, "Or this?" and deepened the kiss.

A minute later he finally spoke. "Those are acceptable terms. So did you want to keep talking, or should I just read your ridiculously fast heartbeat?"

He made me smile. I really did love him. "Mason, I want to tell you that—" My voice caught. I should just say it. Maybe if I said the words out loud, my feelings wouldn't be so scary. I'd just speak and we would figure things out and move on from there. *I love you, you love me, let's see where this goes next.*

Instead I stayed quiet until he said, "Now I'm the one freaking out a little. Say something."

"I'm trying to figure out how to . . ." I still couldn't get the words out. I should probably just show him.

If the ferocity and hunger of my kiss surprised him, he didn't show it. He matched me stroke for stroke, every move I made being met and returned. He made me so aware of the way the blood in my veins pulsed through me and sent prickly, tingling sensations from my lips to my chest, out through all of my limbs until I was shaking with need.

He leaned me back against the floor, following me down. I tugged him close to me. I didn't care if it was a hundred and fifty degrees outside—I needed to feel him against me. We were both radiating heat, which made all of the cells in my body feel like they were boiling with desire and anticipation.

It was too balmy, and my skin was too tight. Everywhere I touched him felt just as hot and feverish, and I reveled in his strength and the way his muscles flexed under my fingertips. I loved having him hovering over me, pressing me down into the hard wooden floor.

With how hot it was, how slick our skin had become, it was impossible to tell if the fire between us was caused by the weather or the combination of the two of us together, burning hotter and brighter the longer we kissed.

I didn't care about the floor or the oppressive heat—nothing else mattered but Mason touching me, kissing me, holding me close.

"You taste like salt," he murmured against me, and I said, "So do you."

Then his mouth was back on mine, and if the goodies in the basket hadn't been melted before, they definitely were now.

"Savannah?" I heard my mother's voice, and we broke off the kiss, both of us breathing hard.

"Shh," I told him.

"What is your mom—"

I clapped my hand over his mouth. "Your voice carries. She's going to hear you!"

When I let my hand fall, his voice dropped deliciously low, and as he nuzzled my neck, he whispered, "I'm not the one making those sexy little noises."

Had I been doing that?

My mom called my name a couple more times, and Mason and I held completely still, locked in each other's arms.

The back door closed behind her, and I let out a sigh of relief that we hadn't been discovered.

"I'm going to have to go back in the house," I told him, full of regret. "She's like a bloodhound. She'll sniff me out eventually."

"How does she know you're home? Did you park in the driveway?"

"Yes."

"Have you never had a secret assignation before?" he said in mock exasperation. "You have to hide your car."

"Did you?"

"Yes! I parked my mom's car down the block."

"You are so smart," I said, admiring him.

"I know." He gave me a quick kiss. "It's a good thing, too. If she knew what we were doing up here, both of our moms would be ordering bride catalogs tomorrow."

"What's a bride catalog?"

He shrugged, not able to lift his shoulders up very far, as we were still intertwined. "I don't know anything about the industry. Don't they have those? Where you order wedding stuff?"

"I think they're called bridal magazines. Or websites. I think a bride catalog is a way to order a bride."

"Don't tell my mother that she can order me a bride," he said. "She'd do it before I got home tonight."

"What kind of bride do you think she'd order for you?"

242

He smiled adoringly at me. "The dark-haired, tall, smart, loving kind with a wicked spike."

"I haven't spiked a volleyball in years," I told him.

"Who said I'm talking about volleyball? I meant your verbal skills." Another quick kiss that felt far too fast.

"I have to go in and see what she wants," I said. "I was all hot and bothered, and now I'm just bothered and hot."

Mason gave me his signature sexy smile that sapped nearly all of my willpower. "I could try to fix that."

"Maybe another time."

"Another time," he agreed, giving me a fleeting kiss. "I'm going to sneak back to my car."

He kissed me about a dozen more times, saying after each one that he had to go, until he finally left. I stayed on the floor, willing my heart rate to return to normal.

It didn't help things when Sierra threw the trapdoor open and said, "There you are!"

I yelped and put a hand over my chest.

She came into the treehouse, taking in my romantic date setup. "Oh . . . what was happening here? Or, rather, is going to happen in the very near future?"

"Mason came by, and we hung out."

"Is that what the kids are calling it these days?" she asked, waggling her eyebrows at me.

I had to tell her what was going on. I needed to vent. "Confession time—we have discussed that the adult and rational thing to do is to take things slowly so that I can trust him again, but every time he gets close to me, all of that goes out the proverbial window, and I pounce on him. He says the most romantic things you could possibly imagine, and he, well, looks like Mason, so there's been a lot of making out."

"It makes sense. The two of you have a lot of pent-up longing to express," she said. "Mom's looking for you."

"I know. I heard. I'll go inside in a minute." I was going to lie here for about five minutes, until all of my nerve endings calmed down, and then I would go into the house.

Where I planned on taking a very long and very cold shower.

"Cool." Her expression shifted, and I realized that there was something she wanted to say to me, but she was worried.

"Out with it."

"When you get the chance, you might want to check out that message board for our high school. In the alumni section. There's something I think you might want to see."

She climbed back down, letting the door shut, and I reached for my phone. I found the board she was talking about, and I felt a strong wave of nausea when I saw why Sierra had brought it to my attention.

Bridget had posted.

CHAPTER THIRTY

I needed a minute to regroup before I read her post. I saw that there were literally hundreds of comments, and no other post on the message board had anywhere near that many. When I went inside the house, I thanked the heavens for the invention of air-conditioning and then took my shower.

I'd nearly forgotten about the online hypnosis session that I'd scheduled, and I threw something on that looked professional, then pulled my wet hair into a bun and hoped my client wouldn't notice.

When the session was over, I reached for my phone and clicked on the post. Bridget had called it "The Actual Truth About Mr. Landry." She had written down everything she'd told me. She took full accountability for her actions, apologized to me, and admitted that she had been wrong. Some other women posted that they had thought he was inappropriate with them, but didn't tell because they thought it was their fault or that no one would believe them or that they had been misreading the situation.

There was a lot of support for Bridget, and I was glad she was getting that. What had happened to her was awful, and I hoped she would find a way to heal and move forward with her life.

The anger and the betrayal were still there, but finding out it was her and not Mason—it didn't feel like such a personal act. What she had done was terrible, but it had come from a place of fear and not out of a desire to hurt me.

When I'd suspected Mason, that felt entirely personal. Like a targeted attack for a reason I didn't understand, and I hadn't been able to move past how big that betrayal was.

I'd already realized that a large part of it was because I was in love with Mason, and so of course it wouldn't feel the same with Bridget, especially because we hadn't even been friends back then.

I wished that this pain could go away—that I could stop being angry, stop feeling hurt. But I didn't know how to just let it go. I wanted to be more of an adult, to forgive, but it was something I was going to have to work on. I wasn't ready to do it yet.

The wound she had caused still ached.

Later that night Sierra found me in my room, where I was reading a book. Whenever I needed to escape the real world, a good book never let me down.

"Did you read Bridget's post?" she asked as she sat next to me on my bed.

I put down my book. "I did. That must have been hard for her to do. It means she probably had to tell her mom first, which couldn't have been easy, either."

She blinked at me a couple of times. "You are handling this much better than I thought you would."

"I am hurt and mad that she did it and angry that she kept it from me, but I also know it wasn't intentional and she was confused and being groomed and preyed on." I wanted to handle this better than I'd handled the situation with Mason. I didn't want to keep making the same mistakes, but I couldn't turn my hurt feelings off.

"She's apparently put posts up on all of her social media accounts, and she contacted the proper authorities to report it. I don't know if the statute has run out yet or not, but she wants to make sure that Mr. Landry stays locked up. She's making an effort to own up publicly to what she did." It confirmed to me that Sierra and Bridget had stayed in contact and were still talking.

"And I appreciate it," I said.

My sister stayed quiet for a few moments, her expression serious. I waited because I could tell that what she wanted to say next mattered to her. "One of the most important things I've learned over the years is about forgiveness. For ourselves and for others. For some reason, we see forgiving someone as a weakness or a failing."

I nodded because I knew that better than anyone.

"It doesn't mean you have to forget or condone what happened. It doesn't even mean you have to ever speak to or see that person again. But forgiving someone means you don't let them control you any longer. You get to replace all the heavy, negative feelings that weigh you down and focus on your own well-being instead. Bridget can't undo this. Neither one of you can change what happened, but you get the choice to change how you relate to it."

"That's really good advice. When did you get so wise?" I asked.

"Therapy. Years and years and years of therapy," she said. "I wanted you to forgive Mason for a long time because I saw how unhappy your anger toward him made you. And I'm saying this because I love you the most, and not just because Bridget is our friend, but I don't want to see you get caught up in that cycle again."

Maybe I wasn't as angry with Bridget because things had changed. Because I had found someone who made me feel more myself, more complete, who pushed and challenged me to do better and be better, and so forgiving Bridget didn't seem like such an impossibility.

"With time, who knows?" I said. "I probably have to work through some things first. It's a lot to deal with."

"If you need the name of a good therapist, just let me know."

That made me wonder if my mentor, Camila, was back in town yet. I made a mental note to send her a text and see if she was reachable. She would be a really good person for me to talk to. "I'll tell you if I need anything."

Sierra nodded and then hugged me. "You are my favorite sister."

"And you're mine."

~

The next few days were filled with work and my clandestine meetings with Mason. We were dedicated to taking things slow, and we were managing fairly well in that area, with a couple of close calls. He really was too sexy for his own good. Sierra was probably right, as she had been about so many things lately, that we just had a lot of pent-up wanting and longing that we had to work out before we could calm down.

I wondered if there would ever be a time when I wouldn't want to make out with his face as soon as I saw him.

He encouraged me to forgive Bridget, too, for the same reason Sierra had given me—that he thought it would be better for me to move on. His words carried a lot of weight with me because he'd been on the receiving end of my anger without it even being warranted. I was pretty growth resistant, but he made me want to try.

It became easier and easier to trust Mason, to focus on how much I was in love with him. It wasn't really a "falling" kind of experience—I had never stopped loving him, and it was more like reading a book I'd forgotten about. We just picked up where we'd left off, the page bookmarked and waiting for us to return to our story.

Camila finally returned and asked to meet me for lunch. The second she sat down, I completely unloaded on her. I told her everything about Mason and Bridget and all the things I'd been dealing with lately.

She was an attentive listener, asking questions here and there, but mostly she just let me tell her what I needed to say. I told her about how Vivian and Mr. Franklin were related and how worried I was about being caught.

"I know you told me that I had to be super careful and not give them any ammunition, but I—" I still hadn't said it out loud, not even when I was the only person who could have heard it. Maybe if I said it to Camila, that would make it a bit easier. "I'm in love with him."

"Are you currently treating him?" she asked.

"No."

"Were you inappropriate with him during the session?"

"I thought about stabbing him a couple of times, but I didn't," I confessed.

She smiled. "Internal thoughts don't count. Just what you did and said. Did you do something that the Board would consider inappropriate?"

"I don't think so."

"And you say he never paid you for your session? Money changing hands is important."

Not unless we were going to count a barter system where he had more than repaid me in kisses. "He never paid me. He was doing research for an article."

It seemed so clear as Camila questioned me. I had been holding on to the whole "he's a client" thing so that I wouldn't have to face the fact that I was attracted to him and very much wanted to spend time with him.

Now that I was admitting at least that much, I was glad that I could put that potential problem aside.

"Then Mason isn't a client and you haven't breached any ethics. If Mr. Franklin mistakenly believes something different, we can set him straight. You were helping a professional journalist in doing research for an article. Do you think Mason would be willing to testify to that, if you were called in?"

I was pretty sure Mason would get up and tap-dance on the Board's big conference room table if I asked him to. "He would show up and tell the truth."

Mason had been right about him not being an official client, which meant the last obstacle I'd put in our way was officially destroyed. There was no reason for me not to tell him that I loved him.

And the thought didn't terrify me the way it had before. I was ready to give him my heart. I knew he'd keep it safe. "It's funny—none of this would have happened if I hadn't been worried that he was in a too-suggestible state and that I had to keep him safe from making potentially harmful choices."

Camila looked confused. "That was never an issue. The second he woke up, he was fine. You didn't need to follow him around."

Oh.

I was very glad that I hadn't known that at the time. While I sat there and thought about how things might have turned out if I'd known, she asked, "Where are things at with your friend Bridget?"

"It's been a shock. I haven't spoken to her since I confronted her. She did apologize to me, and she made some really public statements owning up to what she'd done. She's pressing charges against the teacher, and several other women who went through something similar have joined her." If someone asked me, I would be more than happy to testify.

"That's good. I'm glad she's working on finding her peace and dealing with her past. You know how I feel about radical forgiveness."

I did know. We had talked about it often enough over the last couple of years, especially with regard to Mason.

That made me consider where he and I were and where we wanted to go.

An idea came to me then, and I sent Mason a quick text, asking him to meet me at my house later that evening. He asked:

For a secret assignation? Do you want me to come in through the window?

No, use the front door.

With my plan set in motion, I asked Camila about her trip, and she had a slideshow all locked and loaded, and Peru looked gorgeous. I had always admired Camila so much, looked up to her and wanted to be just like her. She was a holistic therapist, and the conference she had gone to had sounded a bit out there to me. I didn't think I would have enjoyed it.

Did I want to become a therapist? The idea that I could help people like my sister really appealed to me. But I could do that now with my hypnosis. I didn't necessarily have to become a licensed therapist. I could do good either way.

If the only reason I had wanted to become a therapist was because of my concern over how people reacted to my career choice, I had been letting my fears control me. When I did a hypnosis session, I was looking for the underlying reason that kept a person from reaching the thing they wanted to achieve, and mine was staring me in the face.

Mason had called it. I couldn't tell him, given that it might make him slightly insufferable if I admitted that he was right. But I did worry way too much about what other people thought. It had started in high school after that rumor and had stuck with me all these years. I hated when people made fun of my job, and so I had looked into becoming a therapist, not only because of Camila but also because I thought it would make others take me more seriously. And if I was spending all this money and time to get a license just to impress some imaginary audience, was that a good enough reason to be doing it?

It was something to consider.

I thought about it for the rest of the afternoon and into the evening. When I got home, I spent a long time getting ready. I wanted this moment to be perfect.

Waiting by the front door, I was the one who answered when Mason rang the doorbell.

He let out a low whistle when he saw me. "You look gorgeous. Like you should be somebody's girlfriend."

"If somebody asks me, maybe I'll consider it," I said, then grabbed him by the hand and led him into the dining room.

It was Mom's turn to host the quilting club, and so Heather, my mom, and every major purveyor of gossip from Playa Placida were seated together. My dad was in the living room reading, and Sierra was in the kitchen making a snack.

Mason's face fell when he saw everyone. "Sinclair, what—"

But I interrupted him with a kiss, in full view of everyone around us.

Heather was the first one to react. She made a joyous sound and ran over to throw her arms around us. My mom stayed put, fielding questions that she didn't have answers to from the rest of the club, but she had a grin so big I was worried her face might split in half. My dad glanced at us over the top of his book, shook his head, and went back to reading.

Sierra just said, "Finally," and went up to her room.

"Does this mean what I think it means?" Heather asked when she finally stopped hugging us.

"Sinclair's my girlfriend," Mason announced, holding my hand.

"Not technically, since he hasn't asked. But we are dating."

"I am so happy!" Heather said and hugged us again. She then went over to my mom and hugged her.

"You do know they're already starting to plan a wedding," Mason said.

I shrugged. They could have the moment that they'd been hoping for since the two of us had been born twenty-four years ago.

"What brought this on?" he asked, kissing my hand.

It was something I adored about him, how he always found a way to make a physical connection with me, to let me know that he was there, close by, ready to support me in whatever I needed.

"I spoke to my mentor, Camila, this afternoon. We have the all clear."

He grinned. "So we can be official?"

"That's still not asking," I reminded him.

Mason slid both of his arms around my waist. "Sinclair, will you be exclusive with me? Given that I'm already in love with you?"

That urge to share my feelings with him hit me full force, but I didn't say it. The first time I told him that I loved him was not going to be in a roomful of overly excited middle-aged parental units watching our every move. "Exclusive, huh? I'll take it under advisement," I said.

"That's all I can ask for," he said before he gently kissed me.

It was a perfect moment.

I should have known it couldn't last.

CHAPTER THIRTY-ONE

"My mom is going to visit her sister in Orlando," Mason said on our phone call, a week after our public debut.

"Is she?"

"Yep. And I'm going to be here all alone."

"That sounds tragic," I said.

"So I was thinking that maybe you could come over, like at seven o'clock, and I would make you dinner. What do you think?"

I thought it would take an actual herd of wild horses to keep me away from him, because I understood what he was asking. A romantic dinner with no possible interruptions. I would tell him that I loved him, and I supposed we'd see how slow he wanted to take things then.

"Maybe I could bring dessert," I said.

There was a long pause, and I wished more than anything that I could see his face so that I could judge his reaction for myself.

"If you're offering what I think you're offering, you're far more savory than sweet."

"You like savory desserts."

"You're right. Come over right now."

I laughed and said, "I'll see you at seven o'clock."

"On time, Sinclair," he growled, as if he couldn't wait a minute past that.

"I'm always punctual," I reminded him and then told him goodbye. This time when I got ready, I put on the good, matching underwear.

When I got to Mason's place, he opened the door before I could even knock, pulling me into a hungry kiss that left me completely dizzy and breathless.

"Do we have to have dinner?" I asked.

"I worked hard on it," he said. "Good things come to those who wait. Besides, there's something I want to show you."

"I heard. That's why I came over."

He laughed and took me into the living room. His laptop was on the coffee table. "Have a seat."

"This isn't going to be something weird, is it?" I asked, sitting down cautiously.

"No. I was thinking the other day about that guy who filed a false claim against you."

"Timothy?"

"Yeah. And how he was making multiple accounts to give you bad ratings. I'd bet good money that cretin never bothered to try to hide his IP address and that if we get somebody on the other end to look into it, they'll see that all the reviews are coming from the same person."

"Your plan tonight was to help me?"

"Of course," he said before kissing me. "Your fight is my fight, Sinclair." A timer buzzed in the kitchen. "I'll be right back, and then we'll get to work on uncovering this troll."

I watched him leave and felt an indescribable joy, a happiness that was beyond anything I'd ever experienced before. I felt so incredibly lucky to have him back in my life.

As if a piece of me had been missing for a long time and I'd just found it.

His laptop dinged, and I glanced at the screen. I noticed a folder in the center labeled "Sinclair." What was that for?

The article, maybe? Or something else?

It was none of my business. Mason was in the kitchen, humming to himself as he worked on dinner.

But resisting my desire to know things had never been a strength of mine.

Without thinking about it further, I reached for the keypad mouse and hesitated, my fingers hovering just above it. My curiosity was overwhelming, and I touched the mouse, moving the cursor and double-clicking on the folder.

There was a single Word document.

I opened it and started to read.

> Hypnosis has been around for hundreds of years, and scam artists have been conning people into giving them money by promoting the belief that someone saying magical words will help them lose weight or sleep better or feel less anxious.

My stomach dropped down to my feet. My heart started to beat hard and fast, and there was a sour taste in my mouth.

> Some of these quacks have the audacity to add the word "therapist" to their title as they fleece their clients, convincing them to sign up for years of hypnosis with a false promise that all of their worst problems will be solved.

Blood rushed through my ears, drowning out sound. That was a question he had specifically asked me—how long hypnosis would take, if it took years to complete. I remembered. I had told him that wasn't true—that my goal was to help people as quickly as possible. The more I read, the more my heart failed me.

How could Mason have written these things? Did he really think so little of me?

I covered my face with my shaking hands, unable to keep reading. I tried to breathe, in and out, but I couldn't get my lungs to work right. I felt like I was going to throw up.

Ever since I'd found out about Bridget, there had been this dull, throbbing ache that never seemed to go away.

But that ache that I'd been able to ignore was now turning into a gaping, sucking wound that made it so I couldn't catch my breath.

How could he do this? How could he be this cold, this selfish?

I had kept warning myself that he was going to do something like this. That he would use me and break my heart just to further his own career.

Some part of me didn't want to believe it—wanted me to allow him to explain—but it was quickly overruled. The evidence was right in front of me, with his cruel and spiteful words. All the things I worried about, the ways that I thought people might see and judge me—he had put them in an article for entertainment. My head spun; my stomach roiled.

This was why I hadn't been able to tell him I loved him. It was like some part of me had known and kept the last bit of pride I still had safe.

Mason was writing a horrible exposé on me. Writing things that I had told him weren't true. I'd been worried that he might use me for his job, and here was proof. In black and white.

He'd only told me he loved me to get dirt on my profession so that he could write a viral article, and I had been stupid enough to fall for it.

Jittery adrenaline coursed through me, and I was either going to pass out or throw up.

Mason came back into the room carrying two wineglasses. The smile slid off his face when he saw me.

"Sinclair? What's wrong?"

"What's wrong?" I repeated, standing up, not sure if my shaking legs would support my weight. "What's wrong? I saw your article. What kind of hatchet job is that?"

He looked confused. "I haven't written—"

"You wrote bald-faced lies. When that thing gets published, my reputation will be ruined. I told you—no, I *confided* in you—how important my career is to me, and the fact that you would betray that trust just to get ahead, to make sure your next book sells, is so despicable."

Understanding finally dawned on his face, and he set the wineglasses down. "You don't understand, I wrote—"

The anger I used to routinely feel around him flared back to life, like a dragon roaring awake inside me.

My voice was shaking nearly as hard as my hands. This was why I had resisted. Despite all his smooth lies and supposed perfection, he had been playing me the whole time. "You told me that you loved me. You used my teenage crush against me so that I'd share secret things about my life for your clickbait article. You'd put my job in jeopardy just to advance your own career?"

"Look, you don't understand, and if you'd just let me—"

He was being so calm and rational that it made me even more infuriated. "You promised me you wouldn't lie to me, and you did. You used me. You're the scorpion!"

That seemed to stop him from trying to rationalize what he'd done. "The what?"

"That story! About the frog who takes the scorpion across the river when the scorpion promises he won't sting him and then he stings him and they both drown and you're the scorpion. I knew what you were, and I took you across the river anyways! I can't believe I did this."

I walked into the front entryway and grabbed my purse.

Mason's hands were on my shoulders, trying to get me to turn around. "Please let me explain."

I jerked away from him. "No. No more explanations or lies or justifications. There's nothing else to say."

This time he kept his hands to himself. "Look, I know that you're scared—"

"You think this is about me being scared?"

His hands were in his pockets, and he was still calm, his voice even. "Yes, I think you're looking for an excuse because you're scared."

I'd spent all this time thinking that Mason knew me better than anyone, and it turned out that he didn't understand me at all.

Without saying another word, I walked out his front door and back to my car. I could hear his footsteps behind me and him calling my name. I broke into a run.

"You promised you wouldn't do this!" he said, and his words both hurt and infuriated me. He didn't get to play that card with me right now.

I ignored him and was alone when I reached my car. I hurried to put it into drive and went home.

I stewed in my anger, so furious at him for doing this. For making me care about him when all he wanted to do was use me.

Never again. I was never going to trust him or any other man ever again.

Rage fed me the whole way home. I heard my mom call my name when I went into the house, but I rushed upstairs. I wanted to be alone when the dam broke, and as soon as I set foot in my bedroom, it happened, and I started sobbing uncontrollably.

After finding out about the way Bridget had lied to me, I had thought that I didn't have any more tears to cry.

But this was worse. So much worse. I collapsed into a heap on my floor and cried my heart out. Because coming down from anger, I found that there was nothing but despair and heartbreak waiting for me.

I had trusted him. Loved him. And he had been scamming me the entire time.

"Savannah?" My bedroom door opened, and I was so relieved to see that it was Sierra.

"I thought you weren't coming home tonight," she said in a playful tone before she realized that I was crying. She got down on the floor next to me and wrapped her arms around me. "Oh no, what's wrong? What did he do? Do I need to go over there and slap him around a little?"

In between sobs I told her the whole story, and she held me while my body shook and my chest ached and my whole world fell to bits around me.

He'd been so diligent in knocking down all of my defensive walls, and now that I needed them to guard my heart, they were just a pile of rubble, and all I could do was feel hurt and betrayed.

"What did he say when you confronted him?" she asked.

If I could have laughed, I would have. My initial instincts when he first came back to Playa Placida had been right. Why should I let him explain anything? He would just lie in that smooth, calculated way of his, and I was done with it. Done with being used, done with being made fun of, done with being lied to. "I didn't let him explain. He always has an excuse."

"Or a reason," she said.

"Excuse," I repeated. "He tried to deflect and say that my reaction wasn't because of that trashy article he'd written but because I was scared."

My sister raised both of her eyebrows, and I saw in her expression what I was hearing in my own head—that maybe he was right. That I was scared and had been looking for an exit so that I wouldn't let myself get too close to him.

That I was the one making excuses.

All of my self-doubt and insecurities rose up inside me, making me question what I'd done and said in that moment.

I'd focused so much on how hurt I was feeling that I hadn't behaved rationally, and now I was wondering if that had been a mistake.

Sierra made it worse when she said, "I love you and I know you're in a lot of pain right now, but haven't you learned to let people explain yet? To not jump to conclusions? You didn't even let him tell his side of it."

"What side can he have?" I asked, wanting to put those defensive walls back up. Mason couldn't have a side. He'd written the article. I'd seen it. Discussion over.

"I don't know," she said with a shrug. "That's why you need to ask."

"No." And whether that was because I couldn't admit that I might have been wrong or because I couldn't deal with the pain of him admitting that he'd hurt me deliberately, I wasn't sure.

"Sometimes you are more stubborn than a stain in a laundry detergent commercial," she informed me, sounding exasperated. "Not now, but maybe when you've calmed down a little, you could go over there and hear what he has to say about it. I'll go with you. Or I'll go over there and pretend that I'm you and—"

"He'll know," I said, weakly. *I could be robbed of every single one of my senses and I would still know you.* His words reverberated inside my head. How could he say those kinds of things and then write such a horribly mean and false article? One meant to destroy me?

My heart hurt, twisting back and forth in pain while my head throbbed.

"So you talk to him, then," she said.

"I saw the proof in black and white. There's no explanation, no way to dispute it. I'm not making this up."

"I believe you," she said.

The problem was, I didn't know if I believed me. If I was sure of what had happened at his place tonight. Had I been scared? Trying to run away from him?

But that wouldn't explain the article and the pain he had deliberately inflicted on me, just for the sake of his job.

Then I thought of his parting words—how he'd called out to me, reminding me that I had promised not to jump to conclusions where he was concerned.

And I couldn't even begin to process all the feelings I had surrounding that. There was definitely anger but also something else that felt a bit like guilt.

It was all too confusing.

Exhaustion racked my entire body, and all I wanted to do was sleep. "I'm so tired. I need to go to bed."

Sierra helped me up and tucked me in.

"Will you stay with me?" I asked her. "I don't want to be alone."

She got into bed beside me. "I'm not going anywhere. Get some sleep. Things are going to be okay."

The problem was, I didn't think I would ever feel okay again.

CHAPTER THIRTY-TWO

The pain I felt at losing Mason was this ever-present, thrumming ache. I could never forget about it. Even when I was at work, I was still thinking about him. I knew time was supposed to heal my wounds, but all time was doing was reminding me on a constant minute-to-minute basis how empty everything felt without him in it. How broken my heart was, and how the entire world felt dark without him. Like he'd been the sun and I hadn't realized it until he was gone.

My parents knew something had happened. Heather and my mom had obviously held some kind of summit about it, but no one asked me what was going on. I wondered if Mason had told them.

Or Sierra.

I felt like a ghost in my own life, drifting from place to place, not feeling entirely real or even visible. A shadow instead of my full self. I tried hard to suppress my feelings for him, all the good and the bad, but it didn't work.

Sierra's words stuck with me, much as she did. When she wasn't working, she was by my side, watching old movies with me like I used to watch with Mason and handing me tissues while I cried through each one.

Mason didn't try to reach out to me. I ran through a variety of emotions on that one, too. At first I was glad he didn't call or text, because I never wanted to speak to him again. When some of that anger began to fade, I was hurt that he didn't even attempt to check up on me. Then back to mad because I must not have ever mattered to him. Then sad again over what we might have had.

While I recognized I wasn't being rational, it was how I felt.

I also kept doing internet searches for his name, waiting for the article to appear. I didn't know how much lead time a publication or editor would need before putting an article like that up online, but it never showed.

Which made me question myself—had Sierra been right about that, too? Should I have let him explain? Maybe he'd decided not to publish the article. Maybe his feelings weren't fake.

What if I'd made a huge mistake in accusing him?

Or was he holding off for another reason?

I didn't know what to think. And I couldn't hash it out with anyone. My sister and parents would just tell me to go talk to him and I couldn't call Bridget and Camila was busy and I wasn't sure what to do.

Staying in this limbo where I felt half-alive didn't seem like a good plan, either.

"I broke up with Joseph today," Sierra told me as we were eating a container of ice cream and watching yet another Cary Grant movie.

"You did? Good for you."

"Yeah, I figured one of us should be making some progress in our love life and having real conversations."

I had wanted to ask her how it went, what he'd said, but her words kind of shut me down. Because she was moving from being entirely sympathetic and on my side of the scale toward the middle. She might have even moved over to the "poor Mason" part.

"I'm glad that you stood up for yourself," I told Sierra, ignoring her implication. "Like I told you, you deserve better."

She gave me a pointed look, but she didn't say anything.

When she was quiet like this, all it did was give me more time to think about Mason, which I did constantly.

Because the worst part of all of this was how much I missed him. Like someone had removed vital pieces of me and I couldn't function without them.

Without him.

"I'm going to go upstairs for a little while," I told my sister, and she just nodded. I put my spoon in the kitchen sink and then went up to my room.

I had just crawled into bed when I heard a knock at my door. I sat up, surprised. My family had no boundaries, and nobody ever knocked on each other's bedroom doors.

My heart beat low and hard in my chest as I called out, "Come in!"

I realized that I wanted it to be Mason. Wanted it so much I wondered if I could will it into being.

But when the door opened, Bridget was standing there.

I was so surprised to see her that I blinked a couple of times, my mouth slightly open. I finally managed to say, "What are you doing here?"

She looked as anxious as I felt. "I was hoping I could talk to you, if that's okay."

"Um, sure." I gestured toward the chair at my desk, and she went and sat in it, perched on the edge as if she were ready to run away quickly if she needed to. I took one of my pillows and hugged it against my chest. Like it could protect me.

There was a long pause, and one moment turned into two until we'd been sitting there for almost a full minute in silence when she finally spoke. "Again, I'm sorry. I know that doesn't change anything, but I do need you to know that. I really regret my actions, both back in high school and when we met again a couple of years ago. I should have told you the truth, and I'm sorry for the way I hurt you and your family. You didn't deserve that."

"Thank you," I said. I was so emotionally drained from crying constantly over Mason that I didn't have much resistance left. "I saw the posts you made. Sierra told me that you reported it to the police."

She gave me a small smile. "I made it just under the statute. Another two years and they wouldn't have been able to prosecute him."

"I'll testify," I said. "He was inappropriate with a lot of girls. I don't know if it will help, but I'm willing."

"You are?" She sounded surprised. "Thank you. I'll let the district attorney know. But that's not why I came over here today. I was just over at Mason's house."

Even though my heartbeat had calmed back down to normal, Bridget saying his name sent it back into overdrive, and I glanced down, half expecting to see my heart beat its way out of my chest.

"Oh?" I said.

"Savannah, I've tried hard to make things right between us. I hope you don't mind, but Sierra told me about the article and how you and Mason broke up. I know I can't go back in time and change the past, but I thought maybe I could fix your relationship with him now."

My immediate instinct was to object, to tell her that there was no way that was possible, but I held my breath as I waited to hear what she'd say next.

"I apologized to him, and he was really gracious about it and forgiving." I knew Bridget didn't mean her words to be an accusation, but they almost felt like one, stinging and barbing my still rapidly beating heart. "I asked him about the article. He told me that he had written it before he came back to Playa Placida. That he had a lot of wrong ideas about hypnosis and how it works, and that the editor who hired him had intended for it to be a hit piece. So Mason wrote what he was supposed to write."

That didn't make things better. It just confirmed what I'd suspected—that he was willing to put his career before mine.

"Then he came back home and realized that he was wrong in his assumptions, and he told the editor he wouldn't write the article that the editor wanted. He said he realized that everything he believed about hypnosis was incorrect and that he would never write anything that would hurt you."

White light burst behind my eyes, silencing all of my thoughts and making me go still, my ears ringing. Mason had already told the editor he wouldn't write the article?

Her words shocked me, like someone had punched me in the stomach. My head started to spin with panic as I took in what she was saying. "So what I found was an early draft of an article he refused to finish writing." The words felt thick in my mouth.

She nodded. "Yes. He loves you. And Sierra thinks you love him."

"I do love him," I said as tears began streaming down my face. "I'm sorry. I can't stop crying. I'm like some kind of faucet."

Bridget got up and went over to my nightstand and grabbed a box of tissues. She handed them to me. "Don't be sorry," she told me. "Just don't make a mistake and lose someone you obviously care a lot about. You wouldn't be crying like this if you didn't."

She was right, and I nodded.

"Don't let another six years go by," she said. "I think you'll regret it."

I nodded again and then blew my nose. "What if he's lying?"

She gave me an incredulous look. "Why would he lie to me? As far as he knows, you and I aren't speaking to each other. The bottom line is you either trust him or you don't. I know I'm no relationship expert, but you've been afraid to trust him and believe good things about him for a very long time. I understand that it's a hard habit to break, but you need to find a way because I don't think you want to lose Mason."

Sometimes it took another person holding up a mirror to realize things about yourself. I was afraid to trust Mason. I'd been afraid to trust anybody outside my family. Bridget was one of the few people I'd let into my heart, and even she'd ended up betraying me.

But that was no way to live. If I kept everyone at arm's length, yes, maybe I wouldn't get hurt, but I wouldn't get the joy from loving someone, either.

I had jumped to the worst possible conclusion about Mason because of the internal fear I'd had that he was going to hurt me. It became like a self-fulfilling prophecy, almost like I was trying to will it into being. To find a reason to be angry with him, to again falsely accuse him, so that I wouldn't have to trust him.

Especially after I'd promised him I wouldn't do that again. Instead I'd done it the first chance I got. Guilt and shame filled up my stomach, making it turn over.

Things needed to change. I didn't want to keep everyone else in the world outside my walls. I wanted to let them in.

I wanted real joy and love in my life.

"I don't want to lose him," I admitted. "I cut him out of my life before, and it was a colossal mistake. I don't want to keep making the same mistake. I don't have a lot of people that I love, but he is definitely one of them. And so are you."

She let out a short gasp and then said, "I am?"

"Bridget, of course you are. And it's going to take me some time, but I don't want to lose you, either."

Now she was the one brushing tears away from her cheeks. "You won't lose me. I'm willing to wait for however long it takes."

I reached out to hug her and she held on to me so tightly. I had missed my friend.

People made mistakes all the time. Including me. I had made more than my fair share, actually. I had hurt people with them. Who was I to judge Bridget for doing the same thing?

Or Mason, for that matter?

I really had been the world's stupidest person ever.

I had to talk to him and see if I could make things right.

As if she could hear my thoughts, Bridget said, "Just FYI, he's home right now. Don't let him be the one who got away."

He already had been the one that got away, and I'd spent the last six years missing him.

While I was probably going to make all-new mistakes in the future, it was time to try to fix this one.

CHAPTER THIRTY-THREE

I didn't change into something cute. I didn't even bother to wash my face. I told Bridget that I'd text her soon and walked her out to her car. Then I got into my car and drove to Mason's house before I could talk myself out of it.

When I got there, I didn't want to knock on the door. I was worried he'd shut it in my face. I had accused him of things that weren't true after I'd promised him that I wouldn't do it again.

Another mistake.

What if he didn't want to forgive me? I probably didn't deserve it at this point.

Maybe it was my turn to do something romantic and impulsive.

I went around to the side of his house and found the ladder he'd messed around with that night after the alligator restaurant. It felt like such a long time ago. It probably wasn't safe to use, but I was a woman on a mission.

I put the ladder up next to Mason's second-story bedroom window and hoped that it was unlocked. I didn't look down, and thankfully the ladder didn't shake as I climbed. I pulled the window screen out and then pressed against the windowpane, lifting at the same time.

Triumph surged through me. It was unlocked! When I had it up completely, I swung one leg over and leaned into the window. Mason was sitting on his bed, reading a book, looking at me like I was an alien with two heads.

"Hi," I said, and then fell to the floor when I lost my footing. He started to move, but I held up my hands. "I'm okay! Stay there."

It would be better for me if he wasn't close. I was going to forget everything I had been practicing on the way over, and I wanted to get this right.

"Did you notice how I didn't throw a bowling trophy at your head?" he asked, and his tone was light, but I wasn't sure if he was being sarcastic or if he thought me climbing in his window was funny.

"Yes. Thank you. I need to talk to you."

He set his book down, giving me his full attention. Now that I had gotten in front of him and he was looking at me and not yelling at me to leave, my adrenaline finally caught up with my actions and flooded through me, leaving me jittery and unable to catch my breath.

"I know you probably don't want to talk to me, but could you just listen?" I asked him. "Not say anything until I'm done? Because there are a lot of things I have to say."

He cocked his head to the side, as if to indicate that he was listening.

My heartbeat was jackhammering inside me. "Okay. Good. Thank you." Then I wasn't sure where to start or what I should say. "I just saw Bridget. She told me about the article. And I realized that I misjudged you, and Sierra pointed out that I hadn't let you explain, and they were both right. I shouldn't have jumped to a conclusion without letting you explain yourself. It was a huge mistake, especially after I'd told you I wouldn't do that again. And I've been doing nothing but thinking about why I did. Why it was so easy for me to believe the worst about you instead of giving you the benefit of the doubt."

I took in a big breath and wondered if he would defend himself or try to press his case, but as I'd asked, he stayed quiet.

"Then I realized that there was something you said to me that night that was right. That I was scared. I was. I am scared," I corrected. "I'm scared of how much power you have over me. I'm scared of how much I care about you and how important you are to me. Most of all, I'm scared of how much I love you. How much I've always loved you, even before I really understood what it meant to be in love with someone."

He made a slight sound, and his expression shifted, but still he stayed silent.

"I do. Love you. And I'm sorry that I rushed to a judgment. I think there was still a part of me trying to keep me safe. But I don't want that. I want to say yes, to take a risk and be vulnerable and tell you the truth. I'm sorry that I accused you of something you didn't even do. I know how that feels and it kills me that I did it to you. I don't know if there's a way for me to fix this, but I needed you to know how sorry I am. I wish I could promise you I won't do it again. I'll try not to, but—"

"Can I speak yet?" he asked.

I was a bungled-up mixture of fear and relief, and I nodded. He got up and took me by the hand, leading me back over to his bed.

We sat down facing each other, and in that moment, my fear was starting to win.

"I will admit that I was a little bit frustrated and upset with you before I got back to Playa Placida," he said. "Because you didn't want to talk to me and because I'd been dumb enough to listen to Sierra and keep my distance from you, which I shouldn't have done. When that editor offered me the assignment, I took it because I knew it was your job, and I started writing the article without having any facts. It was just all of my own preconceived notions, fears, frustrations, and hurts spilling onto the page."

Oh. I wasn't sure what to make of that.

"Then, the moment I saw you again, all of that went away. I knew I wasn't going to finish the article I had started writing. When I told the editor I was willing to do one with a more positive spin, he killed it."

"I didn't know that."

"Well, to be fair, I didn't tell you. That night at Flavio's? I was still trying to get the editor to agree to my changes, but he refused. Which is why I never mentioned the article again after that night."

I immediately started to think back, trying to remember when he'd stopped talking about writing the article. I'd been so caught up in him that I hadn't even noticed. "I'm just happy that you're talking to me. I thought you might be too angry with me to even speak to me."

"Why would you think that?" he asked.

"Because I did it again. I blamed you for something you didn't do. I told you I'd try to trust you, and then at the first opportunity I screwed it up."

He seemed to consider this. "Again, to be fair, this time you accused me of something I did do and just hadn't bothered deleting, like I should have. But no, I wasn't going to submit it. I would never hurt you like that."

Then Mason reached over and took both of my hands in his, and I was so relieved and thrilled to be touching him again that I didn't question it.

He said, "When I said that I love you, I meant it. I will love you no matter what, even when you get mad at me. I wasn't angry with you over this. And I'd never stop speaking to you. I've already lived through that and it was terrible. I knew you just needed time to cool off and that you needed to figure out that you could trust me and how you felt about me. About us. I backed off."

"Was that why you didn't even text me?"

"Yes." He nodded. "Because I was giving you space. But you should know that I wasn't going to wait six years this time. I planned on giving you a week, and then I was going to sneak in your bedroom window so that we could talk, because I'm not willing to lose you again. You are stuck with me, Sinclair. I will always be here for you. Patient when I have to be but willing to press the issue if I need to."

That made me start crying again. "I don't deserve you," I said in between sniffles.

"When you did that hypnosis session and I asked what you thought I needed to change, it surprised me that you saw me as a negative person. It made me wonder if I'd been closing myself off to things since I'd lost you, and I didn't like it. That session we had . . . It made me feel like you gave me permission to be the person I always wanted to be. Like you unlocked a better version of myself. You help me to be the man I want to be, by keeping me on my toes and challenging me. No one understands me the way that you do, and no one else loves the way you love. I adore your big emotions."

"I'm too much," I insisted.

Then he reached up to cup the right side of my face and looked at me with so much tenderness, kindness, and love that it made me start crying all over again. "Sinclair, you're never too much for someone who can't get enough of you."

I cried harder, and he added, "That someone is me. I can't get enough of you."

He did it to make me laugh, and it worked. I laughed and cried at the same time, my poor emotions all over the place.

When I could breathe normally again, I said, "I should have told you that I was in love with you a long time ago."

"Maybe Sierra is onto something about stuff happening when it's supposed to. We can't live with regrets. We have to be here in the present and do the best we can going forward. I'm glad you're telling me now. But I've always known."

"What?" I asked in surprise.

He looked at me like I was silly. "I knew that you loved me from the way you kissed me, the way you touched me, the look in your eyes whenever you'd see me. I didn't need the words, Sinclair. But I'm glad I have them."

Then he leaned in toward me until our foreheads were touching. We breathed in and out together, and it calmed my soul in a way that I didn't know was possible. "Me too."

"I'm on your side," he said. "I always will be. Even if I'm the one you're mad at, come and talk to me. I want to hear everything you're thinking and feeling."

"I will," I promised him. "Because Mason? I trust you."

That made him pull back, searching my face like he was looking for something. "You do?"

Why did it seem like my trust was more important to him than my love? "I do. I will."

His mischievous grin that turned my insides liquid was back, and he said, "You know, you offered once to make it up to me when you accused me of something I didn't do."

Seeing where he was going with this, I said thoughtfully, "You're right. I did make that offer."

Then I started kissing him, and he seemed more than happy to accept that as payment.

"So you love me?" he asked, pressing gentle kisses along my cheeks.

"Yes. I love you," I responded as I ran my fingers along his broad shoulders.

"I bet you'll love me doing this," he said as he started kissing his way down to my throat.

It was then that I realized what he was doing—recreating our time in the study, only we were speaking of love instead of hate. "Yes, I *love* that."

"You say that with so much conviction," he said, sounding delighted.

Then he was peppering my jawline with butterfly kisses. "Do you love this?"

I nodded. "I do love it. And you."

275

Then he kissed me on the lips, locked into place with me for a long time. When he pulled away, he asked, "What about that?"

This time I was the one to look deep into his eyes, to show him how much I adored him, how this was where I most wanted to be in the whole world. I brushed my lips gently against his and then said, "I love you the most."

EPILOGUE

Six months later . . .

Mason refused to tell me where we were going. I had forgotten how big he was on surprises, another fun fact I got to be reminded of while we'd been dating. He wasn't a big-romantic-gesture kind of guy—but he was the type who always surprised me with flowers and told me he loved and adored me every chance he got. It turned out that those little acts of service and reassurance were my love languages, and he happened to be fluent in them.

I had decided to take a semester off school, as I was figuring out whether or not I wanted to continue. Mason had told me he'd support me either way, and I knew that was true. My hypnosis practice had taken off to such a degree that I had to add another hypnotist to help me with the workload. It was a good problem to have, and I was glad that I had taken the time off so that I could focus on building the business that I loved.

Mason would constantly tell people about my job and how good I was at it. He made it so that I didn't feel quite so embarrassed about it. Even when people did give me funny looks, he was there to whisper in my ear that their opinions didn't matter because he thought I was amazing.

It turned out that this was all I really needed. The confidence and love of a man who had been made for me.

Things had been going well professionally for him, too. Mason found another outlet willing to print a positive take on hypnosis, and someone did a video about the article, and it exploded all over social media. Which led to him getting tens of thousands of followers and having a much bigger platform. He finished up the novel he was working on about twin sisters who switched places to commit the perfect murder, and it went to auction. His new publisher had promised to put all of their marketing might behind him, and I just could not have been prouder of him.

"Where have you brought me?" I asked him, as it had started to get dark and was relatively cold for Florida. That only meant, like, seventy degrees for us, but it was cold enough that I had to wear a sweater. He parked the car and turned the engine off.

"Before you get out, you have to put this on," he said and held up a blindfold.

I raised my eyebrows at him, and he laughed.

"Come on," he said. "Don't you trust me?"

"Yes, I trust you," I said in an exasperated tone. "I never should have admitted that to you."

"Probably not," he agreed cheerfully. "Turn around."

I did as he asked, and he put the blindfold on and told me to stay put. I heard him get out of the car and run around to the other side and open my door. He reached in to help me get out and tucked his arm through mine. "This way."

"If this winds up someplace weird, I'm leaving," I told him.

"I'm the one who drove," he reminded me. "I have the keys, so you won't get very far."

"That's what you think. I can walk. I'm not the one who is afraid of alligators."

He kept me tucked close to his side, which was where I always wanted to be. We hadn't gone a single day without seeing one another since I'd climbed in his bedroom window to apologize.

"How is Sierra doing?" he asked.

"She's almost got all the money she needs to qualify for her own condo. She's hoping to get one down on Harper Street so that she'll be close to the beach. And apparently her real estate agent is pretty cute, and so she's been flirting with him a bit. He seems like a nice guy."

I knew what Mason was doing. He was distracting me so that I wouldn't figure out where we were. Because I was going to start asking questions and looking down through the bottom of my blindfold. It was clever of him.

"And Bridget?"

"She's still dating the same guy. It's been two months now! We're not sure if she's in love with him or if he's emitting some kind of pheromone that keeps her from looking at anyone else." Bridget being in a committed relationship was throwing all of us for a loop, her most of all.

After Mason had extended me forgiveness for my boneheaded mistake, it felt wrong not to give it to Bridget in return. After a few weeks, I called and asked if we could all start hanging out again, and we did. Bridget, Sierra, and I met up for our daily coffee chats again, and it felt like nothing had changed between us.

"What about Bridget's mom?"

The funniest thing about his plan was that he already knew all this information and was just having me repeat it to keep me from asking him questions. "She just qualified for a clinical trial, and they have high hopes for it. Are you going to ask me about Vivian next just to distract me?"

"I didn't know you realized what I was doing."

"Ha. I know you better than anyone," I reminded him.

"You do."

The ground beneath my feet shifted from a concrete feeling to a wooden one. We walked along planks while I wondered where he'd brought me. Back to Murphy's Alligator Emporium and Restaurant?

That would have been sweet of him. Our first sort-of date.

"Okay, sit here," he said and helped me to sit on the wooden planks. I felt him take a spot across from me, and then he reached for my blindfold.

I kept my eyes closed for a second. My curiosity was driving me bonkers, but if there was anything Mason had shown me over the last few months, it was the power of anticipation. Of waiting for just a moment longer to prolong the excitement.

My eyes opened and I gasped.

We were in Mason's happy spot.

The dock where we'd talked all night as teenagers. I drew in a big breath, my lungs filling with both fresh air and utter bliss. He was so thoughtful and romantic.

He said apologetically, "There's no fireflies because it's not the right season, and no bonfire because no pyromaniac teenagers, but other than that—"

I smacked him on the arm. "Shh. This is perfect."

There was even a little rowboat tied to the end of it, just like before. It looked exactly the same.

No, it was better. Because I was here with the man I loved.

"This is where I realized that I was in love with you," he told me.

"I knew a long time before then," I said.

Now he was the one shushing me. "You don't have to make everything a competition. I'm doing something here."

He reached into his pocket, and my heart stopped functioning entirely. I cursed the fact that I hadn't had a manicure recently.

Which was ridiculous because obviously it was far too soon for him to be asking me to marry him.

Mason pulled out something round and silver that fit in the palm of his hand, and I had to push away the disappointment I felt.

"What is that?" I asked.

"A pocket watch." He held it by the chain, letting it dangle down. Then he started to sway it back and forth in front of me. "You are getting very sleepy."

"Am I?" I said with a laugh.

"Yes. You're falling further and further under my power."

"Do you hear yourself when you talk? I just want to know if you're aware of the kinds of things that come out of your mouth," I teased him.

"Just watch the watch," he told me.

"See? Nonsense. Plus, whatever you think is going to happen is not going to happen."

"I'm going to make you quack like a duck."

"Doubtful," I said. "I've never quacked in my whole entire life."

"You shouldn't doubt my powers of persuasion."

That made me grin. "You're right. I shouldn't."

"What is it you secretly wish for?" he asked, as he still swung the pocket watch back and forth in front of me.

I thought about his question seriously before I answered. "Nothing. I have everything I could ever want."

"Everything?"

"Yep." A loving family, a job I adored, and my soulmate sitting across from me, trying to do an old-timey hypnosis trick on me. Everything.

"Are you sure?" he asked.

"Pretty sure."

He kept the watch swinging. "Do you feel sleepy yet?"

"Nope. Just very in love with you."

Mason put the watch down and leaned in to give me a quick kiss. "You know that this is my happy place, where I feel safe and loved. When I imagine this place in my mind, this is what I think about."

"Swinging a pocket watch in front of my face?" I asked.

"No."

There was movement, and I realized that he had a ring box in his other hand. I hadn't even seen him reach for it.

Maybe he really had hypnotized me.

My hands flew up to my mouth as pure exhilaration and joy filled up every cell in my body.

"I think you should be my wife, Savannah Rose Sinclair. Because I love you, and I want to be with you every single day of my life. I want to wake up to your snoring and go to sleep with your cold feet against me. I want you to challenge me and one-up me and remind me to be my best self. I want to come back here sixty years from now and hold your hand while we sit on this dock together. I want children and joy and a messy, full life."

Of course I cried. Big happy tears, but I cried.

"Is that a yes?" he teased.

I calmed my breathing down so that I could speak. I had to give him a hard time. "Six months is too early for us to get engaged, and also you're supposed to ask."

His eyes sparkled, aware that I was teasing. "I was ready to ask you six days after I came back home. I feel like waiting six months was very big of me. And, Sinclair, will you do me the honor of being my wife?"

"Yes," I said and then launched myself at him, wrapping my arms around his neck, kissing him everywhere I could reach.

"Careful!" he said with a laugh. "We don't want to fall in this water. Who knows what's in there?"

I pulled back so that I could smile at him. "It's okay. I would save you."

"Not if I save you first," he said.

"We'll see," I said. "And I think your hypnosis worked. You got me to agree to marry you."

"I told you it would work. Never doubt my skill. Now we're just missing one more thing," he said.

So I smiled, kissed him, and then said the words he most wanted to hear. "Quack, quack."

AUTHOR'S NOTE

Thank you for reading my story! I hope you liked getting to know Mason and Savannah and enjoyed them falling in love as much as I did. If you'd like to find out when I've written something new, make sure you sign up for my newsletter at sariahwilson.com, where I most definitely will not spam you. (I'm happy when I send out a newsletter once a month!)

And if you feel so inclined, I'd love for you to leave a review on Amazon, on Goodreads, with your hairdresser's cousin's roommate's blog, via a skywriter, in graffiti on the side of a bookstore, on the back of your electric bill, or any other place you want. I would be so grateful. Thanks!

ACKNOWLEDGMENTS

For everyone who is reading this—thank you. I've been able to do this job for eight years now, and it has been an incredible experience. I'm so grateful when you reach out and let me know that you enjoyed my books. Thank you so much for your support and helping me to keep the lights on at my house.

I always thank my editor Alison Dasho first—this wouldn't be possible without you and your guidance and enthusiasm. Thank you for supporting me and loving my stories as much as I do. I hope we get to work together for a very long time. I'm also particularly grateful to the team at Montlake for doing everything you can to make my books successful. Charlotte Herscher—it always makes me feel amazing when I get your notes. I've actually started to look forward to them—to finding a way to make my stories the best they possibly can be. I'm also very happy that you loved the ending lines in the final chapter and the epilogue. Your feedback is invaluable to me.

Thank you to the copy editors and proofreaders who find all my mistakes and continuity errors and gently guide me in the right direction (especially Kellie, who seems to get what I meant to say and shares a love of one of my favorite TV shows). A special shout-out to Caroline Teagle Johnson for my absolutely gorgeous cover.

For my agent, Sarah Younger—I couldn't ask for a fiercer warrior to be on my side. Thank you for always going to bat for me and holding my hand when I am absolutely freaking out about something, for always being understanding and supportive. I look forward to years and years of us working together.

Thank you to Jessica and Kristin of Leo PR. I'm grateful for your efforts and guidance!

I have to send a special thank-you to Janece Hoopes of Utah Hypnotherapy for sitting down with me and telling me all about hypnosis, how it works, and what it can do. Any hypnosis-related mistakes in the book are entirely mine or were fictionalized specifically for this story. Thank you for allowing me to share your methods and words and for explaining the difference between stage hypnosis and actual hypnosis.

For my kids—you bring me so much joy and love, and I'm so thankful that I get to be your mom.

And for Kevin—quack, quack.

ABOUT THE AUTHOR

Photo © 2020 Jordan Batt

Sariah Wilson is the *USA Today* bestselling author of *The Chemistry of Love*, *The Paid Bridesmaid*, *The Seat Filler*, *Roommaid*, *Just a Boyfriend*, the Royals of Monterra series, and the #Lovestruck novels. She happens to be madly, passionately in love with her soulmate and is a fervent believer in happily ever afters—which is why she writes romance. She currently lives with her family and various pets in Utah and harbors a lifelong devotion to ice cream. For more information, visit her website at www.sariahwilson.com.